Paradox

Soul of the Witch Saga - Book 5
C. Marie Bowen

Pixler Publications

Paradox
Soul of the Witch Saga – Book 5
by C. Marie Bowen
Copyright © 2017 C. Marie Bowen

This book was previously published as *Soul of the Witch, Book 3*.
ISBN-13: 978-1-945215-049 – Paperback

ISBN-13: 978-1-945215-056 – EPUB

Edited by Liette Bougie

Cover Design by C. Marie Bowen

Published by Pixler Publications

Discover other titles by C. Marie Bowen at www.cmariebowen.com

Contents

Chapter 1

Morago

—

The broad-winged hawk soared across the empty blue Colorado sky. Anger and frustration beat in the bird's chest with every downward stroke of its wings.

Morago, the demon entity in possession of the feathered raptor, fumed with impotence and abject failure.

The demon-servants Morago held in thrall were unusually quiet in the aftermath of their master's defeat. Only the old woman's soft laughter remained to mock his fury.

Quiet!

Morago struck his prisoner's soul with his thoughts, lashing her battered spirit.

In the silence that followed, the master inside the gold-breasted bird could sense the hawk's gnawing hunger.

Desperate for nourishment, the young raptor had attacked Morago's primordial snake form as he fled the witches across the prairie.

Pinned beneath the bird's talons, Morago had transformed into a mist and passed into his new host's mind, possessing the predator's healthy young body.

Deprived of its meal, the hunger inside this body remained.

Never before concerned with his host's needs, Morago paused to reconsider.

I will need living slaves. Corporeal fighters to defeat the witches' allies.

He loosened his grip on the hawk, riding behind the bird's instinctual mind instead of exerting complete control.

The broad-winged hawk dropped from its lofty height and slowed, surveying the ground.

A peep from a prairie dog below warned the entire animal village to scurry for shelter.

The hawk banked and skimmed the prairie sage, uttering a sudden piercing shriek. Its keen eye focused on a dove his cry had flushed from the brush. Talons extended, it plucked the smaller bird from the air and forced it to the ground. The raptor's ravenous appetite took control and it ripped the flesh from the tiny creature. The hawk's curved beak slashed at tissue until feathers scattered and blood soaked into the hard soil.

Morago delighted in the rending of flesh and the bird's satiation as the raw meat slid down the hawk's gullet to fill the emptiness inside.

Giving this raptor the strength to serve me further.

The bird ate its fill from the downed dove, then lifted into the sky. Gorged, it searched for a place to roost for the night.

Not yet, Morago conveyed with his mind, imposing his will. *Fly West.*

A slight adjustment to its feathered wings and the hawk turned toward the distant hills.

An inkling of a plan took shape in the demon's mind. With renewed enthusiasm, Morago fed the bird a new destination—a house in the human settlement along the mountains. The place where he had possessed his last human host, the dead man who thought of himself as Hunter.

***

Nichole Harris-Shilo

—

After the group of witches and gunmen had beaten back the demon and revived Hunter, Nichole and Cat escorted the weakened man into the ranch house, out of the sun.

Amy and Alyse followed them inside.

They gathered at one end of the large family table, exhausted from their ordeal.

Nichole leaned forward in her chair and placed her elbow on the edge of the long table. Her chin rested on her palm while her gaze stayed glued with fascination on Hunter.

The fatigued man acted on her like a magnet, focusing her attention as though he were the only other person in the room. She'd read about Alexander Veau, the man known as Hunter, in her father's genealogy research. In fact, she'd slipped Catherine Veau's postcard to her husband from a pile of her dad's old documents and hid the frayed card inside her personal treasure box as a young girl. She'd read the short missive, again and again, always wondering who Alexander Veau was, and why the Veau family history dead-ended at Alexander and Catherine Veau.

And now he sits across from me. They both do.

Nichole couldn't look away. She pressed fingers to her lips to hide a fangirl grin as she took stock of Courtney's ancestor.

At first, Hunter's eyes appeared as black as their pupils, but when the light fell across his face, they were the darkest blue she'd ever seen. His eyes were only slightly less fascinating than the jagged scar that ran from the outside of his left eye down his cheek to his chin. He probably wore his long hair tied back the same way Nichole's husband wore his, but right now Hunter's dark strands hung in dusty tangles across his shoulders and down his back.

Dehydrated and exhausted from his horrific ordeal, Hunter downed a third glass of water and nodded his thanks to Cat.

"Thank you," Hunter spoke to Cat as the tall brunette placed yet another glass of water on the table near his hand, but his gaze darted to Nichole, catching her stare. "You implied we had met, Mrs. Shilo. I apologize, but I'm at a loss to recall where that might have been."

Amy and Alyse sat to Nichole's left. The identical twin witches were dust-covered and drained by their recent efforts against the monster.

Catherine Kline, equally bedraggled, hovered beside Hunter. She tracked each shift and gesture of the bounty hunter. A slight blush colored her cheeks.

Nichole couldn't remember a striking resemblance to Hunter in any of Courtney's family photographs. Hunter's dark skin and hair must have lightened with each passing generation. But Nichole had seen Catherine Kline, or her near image, in Courtney's makeup mirror every day.

Before the car accident. Before she returned to her past life as Nichole Harris.

"Where we met?" Nichole raised her eyebrows and shrugged. "I'm not sure how to describe it." She paused and studied his profile.

I'm going to sound like a complete psycho to him.

Beside her, Amy lowered her head into her arms on the table and closed her eyes.

Alyse relaxed back and grinned at Nichole giving her a nod of encouragement.

"All righty then." Nichole cleared her throat and lowered her chin to address Hunter. "When Jimmy Leigh shot you, well—shot the demon inside you—your death put my future existence in jeopardy. As I expected, that act knocked a portion of me into what I call *The Passage*. I knew it would."

Cat sank into the chair next to Hunter, hand over her mouth, her gaze now fixed on Nichole.

Hunter narrowed his eyes. "Go on."

"Anyway, in this passage, I don't look like I do now because—" Nichole searched for a clear and concise explanation. Not finding one, she held out her hand as though in supplication for Hunter's trust. "Because Nichole, the person seated before you, would have remained alive even if you died. But the reality of Courtney's life would have ended with yours." She glanced at the sisters. "I had to give Amy and Alyse a chance to heal you by stopping your spirit from moving out of reach."

Hunter's brow furrowed as he rested his arm on his knee and leaned forward, searching Nichole's face and eyes. "Then—that was you."

"Yes," Nichole whispered.

"How did you change your appearance?" His voice lowered. "How did you know the resemblance to Cat would make me hesitate?"

"I didn't. I appeared as myself." Nichole shrugged and exhaled through tense lips. "I'm also Courtney Veau. Your descendant. I-uh, returned to my past life, my life as Nichole Harris, to be with Merril. In my future life, I bear a strong resemblance to one of my ancestors." Her gaze flicked to Cat and back to Hunter. "Apparently."

Hunter raised a brow as he looked from Nichole to Cat, then he leaned back in the chair and ran a tanned hand over his face. Although he'd washed the blood and grime from his skin, his clothes remained tattered and stained from his ordeal. "You claim to be my descendant. And you're here because you spirit-walked into this life and chose to stay. You gave up your future existence to return here."

Nichole closed her mouth. *He understood.* "To be with the man I love. Yes."

"Who taught you?"

Nichole's mind went blank. "Who taught me what?"

"To spirit-walk. That is a difficult and dangerous skill. Someone must have guided you, showed you how." He wasn't angry, only exhausted and curious. He pushed back his thick black hair and reached for Cat.

She grasped his hand with both of hers and tucked her fingers under his palm, resting his hand and her elbows on the table.

Nichole shook her head. "I didn't have a teacher. My father would have, I'm sure, but my parents died when I was young. My grandmother raised me. My mother's mother. Grandma Curtis knew nothing of my father's skills." Nichole's spine straightened as a thought occurred. "But my father spoke with spirits. And I saw Kevin Shilo." Her attention darted to the sisters and found both sets of identical eyes on her. "Kevin was Merril's brother. He died in this house."

Hunter closed his eyes for a moment. "He's not here now."

"Exactly. I showed Kevin *The Passage,* so he could move on."

The conversation ended when the front door opened. Merril and Jason removed their hats as they entered the dining room.

Merril rounded the table and dropped an easy kiss on Nichole's forehead. "We're going to head back to the Highlands." He addressed Amy and Alyse, "Most of the small animals and insects are burning in a fire your uncles started in the corral. The large animals are too heavy to move." He shook his head. "I'm not sure what we'll do. Butcher them where they fell, I suppose."

Jason squeezed his wife's shoulder. "Amy, would you and Alyse care to ride back to the ranch with us? Whatever Jim decides, he'll need help. Merril and I plan to return with men from The Highlands once everyone at home knows the threat is over, at least for now."

"Wait a minute." Nichole held up her hand. "Go back to what you said about the large animals." She raised an eyebrow at Amy. "Why don't you sink them into the ground?" She grinned at their various expressions. "I'm serious. You and your uncles manipulate earth. Why not change the density of the ground underneath the bodies and quicksand them underground? Suck 'em right down."

Amy rose from her chair. "I'm not sure it would work." Her gaze circled the table. "But it's worth a try." Chairs scraped back as Amy turned and led the group to the front porch.

In the yard, Jimmy Leigh, the Highlands' foreman, and Marshal Sam Kline worked together to drag a deer carcass toward the fire pit in the corral. They paused when the group filed onto the porch.

Jim pushed up the brim of his hat with his thumb, setting it back on his head. "What's happened?"

"Nichole has an idea," Merril explained.

"A good one," Amy added. "We're going to sink the large animals into the ground where they lie or at least make an attempt."

"I'm not." Alyse passed Jim and Sam on her way into the corral. Her smile lingered on Jim. "This *Fire* and *Air* witch will tend the flame."

"What's this?" Bayard wiped an arm across his head and reset his bowler hat. "Sink the animals?" He leaned his arms on the split rail fence and stared at the group on the porch.

"I never considered that." Bernard joined his twin at the rail.

"It should be possible," Bayard agreed. He gestured toward the deer at the foreman's feet. "Let's try with that one."

Jim and Sam stepped back as the brothers approached the carcass.

After a few moments, the twins held their hands out, palms down, and closed their eyes. Each movement, including the rise of their chests, mirrored the other.

By infinitesimal degrees, the carcass sank into the ground. The area where the animal had lain shimmered for a moment, appearing liquid, then hardened, leaving no trace the hard-packed yard had been disturbed.

Bay and Bern continued to concentrate for several minutes after the animal disappeared, then lowered their arms.

Bay leaned over, hands on his knees. "Not as easy as it looks, folks."

"That doesn't look easy at all," Jason replied, shaking his head in wonder.

"If Amy wasn't tired, she could do this by herself." Bernard pointed at a two-year-old heifer across the yard. "That one next."

"I want to help." Amy gripped Nichole's arm and pulled her along as she followed the brothers across the yard. "You don't mind, do you?" she asked Nichole. "I want to watch what they're doing."

"No problem, just glad I can help."

"How do you assist them?" Hunter called.

Both Amy and Nichole looked back, but it was Bernard who answered. "She acts as a bridge between us. Although Bayard and I can twyne our magic together, Amy would not be able to observe how we use our gifts. Our white candle makes that possible."

"They could see Kevin's ghost when they touched me," Nichole called to Hunter.

Nichole placed her hand on Bernard's shoulder and held Amy's hand.

"Wait." Hunter hurried to the group. "I want to observe their work."

"Unless you have their type of magic, you won't witness anything," Nichole explained.

"That's all right." Hunter's hands rested lightly on Nichole's shoulders. "I want to watch what you do."

"Okay." Nichole shrugged. "But there's nothing to see."

A throaty French scoff, deep in Hunter's throat, sounded behind her.

"Now." Bayard and Bernard said in unison, and the heifer lowered into the ground.

Several moments after the animal sank beneath the yard, the brothers broke their twyne and dropped their hands.

"Do you understand what we did?" Bayard asked Amy.

"Yes, I do." She pointed to a large steer on the far side of the corral. "I'm going to try that one."

"You go girl." Nichole waved her on. "Did you learn anything?" she asked Hunter.

Hunter shook his head. "Not a thing."

"Yeah, I don't understand how I help, or what I do." She shrugged. "But if I can lend a hand, even a little bit, it's cool."

Hunter's brow furrowed at her words.

"Oh, sorry." Her face warmed under his stare. "The Courtney side of me is super jazzed to meet you. I know better than to use her words. Amy says I freak her out when I talk like this." She rolled her eyes. "And now I chatter like an idiot, saying things you won't understand."

"You are no idiot, *ma chère*."

Nichole's gaze met Hunter's.

His grin stretched the scar on his cheek, and his eyes danced. "And I do understand your meaning, if not your words." He tipped his head. "I am flattered." He walked beside Nichole as they returned to the porch. "Unfortunately, I continue to suffer symptoms from my ordeal. The afternoon heat has made my head swim." His face paled beneath his tan and perspiration dotted his forehead.

"Go inside and rest," Nichole advised. She caught Cat's watchful eye and tipped her head at Hunter.

Cat stepped up and took Hunter's arm, escorting him into the cool interior of the ranch house.

In the yard, Alyse spoke with Merril near the corral fire, then left the pen and headed toward her sister.

Nichole put her concern for Hunter aside and hurried to join the twins. New to *twyning*, the twins would appreciate the help a spiritual bridge would provide.

It's the least I can do. The only thing I can do.

By mid-afternoon, the teams had cleared the animals from the yard, either by sinking or burning them.

Jim and Merril saddled the horses and hitched the wagon for their return home.

Few had slept before the battle with the demon, and the work of clearing The Shilo showed on everyone's face.

"We look like a horde of zombies," Nichole commented to Amy as she mounted her gelding.

Amy blinked at Nichole. "I'm too tired to ask."

Chapter 2

Morago

—

The hawk perched on the balcony rail of a familiar house. It overlooked a small yard facing west into the sunset. Although the bird slept, the entity inside remained awake.

Morago considered the talents of his adversaries and everything he'd learned in defeat. The witches were formidable. Together, they displayed more elemental power than the old woman had possessed, which was considerable. Two male witches had fought beside his targets, but that alone had not defeated him.

It had been the human servants and their weapons that brought me down.

The encounter had been uneven from the beginning. Morago knew that now.

But that would change.

The bird's head swiveled, and its keen vision focused on a thin older man rounding the side of the house.

"Well, I'll be damned if she wasn't right." The stranger paused and lifted his hat with one hand and scratched his balding head with his fingers. "Wilma said she saw something big fly back here." He settled the hat and threw out his arms. "Scat, ya filthy vulture. You'll eat Wilma's little finches." He jumped forward. "Scat, I say."

The broad-winged hawk cocked its head.

The man picked up a stone. "Now, off with you." His arm froze, and the rock fell from his fingers.

Take Albert Fielding back to his wife.

Morago instructed the lesser demon that now dwelt inside the neighbor.

Tell her you chased the raptor from the yard.

The old man tottered around the side of the house, but Morago's demonic magic allowed him to look through the eyes of his slave with only a thought.

You may watch through your vessel's eyes, Morago instructed his servant, but allow him the freedom to go about his daily tasks. Report to me all you learn.

With a cry, the hawk rose into the evening sky. This body was too unusual within the human settlement. He required a less remarkable host. Beneath the hawk's watchful eye, Albert Fielding returned to his house.

Behind Albert's house, several small, colorful birds chirped at a feeding area.

The broad-winged dipped toward the tiny birds, frightening them into the air. With a single thought, Morago released the hawk and rose inside a little yellow finch above the rooftops.

***

Hunter

—

Hunter stifled a groan as the wagon bounced over another rut. The magical care provided by the dark-haired twin sisters had returned him to life, but in their exhaustion, the healing had remained incomplete.

Or perhaps my soul is scarred, forever marked to show my failures, like my face.

The brother witches, another set of twins, introduced themselves as Bayard and Bernard and shared the wagon bed with Hunter and Cat. They spoke in hushed tones about rescuing their mother from the demon. They were worried for the old woman's soul.

With good reason.

At Hunter's back, a light-haired man, who resembled the blue-eyed, golden-haired Nichole, drove the wagon. On the buckboard seat beside him sat Amy, and her twin, Alyse.

The witches I was hired to kill are the ones who saved my life.

The towering man who fired the rifle, freeing him from the demon, rode beside Alyse, never straying far from her side.

There were so many people. Far too many for a solitary man like himself to recall their names, especially with his physical and spiritual injuries.

Riding behind the wagon were the Shilos, Merril and his wife, Nichole, who had magic in her soul from another life. His descendant, if she were to be believed.

And do you believe her? Noticeably absent since the demon possession, the voice in his head had returned.

I can't doubt her. I've seen the evidence of her power with my own eyes. Hunter's gaze flicked to Cat.

On the other side of Nichole rode Marshal Sam Kline, Cat's older brother, and Hunter's friend. Sam narrowed his eyes as his little sister grasped Hunter's hand.

He worries about the demon.

Cat held firm to Hunter's hand and glared defiance at her brother.

Hunter closed his eyes and leaned close to her. "*Mon amour,*" he whispered in her hair. "It does no good to make your brother angry. Give him time, *mon beau petit chat.*"

"I don't care what Sam thinks."

"Yes, you do. And so do I." He set aside her hand and listened to the murmured words between the brothers, what he could hear. His eyes closed, and the wagon rocked him to sleep.

A sharp jolt woke him as the wagon pulled up a low incline and into a wide yard. They rolled past a white clapboard house. A long, covered porch wrapped the front entry and continued along the side of the building.

Faces peeked from behind the curtains, and then the back door opened. A portly gray-haired woman in an apron hurried down into the yard waving her hands and following the wagon. "Is everyone safe? Is it over?"

Merril and Nichole reined their mounts to speak with the woman as more people spilled from the house into the yard.

"How many people live here?" Hunter asked Cat.

The wagon stopped, and Cat pulled herself to her feet. She slapped at her skirt with a sharp left to right motion and lifted her chin to push several strands of dark hair from her face. "I'm sure you'll get the full tour and introductions. Although, I don't know where they'll put you. All the rooms in the house are taken." Her words were polite and distant.

I've hurt her feelings.

"Cat—"

Two workers from the large stable unlatched the back of the wagon and helped Cat to the ground. She walked to Nichole and Merril without turning around.

"She's right about the house."

Hunter tore his attention from Cat and looked at the tall, muscular cowboy who had put a bullet through his chest.

"We weren't introduced before. I'm Jimmy Leigh, Foreman here at The Highlands. Most folks call me Jim."

"Jim." Hunter stood in the wagon bed and held out his hand to the tall, mounted man. "I'm Hunter."

"So I understand." Jim shook his hand. "Sam and Cat spoke of you before we battened down the ranch and rode to The Shilo."

Hunter hopped over the side of the wagon as Jim dismounted. Normally the tallest man in the room, except for Sam, Hunter had to tip his head back to meet Jim's eye. "Six foot four?"

"Just shy of six five." Jim pointed at the house. "Like Miss Kline said, the guest rooms are filled. If you don't mind, I'll settle you in the bunkhouse. There's only Kelly and Bill in there now, though I've no doubt we'll need more if Merril decides to drive to market."

The workers, father and son, by the look of them, led the animals and wagon to the large stable as soon as Hunter stepped away from the wheels.

"That's Lloyd and Tom Baker. They take care of the livestock and equipment." Jim waved back at the men then held the door to the dormitory for Hunter.

Inside, the long building housed a dozen or more bunks with a small storage box beside each bed. Jim opened an inside door beside the entrance. "My bunk's in here. Bill and Kelly have the first two beds, but you have your choice of the remainder."

"I don't know how long I'll be staying. My things—" His heart rate accelerated. "I've left important items at my hotel in Denver. I'll need to retrieve them."

"Denver's a fair distance. We can make arrangements if you want to head back, but you won't be leaving today." Jim walked down the aisle between rows of beds beside Hunter. "It would be quicker to send a telegram from Kiowa Crossing. The hotel could hold your things until you return."

Hunter nodded and pointed to the last bed. "I'll take that one."

Jim gave Hunter a nod and retraced his path through the bunkhouse. "Cookie will have dinner early, I expect, and the James family will return to The Shilo before sunset." He paused at the door. "Between dinner and their departure, they'll want to make plans."

Hunter lifted his chin. "Am I to have a part in these plans?"

"That would be up to you." Jim shrugged. "You have a unique perspective." Jim's lips thinned. "I know they could use your help, and if it were me, I'd want a bit of revenge."

You'll stay, came the voice in his head.

Hunter nodded to Jim. "You're right."

"There's a large metal tub out back with a hand pump for washing up." Jim pointed to the door across from Hunter's bunk. "I'll talk with Sam and Merril about a change of clothes for you. They're about your size."

Hunter examined the long room after Jim had left and scrubbed a hand down his face.

I'll be no help to them without my pendulum.

Your pendulum won't help with this. You'll have to delve deeper. Dark times call for dark magic.

Do you use my grandmother's words against me?

They were my words before they were hers.

"And what does that mean?" Hunter's voice echoed back to him from the empty room. "*Mon Dieu,* now I talk to myself." He half expected the voice to respond, but this time, the whisper inside his head chose to remain silent.

Later that evening, after the dishes were cleared from the dining room table, the family and guests grew quiet, and their gazes turned to the head of the table—to Merril and Nichole.

Hunter sat nearer the other end, beside the James family.

Bayard, the more outspoken of the brothers, leaned forward. "Has anyone given any thought to what we're going to do next? That monster holds my mother's soul." He looked at Hunter for confirmation.

"He holds the soul of a woman," Hunter replied to Bayard. "That much is true." He lifted his voice and spoke to the rest of the table. "Her soul is captive but not broken. I could hear her taunts but did not communicate with her." He shrugged and stared at his hand. His knuckles whitened as he pressed hard on the table beside his water glass. "While he possessed my body, I remained a prisoner inside my mind. The woman, your mother, for lack of a better description, appeared to be a prisoner inside the demon's—"

"We need to go after him!" Bayard pounded his fist on the table. "We must avenge our mother's murder and free her spirit."

"How will you find him?" Jim asked from beside Merril. "He could be any-where. The only thing you know for certain is he will return for your nieces." A look, heavy with significance, passed between Alyse and Jim. "He wants them more than anything, am I right?" Jim asked Bernard. "According to this Prophecy, he'll have to come after them. I say we lay a trap."

"We laid a trap last night," Amy countered. "And he nearly had us."

"Where does he get his magic?" Merril asked. "Why would he desire your elemental magic if he already has those abilities?"

"He has our mother's magic," Bernard said.

"And her knowledge," Hunter added. "I've no doubt this demon can pillage her thoughts as he did mine. He learned where to find you because I knew where you were."

Beside him, Sam nodded as if it all finally made sense, and his eyes widened. "Then he has your skills as well?"

"He wasn't interested in my gifts," Hunter admitted. "Only where he could find the twin witches. But now that you mention it, his actions make no sense. If he covets magic, why not take mine?"

"Maybe he already has yours," Jason said.

"No." Hunter shook his head. "If that were true, he wouldn't have needed my insight to their location, information I gained by the use of my skills."

"It could be because of the Prophecy." Alyse ran her finger around the rim of her glass. "If he had killed you like he did grandmother, the demon would have inherited your power, but the only thing he wants is the magic of the twins." The sisters stared at each other.

"How long do we have until the demon comes back?" Jason asked.

All eyes turned again to Hunter.

They wait for you, the whisper prompted.

I don't have their answers.

No. But you know more than you say. They need you.

I swore never to use the dark arts.

Even to save those you love?

Hunter's gaze lifted to Cat, and then grudgingly slid to Nichole. "I would say you have time. He must make plans, gather his strength, and prepare for his next assault. Your advantage is familiar ground. You should wait for him to come to you."

"Like Amy said, a trap didn't work last night. What's changed?" Bernard asked.

Hunter swallowed and acquiesced to the voice gone silent inside his head. "Now you have me."

Chapter 3

Morago

—

Near sunset, a small yellow finch bearing Morago circled high above a boarding house. The bird's keen eyesight had allowed the demon to retrace his journey through the human settlement to reach this particular dwelling. Satisfied he'd found the right place, the little finch fluttered to the windowsill beside a closed pane.

From his perch on the sill, Morago scanned the thoughts and listened to the words of the middle-aged woman inside the room. Although he had only caught a glimpse of her as he'd ridden into town behind her wagon a few days ago, the bitter hate that had radiated from her mind impressed the demon.

Now the woman's thoughts flickered between her disgust at the bordellos and gambling houses she'd heard discussed at dinner with the other boarders, and her current, unacceptable situation. The rocking chair's rapid pace displayed her agitation.

She counted on her fingers the people she hated the most in the world as she spoke angrily to herself. "The Harris girl." She pursed her lips and spoke the hated name with a mewling tone, "Nichole Harris." Her voice became a snarl, "She was a whore from the minute she arrived from Boston. I never did like the arrogant little bitch. Always wearing her fancy city dresses and putting on airs like she was better than decent, hardworking folks."

Her voice rose in anger, "How dare she turn me out!" Tears of rage festered in her eyes as her lips thinned into a hard line.

On the sill, the little bird hopped with glee. Morago bathed his battered spirit in the woman's bile and hatred.

Her bitterness is splendid.

"And that Shilo boy? Sniffing around that Harris girl like she was a bitch in heat. They'll both come to a sad end, mark my words." The woman spat on the floor then wiped a thin trail of spittle from her chin with the back of her hand.

"Mrs. McKay?" A male voice called from outside the door along with three soft knocks.

June's hate-filled and angry voice became a pitiful whine. "The door is open, Mr. Bramer." She pulled a shawl close around her shoulders despite the beads of perspiration on her forehead.

The boarding house owner peered around the door. "I was passing by and heard you call out. Is everything all right?"

June McKay sniffed. "As well as it can be in such a heartbreaking situation."

"I understand, ma'am, I surely do." Vern Bramer began to close the door, then his shaggy white eyebrows rose, and he leaned in again. "My wife asked me to tell everyone she baked a blackberry pie this afternoon. If you'd like a piece, you can get one in the dining room. But I wouldn't wait too long."

"Thank you, Mr. Bramer." June dipped her head and attempted a smile. "Bless your wife for the caring woman she is."

"Thank you, ma'am."

The door closed, and June's face distorted in a sneer. "I'd rather eat my foot than your wife's nasty pie." Her rocking stopped, and her face showed genuine sadness. "Miss Amy now, she could bake a berry tart worth eating."

The finch hopped closer to the glass. The image in the woman's mind was of the young witch. The bird's feathers fluffed with excitement.

The demon horde at the back of Morago's consciousness begged to be allowed to possess the old woman, but the master's firm, *"No,"* stopped the babbling.

This woman is perfect, the way she is. June McKay's misery inspires me.

Morago tapped on the glass with the bird's small beak.

"Huh?" The rocker stopped. "What's this?" She approached the window with caution; her eyes locked onto the little yellow bird.

Morago tapped again.

"You're an anxious little thing." She raised the sash. "Don't fly away now."

The bird fluttered its small yellow wings and resettled on the sill.

June took a pinch of stale bread from a food tray on her dresser, "Are you hungry?" She tossed the bread onto the wooden ledge outside the window and smiled as the finch pecked at the crumbs. "Now you need to leave Mr. Bramer a little present on his front doorstep." Her laughter was strained and tinged with insanity.

Morago shivered in ecstasy.

June closed the window and discarded the shawl on the bed. "Well now, little birdie. I think I'll go try some of that free blackberry pie and see what's what with the other boarders." She shut the door firmly behind her.

The possessed finch found a bush nearby and settled in for the night. Inside the bird's sleeping body, Morago chuckled along with his snickering horde. The woman's pure hatred had revitalized him with determination. June McKay knew the witches and their champions. He'd find their weakness and take what was his by right.

***

Merril Shilo

—

Merril studied the people slumped around his wife's dining room table. Exhaustion etched every face. He rested his hand on Nichole's and squeezed slightly to catch her attention.

She turned her tired blue gaze to him and gave him a weary smile filled with love. Then her attention returned to their newest guest.

"What do you mean we have you?" Bernard asked. "I'm not one to discount the assistance of our spirit bridge and white candle, but if that's the limit of your abilities—"

"It's not." Hunter clenched his jaw and shook his head. "Nichole, although gifted, is untrained. Her innate abilities have served you well and will continue to do so." He closed his eyes and swallowed. "But there are other skills, beyond divination and communion with phantoms, which have been passed down from my mother and grandmother." His eyes opened, and his intense gaze rested on Cat. Pain and apology shimmered in his dark blue eyes. "There are dark and dangerous arts I command, *mes amis*. The type of magic I swore never to use against another human."

"This thing we fight is far from human," Bayard countered. He no longer slumped in his chair but sat forward with eagerness. "I'm not familiar with spirit magic. How does it differ from ours?"

Hunter sipped from his glass of water as consideration furrowed his brow. Then he shrugged. "Far different." He returned the half-filled glass to the table. "From what I can tell, your power is based in the corporeal world. You manipulate elements in the material universe." He rotated the glass with his fingertips, never looking away from the water. "My abilities stem from the incorporeal world. Spirit magic. Soul magic." His voice lowered. "Death magic. The application of the darker aspect of this art, the things I've seen, well, they would shock you. Horrify you."

Merril felt Nichole shiver. Although she barely spoke, he knew what she muttered.

"Holy shit."

"But your skills, your abilities, could be used in coordination with our own?" Bayard pressed.

"I believe so. Yes." Hunter's shoulders slumped with fatigue or resignation. "One of the demon's greatest strengths is that he is unbound." He stared solemnly at his hands, then flicked his gaze to Bayard. "The words are difficult for me to find." He sat forward and emphasized each word with his finger on the table. "Even though you killed me—the demon's host—he was able to run away. To retreat. He can jump from one living beast to another or escape in his basic form."

"The snake," Alyse said.

Hunter nodded as he met her gaze. "Because binding the demon long enough to finish him will take great strength and strong, dark magic, it would be best for me to work in a pair or group, as you do. However, the only practitioners of Voodoo I know are my grandmother, who is too ill to travel, and my mother, who is too—preoccupied."

"You have me," Nichole offered.

"Willing, but untrained." Hunter's gaze softened as he nodded to Nichole. "The best place for you is where you already are. To act as a spirit bridge for your elemental friends."

"I may know someone who could help," Merril spoke, then shook his head. "Although I doubt we can locate him."

"Who?" Nichole asked.

"Do you remember White Eagle?" Merril replied, then addressed the rest of the table. "An elderly Indian shaman who travels with his grandson. They were camped east of our property, along Box Creek, less than a month ago. They planned to move north."

"They won't be easy to find," Jim commented.

"I can send a telegraph to the Bureau of Indian Affairs," Sam offered. "There are several army forts north of here that monitor tribal movement. Perhaps they've been seen."

"The closest telegraph office is in Kiowa Crossing," Merril said. "A four-hour ride from here, on the same road we take to The Shilo."

"Good." Sam nodded. "I can telegraph the hotel at the same time. I need to let both the hotel and stable know we're extending our stay with friends." He spoke to Hunter, "I could advise them both on your behalf if you like. I assume you've decided to remain."

Hunter nodded.

Jason cleared his throat. "I understand we're focused on what happened at the other ranch." He sent his wife an apologetic glance, then spoke to Merril. "But we need to discuss regular ranch business for a moment. Our cattle need to be driven to market, as well as the remains of The Shilo herd. We'll need those funds to see us through the winter."

Merril ran a hand through his hair. "I haven't thought about that at all." His gaze caught Nichole's. "I'll only go if the ranch is secure while we're gone."

Damn.

"But Jason's right," he continued. "If not for winter supplies, then for safety. We don't want a repeat of what happened with the stampede."

"We'll have to hire at least a half-dozen men and a cook," Jim reminded him.

"I'll be your cook." Henny stepped out from the servants' alcove. "Now that Miss Amy is here for the garden, and Cookie has all the help she can use in the kitchen, I'm not as useful as I was. I'd like to go with y'all."

"What about Katy?" Nichole asked. "If you trust us to take care of her, we could use your daughter's help with baby Hope-Anne."

"She would be a great help with the vegetable garden also," Amy added.

"Yes, ma'am. That's what I was thinking." Henny firmed her chin. "I know I can drive the cook's wagon, Mr. Jim."

"Well, there's one less for you to hire," Merril said to Jim.

"It's one of the most important positions on a drive, Henny. A position of authority," Jim grinned at the anxious woman. "There's no one I'd rather have than you. Thank you for your offer. You're certainly welcome on our drive."

"Which stockyard are you considering?" Jason asked.

Jim rubbed his jaw. "The larger markets are east of here, either Ellsworth or Wichita. Ellsworth is the closer. But even then, it would be a week or better to drive the cattle after we round them up. A day or two for business, then the return trip." His gaze strayed to Alyse. "If we can settle for less per head, the stockyard in Cheyenne is considerably closer."

"What about the one in Denver?" Amy asked.

"The Elephant Corral? They're small and mostly trade in horseflesh and mules," Jim said.

"Yes, but they do buy some cattle. Also, before I left town, there was talk of a new location, larger and closer to the rail line." Amy shrugged. "The paper said they were already purchasing livestock with a temporary packing facility set up on site."

Merril took Nichole's hand. "I want to be away for as short a time as possible. Let's try Denver first. If they aren't interested in our stock, we'll take the trail north to Cheyenne."

"Our plans are set." Bernard rose from his chair at the foot of the table. "While you drive your stock to market, Bay and I will continue to work with our nieces and Miss Nichole. For tonight, it's time for us to head back to The Shilo and find our beds." Although he didn't mention Hunter, his attention remained firmly planted on the newcomer.

Hunter's gaze rested on Sam and Catherine. "I hope you can locate the other spirit caster, Sam. Any plan I devise will need a second man."

"I'll do my best." Sam stood and held out his hand to his sister. "I'll leave for the telegraph office first thing in the morning. Do you want your bags and pendulum forwarded? I'm certain that could be arranged."

Hunter grinned then grew solemn. "Yes. Having my own clothes would be nice, but my pendulum is a child's toy compared to what will be needed here."

Chapter 4

Jimmy Leigh

—

Jim made his way outside as the others said their farewells to the James family in the dining room. His long legs carried him across the compound to the stable. Inside, he found Tom Baker seated in the doorway, mending a harness.

"Amy's family is ready to return to The Shilo. Could you hitch their wagon and take it up to the house?"

"Yup." Tom set the leather beside his stool and hurried to lead two horses through the back exit to the buckboard.

Jim found his saddle in the tack room and took it to the brown gelding he favored. Resting the saddle on the divide, he shook out the saddle blanket and tossed the cover over the horse's back.

"Why are you saddling up?" Alyse entered the stall and caressed the gelding's nose.

"I intend to ride back with you. I want to know you're safe." The flower scent of her hair enveloped him.

She stepped close and blocked his path to the saddle. "Barring demons or acts of God, I'm one of the safest people you've ever met." Her gaze sought his. "There's nothing in the night that can harm or frighten me. Besides, you're as exhausted as the rest of us." Her skirt brushed his legs, and she tipped her head back. "I'd sleep better knowing you were tucked safely in your bed and not riding back in the night."

"Don't worry for me." Jim lifted his hand toward her face. "Besides, how safe you believe you are doesn't matter. I couldn't bear the slightest chance some harm might come to you. Not when being beside you could make a difference." Too many years alone made him uncertain. His fingers hesitated to touch her cheek.

Alyse captured his hand. "How do I know you, Jimmy Leigh?" She searched his face in the shadows. "I can't shake this feeling of familiarity." She scoffed softly. "Perhaps I sound like a confused schoolgirl, but there's something here, just beyond my senses." She tipped her head to the side. "It makes me wonder if we've met before. But that's absurd. Isn't it?"

Jim caught his breath as she caressed his palm with her tender cheek. Her eyes shone in the semi-darkness, curious and alive. Watchful.

How long have I waited to find her? The truth would chase her away in disbelief.

His pulse quickened. "You're beautiful." The tremor in his voice caught him by surprise, and he swallowed. "I can't say why you feel you know me, but I'm forever grateful you do." He lowered his lips to hers.

Her lips were pressed tight and sealed against his.

He straightened and opened his eyes, blinking in confusion at the change in Alyse.

Warm and open a moment before, now her eyes glittered with suspicion and disappointment. Light flared as she called a wisp of a flame to her hand. "Tell me again you know of no reason for my feelings." Her brow rose. Her gaze had become penetrating and cold. "But I warn you, speak only the truth."

What did I do?

"Alyse, I'm sorry." He moved back and shook his head. "I shouldn't have kissed you—"

"This isn't about a kiss. Under any other circumstance, a kiss from you would be welcome."

Such distrust, but for what reason? "I don't understand what you mean."

"Alyse?" Her uncle called from the stable door. "Are you in here? We're ready to go."

"Answer my question, Jim." Her attention never wavered from his face. Her voice soft and urgent, her eyes sparkled in the flame. "Why do I find you so familiar?"

He shook his head. "I can't say."

The flame disappeared, leaving him blind in the sudden darkness.

The scent of flowers departed as she swirled away from him and raced from the stall.

***

Hunter

—

Hunter lay in the bunkhouse, his fingers laced behind his head. At the other end of the long room, two men snored a duet.

The moon had long since set. Beyond the window, the sky held the first gray glimmer of dawn. He sat up and pulled borrowed boots onto his feet.

Outside the back door, he stood motionless in the silence and felt the edge of night. A ghost of a breeze lifted the hair from his neck—the scent of prairie grass, dry and crisp in the chill night air.

Hunter splashed water on his face from the pump and ran a wet hand through his thick black hair. He rounded the bunkhouse and strolled to the empty corral. The house across the yard remained dark. Curtains fluttered from half-open windows. He hooked his boot heel on the lower rung of the split rail and scanned the predawn sky.

How do I trap a demon?

Even if Sam discovered the location of Merril's shaman, there would be no guarantee the man would agree to help them. Without a coven or even a pair, he could not obtain the power to bind a person in place. But it wasn't a person. Only a shell. The demon would ride within. And the shell would be discarded without thought or care by Morago.

You call him by name. Is that power or insolence? the voice asked.

It's knowledge. That I can name him gives me power.

As he can name you.

The slap of the back door brought his head up.

Across the yard walked Cat. The hem of her white dressing gown floated around her ankles. Unbound auburn hair lifted from her neck and danced across her shoulders in the morning breeze.

"Seigneur Dieu, sauvez-moi!"

He tore his gaze away from her voluptuous body and looked at the ground, listening to her approach.

"Good morning." Her voice, soft and sweet. Innocent.

"*Bonjour, mon petit chat,*" his response, little more than a whisper.

"Couldn't sleep?"

"*Non.* Too much on my mind, I'm afraid."

"I understand." She rested her arms on the top rail beside his. "I'd never been so terrified in my life as in that circle with the James family. The insects. The animals. But that was nothing compared to how I felt when I saw you."

"That was not me, *ma chère,* any more than it was me who ran the horse to death or clawed its way across the prairie. That was the demon." He met her gaze. "Like you, I only watched."

"When Jim shot you—shot the demon—I realized I couldn't face a future without you in it." Her voice wavered, and she hung her head.

"*Mon amour,*" Hunter turned to face her and gathered her into his arms, resting his scarred cheek against her soft hair. "And when I saw you in the circle, I knew I would forfeit my life, a thousand times over, to keep you safe from harm."

Cat wrapped her arms around his waist and pressed her lips to his chest through his unbuttoned shirt. "I love you, Alexander Veau." She tipped her head back, and with closed eyes offered her lips.

In the far reaches of his mind, Hunter heard a snicker.

Morago! It can't be.

It's not, the voice assured him. *It's your imagination. Your worst fear speaking. Morago does not remain within you.*

I cannot take that chance. Not with someone so precious.

He held his hand beside Cat's face.

Her eyes opened in confusion.

"The ranch awakens, *mon amour.* I would not have you found in the yard in a *déshabillé.*"

Cat pulled away, clutching her dressing gown tight across her breast. "Of course." Her eyes sought his. "I should return to my room." With quick, graceful steps, she hurried to the back door stoop. She paused and looked back for a moment, then disappeared inside.

Hunter clenched his fist above the rail.

It is more than fear that some vestige of Morago's evil remains hidden in my soul. He spoke to the voice. *You know this.*

But the voice remained silent.

I've misled her and lied to myself for long enough. She needs to understand. A marriage between us would never be allowed.

Nichole stepped from the veranda and waved to Hunter. Her grin wide and eyes creased with delight as she crossed the yard toward him.

And yet, there is evidence to the contrary, the voice whispered.

Chapter 5

Morago

—

The rustle and chirp of a dozen tiny birds brought Morago out of his reverie. A new day had dawned, and with the flutter of wings, an entire flock of sparrows burst from the bush around him. Uncontrolled by the demon inside, the little yellow finch launched skyward, a bright flash of yellow in a sea of gray and brown.

Beneath the birds, the town had already awakened. Horse-drawn wagons rolled up dusty streets, and the call of a steam whistle split the air.

Morago allowed his host to scavenge for a time, pecking at seeds and ripening fruit. After the bird had fed, he imposed his will and directed the finch back to the window ledge at the boarding house.

Inside, June twisted her gray-streaked fawn-colored hair into a bun. She retrieved a brown felt hat decorated with colorful green fringe at the front and a long yellow and green silk scarf tied around the crown to hang down the back.

The bird tapped its beak against the window.

June paused, hatpin in hand. "You came back." She pushed the pin through the side of the hat and wove the needle into her bun. "I suppose you'll want something to eat." The bitter twist to her lips turned her comment into an accusation. A piece of crust from last night's blackberry pie waited on a plate beside the window. She broke off a small piece, raised the sash, and crumbled the crust along the sill.

"There you go. You little beggar." She settled in the rocker, which now sat beside the window, and watched the yellow bird peck at the crumbs. "I'm glad you like that awful pie. I could hardly stomach it myself."

Morago waited for the woman to speak. He could read her thoughts if he so desired, but he enjoyed the anticipation of her bitterness and hatred, the mystery of what malicious word and tone she would use.

She leaned toward the window. "Some of the men at this boarding house whisper of a gambling club in town. They didn't think I could hear, but they go there to drink and meet women." She raised an eyebrow and nodded her head knowingly. "The unsavory kind." Resting back against the chair, she fanned herself with her hanky. "I've been thrown into a den of wickedness by that bitch. A corrupt city, rancid with the reek of animal fornication."

The little bird hopped closer and ruffled its feathers, shaking all over.

June used her handkerchief to dab the perspiration on her upper lip and forehead. "From what I overheard, this town has become the whorehouse of the plains. Lord, help us all! The men who run that gaming house and saloon, they're just as bad as whoremongers. They compete against each other and bribe our public officials. They're all crazed with money and power."

Her eyes opened, and she sat straight. "I'm late." She rose and tucked the hanky into the sleeve of her blouse. "The compensation Mr. Harris gave me won't last more than a month." The woman tucked a stray curl under her hat and stomped to the door. "And here I am, begging for work after how many years with the Harris family?"

The bird fluttered as the door slammed, shaking the windowsill. Instead of resettling, the finch took flight across the city.

***

Jimmy Leigh

—

Jim dismounted in front of the Kiowa Crossing Post Office and draped his reins around the hitching post. "The telegraph office is next to the train depot." He waved south down the street then shaded his eyes and looked up at Sam Kline.

"I'll find it." Sam had remained mounted. "I may be awhile, though. I have several messages to send."

"When you're done, meet me at The Thirsty Mule. We can find a bite to eat and have a drink before we head back." Jim pointed at the restaurant across the street. "I'll buy lunch."

"Sure thing." Sam tugged his reins and directed his borrowed horse toward the train depot and telegraph office.

Inside the post office, Jim scanned the notices tacked on the wall.

The postmaster glanced out the half-door, then turned back to sorting the mail.

Jim pulled a long leather wallet from his vest and withdrew a written notice.

EXPERIENCED WRANGLERS WANTED FOR SWING, FLANK AND DRAG POSITIONS
PAY BASED ON EXPERIENCE—HARRIS-HIGHLANDS RANCH
JIMMY LEIGH, FOREMAN

He hooked the notice on an empty nail, then tipped his hat to the postmaster and headed for The Thirsty Mule.

The darkened restaurant cooled his skin as he entered out of the midday heat. Half-full with lunchtime patrons, Jim stopped at a table in the corner near the door.

"Good afternoon." A young woman in a long brown skirt and apron spoke as she crossed the room. "If you've come for lunch, we're serving butter beans and cornbread today."

"That sounds mighty good." Jim hung his hat on a hook behind the table. "But I'm waiting for a friend. Just bring coffee for now."

The waitress gave Jim a nod and a smile before she moved away.

Jim backed his chair against the wall and considered the other noontime customers. His thoughts were far from roundups and trail drives.

Alyse, my eternal love.

How could she recognize him? She never had before. Throughout their many encounters which spanned centuries, she'd never been so sure she knew him.

And why did she turn away?

At a table beside the long, polished bar, three wranglers enjoyed the beans and cornbread.

Along the far wall, near the back, two men in suits spoke in quiet tones over lunch. The rounded man with a bald head had his back to Jim. Thick white hair brushed the man's shirt collar and rose over his ears to fringe the side of his face.

From Jim's angle, the man resembled Cecil Cobb, the attorney for the Shilo family.

The waitress brought Jim's coffee and set the steaming cup at his elbow.

"Thanks." Jim eyed the hot cup and let the brew cool.

After a few more moments of quiet discussion, the two gentlemen rose, shook hands, and retrieved their hats from the hooks beside their table.

The large man paused when he caught sight of Jim. He waved goodbye to his friend as he headed for Jim's table.

Jim stood and offered his hand. "Mr. Cobb."

"Mr. Leigh. I swear, it's been an age since I've set eyes on you." He took Jim's hand in his sweaty palm. "How's the summer progressing at The Highlands?"

"Fair to middling, I'd say. We're glad to be done with the rain for now. Of course, we'll be wishing for a drop, come August." Jim released the attorney and hooked his thumbs in his belt.

"What brings you this far from home?" Cecil asked.

"I'm looking to hire experienced men for a cattle drive. If you know anyone who might be interested, send them to me at the ranch."

The attorney nodded. "Will do." Then Cecil's smile faded, and he shook his head, waggling his double chin shaved clean between white muttonchop whiskers. "I heard about your neighbor, Kevin Shilo. Rumor says the younger brother, Merril, had a hand in Kevin's death and hasn't been heard from since."

"No sir." Jim shook his head. "That's an ugly rumor and untrue." He ran his hand through his hair. "In fact, Merril was with us at the Harris house in Denver when the messenger brought the news about his brother. We were all shocked and grieved to learn of Kevin's suicide."

"You were with Merril when his brother died?" Cecil leaned forward. "Is he still in Denver? According to Doc Johnson, except for the bodies of Kevin and that woman, The Shilo was deserted."

Jim pressed his lips in distaste at the attorney. "No, sir. Merril's at The High-lands with his wife." He hesitated then added, "Merril and Nichole Harris married in Denver before they returned to her ranch."

"He married the Harris girl? I'm sure I heard Kevin announced his engage-ment to the very same young lady right before his untimely death." Cecil Cobb's brows rose high on his bald scalp. "The Cattlemen's Association is awash with rumors about the Shilo brothers, but this marriage is one I hadn't heard."

Jim narrowed his eyes. "There are rumors, and there are facts, sir. The two should never be confused."

"Quite true. Quite true." He scrubbed a chubby hand across his chins. "Please extend my felicitations to the happy couple." He tapped a meaty finger against his lips and tipped his head. "I suppose your cattle drive will be a joint venture with The Shilo Ranch?"

Jim nodded warily. "It will." He hadn't known Cecil Cobb to be such a gossip. "Both Merril and I will take part in the drive. If you want to stop by, I'm sure Jason would be happy to speak with you."

"Yes. Yes. The young man from Boston." Cecil covered his scalp with his top hat. "Please tell Merril we spoke and remind him I have legal documents in my office which must be signed to claim his inheritance due, ahem... to the most unfortunate of circumstances."

"I'll let Merril and Jason know." Jim nodded farewell and resumed his seat. He sipped his cooled coffee. *Such ugly rumors.*

An hour passed.

The waitress checked with him a half-dozen times.

Where is Sam?

If they left early enough, they'd have time to stop by The Shilo on their way home. Perhaps Alyse would allow him to escort her to dinner at The Highlands. If so, he might manage a brief conversation and try to discover how he'd damaged their budding relationship.

Jim glanced at the door. It wasn't as though the telegraph office was far. The entire town would fit inside two Denver blocks.

He paid a visit to the outhouse and returned to his table, covering his cup when the waitress brought around a fresh pot of hot coffee.

The wranglers beside the bar had left, only to be replaced by a group of four.

Jim sipped his tepid drink.

Maybe I should check on Sam.

He looked up as Sam tossed his hat on the table.

"You can hang your hat." He tipped his head toward the hooks.

"Ah." Sam hung his tan hat beside Jim's and sat across the table. He signaled the waitress.

"What took so long?"

"Everything." Sam unbuttoned his jacket. "I sent an update to my superior on the Peabody and Pierce investigation and informed him of my satisfactory interview with Jason Harris. I let him know I would remain in Colorado for another few weeks."

"I appreciate your staying, especially since Merril and I will be away from the ranch for an unknown length of time." Jim's heart clenched at the thought of leaving Alyse at The Shilo while he managed the cattle drive.

"I don't mind. I can spend more time with Cat. Once I'm back at work, our visits will be fleeting."

The waitress stopped beside their table. "Two daily specials?"

Jim nodded.

"Yes, please," Sam replied. "And I'll have a coffee." He smiled absently at the waitress and turned back to Jim. "I addressed the first telegram to the hotel in Denver. The telegraph office must be near the hotel because their reply came back while I drafted my report to Judge Anders. The hotel manager said he would send Hunter's trunk and personal belongings to the depot in Kiowa Crossing. I checked with the man at the station, and he assured me they would hold the luggage until Hunter retrieves it." He raised an eyebrow. "For a small fee, of course."

"Of course." Jim chuckled.

"I asked the manager of the hotel to advise the livery I would have the wagon and mounts longer than anticipated." He shook his head. "Hunter's horse won't be returned. I didn't mention that."

"Horseflesh ain't cheap."

"No. It isn't."

The waitress brought deep bowls of beans and a plate of square cut cornbread balanced on her wrist. "Anything else?" She eyed Sam curiously and smiled, displaying crooked front teeth.

"No. The meal looks delicious. Thank you." Sam picked up his spoon and began to eat.

The dark-haired waitress shrugged and went to check on the cowboys near the bar.

Jim grinned at Sam's discomfort with the waitress' attention. "Did you send a telegram to the Indian Affairs office?"

"Yes, I did." Sam nodded. "With all the information Merril provided. White Eagle's name, description, known associates, the date Merril last saw him, and the direction they traveled. We can check back at the telegraph office before we return to The Highlands."

Jim had just scraped the last bit of beans from his bowl when the four wranglers stopped at their table.

"The waitress said you were the fella lookin' to hire a few wranglers."

Jim swallowed his bite, brushed the crumbs from his hand to his napkin, then stood and offered his hand. "I am. Jimmy Leigh, Foreman at The Highlands Ranch. And you are?"

"Clement Stoker, but everyone calls me Stoke." He took Jim's hand. "This here's Hays, Riley and Rodriguez." He stepped back and nodded to his friends. "We stopped by the post office 'fore we came in for grub. I'd sure be obliged if you'd consider hiring us for your cattle drive."

"We have a week's worth of roundup at the ranch before we head to Denver. If we can't sell in Denver, we'll head north to Cheyenne. I'll pay a full month's wages even if we sell in Denver two weeks from today." Jim looked the men over. They were a dusty crew, possibly fresh off the trail for another ranch. "Experienced?"

"Yes, sir. Just back from Dale Green's drive to Abilene." Stoke nodded. "I rode swing with Dale's son. Hays and Rodriguez rode flank and Riley is new, so he rides drag."

"But Dale said I did real good." The sunburned young Riley added.

"I know Dale. Riding with him is as much of a recommendation as I need." Jim returned to his seat. "You can follow us back to The Highlands this afternoon or meet me there. Tell Tom I hired you. He'll get you settled in the bunkhouse."

"Thank you. We'll collect our gear and head out."

"Do you need directions?"

"No, sir. We know the way. Thank you, sir." Stoke tipped his hat to Jim and Sam as he led his friends toward the exit. All four men grinned from ear to ear as they left the restaurant.

"That leaves you with how many saddles left to fill?" Sam asked, pushing his empty plate away.

"Two riding drag. If Dale has released his wranglers, they'll probably show up with this bunch at the ranch. Word spreads fast when work is available."

Jim paid their tab as the waitress eyed Sam, then they stepped into the sunshine and walked across the diagonal to the telegraph office.

Three messages were waiting.

An Indian who matched White Eagle's description had been documented at the Spotted Tail Indian Agency near Camp Sheridan, Wyoming. The clerk had only noted it because of White Eagle's advanced age. He was in the company of a middle-aged woman, perhaps a granddaughter or other family member. However, since the camp was in the process of relocating, no further information would be available.

"Not enough to go on, and we're damned lucky to get this much." Sam folded the missive and opened the next.

A short note from Judge Anders approved Sam's leave of absence. He only asked Sam to notify him upon his return to duty.

The third envelope was addressed to Hunter. Sam tucked it into his vest pocket unopened.

"Ready to head back?" Sam asked as they left the telegraph office.

Jim nodded. "I want to stop at The Shilo and see how the training has gone today."

Chapter 6

Morago

—

Morago demanded the finch sit still at the edge of the roof, ignoring its urgent desire to feed. From the brick structure beneath him, lively music spilled into the street each time the door swung open. And it seemed the door was open more often than not. All types of men came and went from the place of business, for what else could it be but a business of sorts?

He skimmed the thoughts of each individual as they paused to speak with the man at the door. Only males sought entrance. All hoped for success at the contests which took place inside. A few of the arrivals asked after a man called Big Buck. Their faces reflected anticipation, but their nerves shrank from the name.

Big Buck. Respect. Fear.

The guard experienced a sense of relief each time he shook his head and proclaimed Big Buck could be found at his brothel, a few blocks over.

Big Buck. Power. Obedience. Master.

The guard's head came up as another man approached from down the block.

"Vasquez." The man on the stoop greeted the thin, dark-skinned newcomer.

"Perry," Vasquez replied. He rested his hands on the gun belt strapped to his hips and grinned at Perry from the street. "Mr. Buckner wishes to speak with you, amigo." Vasquez's fine-tooled pointed-toe boots shone in the afternoon sun. "I'll warm your seat while you're away." His lips drew back from white teeth that held a toothpick in a mocking smile.

"Did he say what he wants?" Perry rose from the stool and stepped from the boardwalk into the street.

Vasquez chuckled as he brushed past Perry. "No. Mr. Buckner does not tell Vasquez his mind." He lowered himself to the stool and stretched out long legs. "But I would not keep him waiting if I were you."

Curious to see Mr. Buckner—*Big Buck*—Morago passed control of the bird to one of his minions with terse instructions.

Allow the little bird to feed and sleep. You won't like what I do if the animal perishes.

Stay close to June. Report to me all she says and does.

I'll be watching.

With a brush of his regard, Morago slipped inside Perry's dread-filled mind.

***

Nichole Harris-Shilo

—

Nichole twirled the bright yellow parasol she rested across her shoulder, glad she'd taken the delicate umbrella from the stand when they'd left for The Shilo this morning.

Hunter carried chairs from the dining room to the front porch, placing the seats so the three observers could watch the James family work in comfort.

Cat pulled her skirt out of the way and seated herself on the far side of Hunter.

Hunter spun his chair around, crossing his arms on the backrest, his attention on the James family.

Voices from the corral drifted to them sporadically as the James brothers taught their nieces the finer points of *twyning* in the corral.

As Nichole settled in her chair, she glanced past Hunter and studied Courtney's distant ancestor, Catherine Kline.

She's so elegant.

Cat's raspberry-colored gown, only slightly rumpled from the trunk, stood in stark contrast to Nichole's simple black divided riding skirt and boots.

Even her parasol matches her outfit.

Beside her, Hunter rolled his shoulders uncomfortably. Merril's clothes didn't quite fit the dark-haired man. Although much the same height as Nichole's husband, Hunter's broad chest stretched the seams of his borrowed shirt. The white material pulled taut across his back and refused to stay buttoned. His tanned, hairless chest glistened in the afternoon sunlight.

Nichole stole a glimpse at Hunter's muscular pecs, then lifted her attention at the same moment as Cat. Their gazes met. Nichole wiggled her eyebrows playfully, but Cat turned her face toward the yard. A rosy blush stained her cheeks.

Inside the corral, Bernard and Bayard, both wearing their bowler hats, demonstrated how to *twyne* their minds and magic to increase the power of their spells.

Amy reached out a hand, placed it on Bernard's shoulder and closed her eyes.

Alyse crossed her arms and looked toward the road, visibly frustrated with the exercise.

Both women wore wide-brimmed straw hats to keep the sun from their faces. Alyse dressed in her sturdy dark skirt and boots, while Amy wore a bright floral day dress with a small bustle. Only their hats and faces matched.

The brothers raised their hands in unison, and a small dust devil spun from the dry soil into a twirling column and shot into the sky.

"I don't understand the problem." Hunter pointed at the James family. "What are they trying to achieve?"

"Amy and Alyse have only *twyned* a few times," Nichole explained to Hunter. "Since they didn't grow up together, learning this skill has proved troublesome."

"Is *twyning* different than pairing or working with a coven?" Cat asked and lifted her chin at Hunter's sudden regard. "Several girls at school play at magic. They often speak of casting in pairs and attending secret meetings with their coven."

Hunter stared at Cat for a moment, his brow furrowed. Finally, he shrugged. "I hope your friends take care. Magic such as this," he tipped his head at the corral, "is not a game. However, their elemental magic is vastly different from mine—from ours." He glanced at Nichole and shook his head. "Those of us who serve the spirits, or *sèvitè,* work with others like ourselves to accomplish specific goals." He gestured to the yard. "Where they manipulate elements, we interact with the spirit world. Our means and goals are dissimilar. For us, working with another requires cooperation and agreement about what we wish to accomplish."

"*Twyning* must be a twin thing." Nichole turned back to the witches and the large dust spiral. "Amy and Alyse don't *twyne* with their uncles. It's as you say, they discuss what to do and then work together."

Hunter nodded. "And you don't know how you assist them?"

Nichole placed her hand on Hunter's warm skin beneath his rolled-up sleeve. "When I touch two of them, I must serve as a conduit of sorts. Amy could see how her uncles cast the quicksand spell, remember? When I bridge between Amy and Alyse, it helps them connect and sustain their *twyne.*"

"Yes, but how do they connect?"

"Not sure." Nichole's eyes widened, and she shrugged. "Honest. I feel and see nothing."

"Show me again." Hunter came to his feet and offered Nichole his hand, automatically tucking her fingers around his arm. "Cat, would you care to join us?" He held out his free hand.

Cat smiled but shook her head. "I'm afraid I would be of little use with this." She took his outstretched hand and rose to her feet, squeezing his fingertips. "I'd serve better in the kitchen. I'll put together some refreshments with the supplies we brought." She dropped her hand to straighten the fabric of her skirt. "They can't continue as they are in the hot sun without something cool to drink, magical or not."

Hunter tipped his head to Cat. "As you wish, *ma chère.*" Straight white teeth flashed in the sun as he stepped from the porch, Nichole at his side. "Let us see if we can learn how to work with these elemental witches."

"Don't you need another, like us, for your plan?"

"That's true, *fillette,* but we may have only those we see here."

"I'm sorry, but I don't understand how gifts, such as ours, will be of any real help." She pointed at Alyse who lobbed a fireball at Bayard from across the pen. "They're the ones with the real power."

Hunter stopped at the gate and stared down at Nichole, his brows drawn. "Your father was not there to teach you the depth or range of our magic, correct?"

"Courtney's, you mean? No. He never got the chance. He died when I—when she was very young, remember? She watched his TV show on DVD, of course, read his journal, and searched his data files. As far as I could tell, he only spoke with spirits. Like you, he could locate the living. He worked with federal and state authorities to find missing people, mostly children."

Hunter's brow rose as she spoke. He nodded at the mention of missing children. "Yes, there is all of that, but there is more, *ma chère,* much more. If his journal did not touch on the darker aspect of our gifts, perhaps he was unaware of its existence." In a quiet tone, he murmured, "There are many things I wish I did not know."

"The darker gifts are the ones you'll use against the demon?" Nichole matched his whisper. They had stopped walking and spoke beside the open gate.

"I fear it may be necessary."

"Will you teach me?"

Blue eyes, a shade lighter than his pupils, studied her. His head moved slightly as though to say no, then he shrugged. "You may learn by observation. I won't hide what I intend, but to teach another to open their soul to the dark *loa,* especially a child of mine, or nearly so—that, I will not do."

A shout from the corral brought their heads up.

Beyond the storage buildings, a cloud of dust rose along the road to Kiowa Crossing.

"Riders are coming in," Hunter murmured as he straightened and faced the road.

Chapter 7

Morago

—

Perry entered Big Buck's bordello and waited in the parlor with the unoccupied women for Buck to come downstairs.

Morago rode unobtrusively behind Perry's awareness, struggling to understand the reason for his host's sexual stimulation as he spoke with the scantily clad women.

The women on each side of him stroked his chest and smiled, suggesting he take them upstairs for a ride.

Cigar smoke hung heavy above several red velvet settees, lending its sharp scent to the women's floral perfumes. Railed staircases followed the sidewalls to the second floor. Perry recalled the small private bedrooms up those stairs where the working girls plied their trade. A dark mahogany bar ran the length of the back wall in front of a smoke-blackened mirror. To the right side of the bar was a closed door.

A dark-skinned, bare-breasted beauty sauntered over to Perry, raised his palm and placed it over her breast. "I like you, mister. I bet I could make you like me, all night long." She flicked her eyes at the stairs. "For two dollars, you can do anything you want. Take me any way you like." She licked her lips and brushed her pebble-hard nipple against Perry's palm.

A rush of blood shot through Perry's cock, engorging it tight against his denim trousers. "Ah, hell Violet, what are you playin' at? You know I'm here to see Buck."

"He's busy upstairs. We could be busy too." Violet pressed her hand between Perry's legs and chuckled deep in her throat as she stroked his erection with a firm experienced hand. "I feel how much you want me." She ran her tongue over her teeth and smiled. "For one dollar I'll suck you dry." She checked the staircase to her right. "We have time."

For a split second, Morago considered jumping to Violet. Her power over Perry, raw and sexual, was beyond his experience.

Perry would do anything, give anything for what Violet offered.

Perry wanted this female. His thoughts filled with their previous encounters. He knew how she tasted, knew her seductive laugh and quick, strong fingers. He remembered her lips, the painted ones above and the hot welcoming ones below. For two dollars, she could make him forget his barren existence.

Morago prepared to jump to the half-naked whore, leaving a minion to ride inside Perry, when a voice rang out from the stairs.

"Take your hand off Perry's cock, Violet, or I'll have you whipped."

Perry's erection withered. His scrotum pulled tight at Buck's sharp tone.

Morago sent a minion into Violet, waiting with avid interest as Big Buck paused at the base of the steps.

Buck nodded to himself as he surveyed the silent room. Tall with a paunch, Randolph Buckner swept long strands of hair across the front of his receding hairline. His smile displayed two missing teeth, a canine on the top right and the lower left incisor. The remainder were stained yellow. His eyes were small and sharp, the color of pale gray pebbles.

The breathless silence at Buck's arrival thrilled Morago. He could taste the metallic tension in the room combined with Perry's acrid stench of fear. With each of Perry's fearful inhalations, the bitter scent of old smoke and Violet's sweet perfume filled Morago with glee.

Here is a human who wields the power I desire.

"If you can keep your prick in your pants long enough, I need you to round up some of the boys. A damned claim jumper opened a pleasure house one block over." He hitched his tan slacks and took a cigar offered by one of the women. "We can't have that, now, can we? Five guns should convince them to move along."

"Yes, sir. Right away." Perry turned to go.

"Aren't you going to ask where the whorehouse is, Perry? I guess you might already know, is that it?"

Perry spun around on his heel. "No, sir. I was going to get the boys, is all." A trickle of warmth ran down Perry's leg and into his boot.

Buck blew a smoke ring at the ceiling. His grin widened as he eyed Perry's crotch.

Perry's dread decided Morago. He assigned a minion to remain with Perry and sprang into Randolph Buckner's mind.

Morago murmured into Buck's brain. *Have Perry bring the gunmen back here for further instruction.*

"All right. Bring the boys back here, and I'll give them further instructions."

"Yes, sir." Perry touched his hat and ran out the door.

***

Alyse James

—

Alyse couldn't concentrate. Her uncles meant well, but a display of their *twyning* proficiency did her and her sister little good. She focused on Amy, willing her mind to make a connection to her twin, but Amy's eyes remained closed, her hand on Bernard's shoulder.

Nothing.

Alyse crossed her arms in frustration and turned her back on her uncles. Instead, she cast her gaze toward the road. Perhaps Amy would discover some trick to help them *twyne* at will, although Alyse doubted it. She had little hope of finding the ability herself.

Thoughts of last night clouded her concentration. The touch of Jim's warm lips pressed against her own. She should have opened up to him. Convinced him to trust her and to tell her the truth, instead of shutting him out in anger.

But my entire life was based on a lie. No more!

Her resolve strengthened. Regardless of her inexplicable and undeniable attraction to the tall, handsome foreman, Jim needed to be honest with her or leave her be.

How can I possibly know a man I've never met?

Her ability to *truth-read* came with a high price, she continued to discover. The cost of knowing those you loved and trusted acted to deceive you.

I won't let anyone betray me again.

She tossed her head in anger, grabbing hold of her straw hat to keep it on her head.

In the distance, dust hung low in the still air. "Riders!" she called over her shoulder.

The dust devil between her uncles collapsed into the ground.

"Do you know who it is?" She asked her sister.

"No," Amy replied. "How would I know?"

"What good is prescience if you can't use it?" Alyse snapped and crossed the corral to the open gate.

"My, aren't we ill-tempered today?" Bayard commented with a grin as she passed him. He lifted his hat and wiped the sweat from his brow with his sleeve. "It's not your sister's fault you're—" The words died in his throat at the look Alyse gave him.

She paused beside Nichole and Hunter outside the pen.

Two men on horseback cut from the main road toward the house.

"It's Sam and your foreman," Hunter commented to Nichole.

Alyse picked the hem of her skirt and ran the distance to the house. She reached the porch as Cat stepped outside with a tray of refreshments.

"Water or tea?" Cat asked.

"None for me," Alyse replied and entered the shadowed interior of the hallway. To her left, the large library with its forward-facing window afforded a view of the corral and allowed her to watch Sam and Jim dismount. Both men drew their horses to the water trough.

Jim bent to speak with Nichole, and Nichole pointed at the house.

"Damn," Alyse muttered under her breath and left the library. She threw her hat onto the hallway table and hurried into the dining room as she smoothed her hair. Flutters rose from her stomach to her chest, and she gripped the edge of the table as the floorboards in the entryway creaked.

"Alyse?"

Her throat tightened at his voice, and she swallowed before she spoke. "I'm in here."

The tap of approaching boots on the hardwood floor made her catch her breath. She closed her eyes.

"I'd say I'm sorry again if that would help." His deep voice held a familiar tenderness.

Why?

Anger flared. "I can't abide liars, Mr. Leigh. Even when the falsehood is told to spare my feelings." She turned, and her sight climbed from the small indentation that peeked from beneath his silk neckerchief to his dark eyes. She lifted her chin to firm her resolve. "My sister and parents were kept from me by a lie. One told to save Amy and me from the very situation we find ourselves in now." Her lips trembled, and she tore her gaze away from his. "My uncles and grandmother knew, of course, and I never doubted their honesty. I never thought they would lie to me or that it would be necessary to truth-read them." She brushed a tear with the heel of her hand and met Jim's stare. "But I could have discovered their duplicity at any time I desired. Much like Amy's prescience, truth-reading is a gift bestowed on few. My family's dishonesty, however well-intentioned, has apparently made me skeptical of the seemingly honest and easy words of strangers."

Jim's brows drew together as she spoke. He reached out a hand to her in sympathy, but Alyse moved back.

"No. I want to confess and ask your forgiveness for reading you last night. This ability is intrusive. In all honesty, it breaks my heart. I'm sure you have excellent reasons for your deception, whatever those may be. I have no right to ask."

She caught her breath, raised her chin, and waited until the quiver in her lips stilled. "However, Mr. Leigh, I do know you lied to me." Her attempt at laughter fell short and became a hoarse scoff. "Over something I never expected you to answer. A rhetorical question. A query brought on by my inexplicable feelings for a man I hardly know." Her words trailed off, and she inhaled deeply, holding her breath with eyes closed. "However, I cannot, will not, be deceived. I find I am unable to ignore your dishonesty, now that I know. That being the case—"

"Alyse."

Interrupted by his low, steady voice, she opened her eyes and stared at him, willing herself not to cry.

"I lied because I thought you wouldn't believe me. You never have before. How could you?"

"How can I not believe you? I'll recognize honesty."

He gripped her upper arms gently, and she allowed his touch. He leaned close and searched her eyes. "Read me now and recognize the truth." His grip tightened. "I have loved you for a millennium. No—two. Each time we find each other, it's a reunion of our souls. The pounding of my heart, the yearning in my being, overwhelms me. And still, my love for you grows stronger with each passing lifetime."

"Lifetime?" She pulled her head back in confusion and searched his eyes. The pincushion feel of a lie was absent from her heart. But the truth lay beyond her understanding.

"Yes. Each lifetime." He wrapped her in his arms and held her gently to his chest. "That is why you feel as though you know me. You do. There sometimes remains a distant feeling of recognition. A familiar affection. In other lives, there is no recognition at all. But you've never been able to believe our truth, so I've learned to hold that knowledge silently in my heart."

"But you remember?" Again, she pulled her head back and studied his face. "How?"

"I remember everything." He nodded.

Footsteps at the front entry continued down the hall toward the dining room.

Alyse pulled away from Jim.

He dropped his arms. "I'll tell you everything, from the beginning, but a conversation like that will take some time and require privacy."

Chapter 8

Hunter

—

"What did you find out?" Hunter followed Jim and Sam to the water trough.

"Several things." Sam loosened the girth on the saddle. "White Eagle may have been at the Spotted Tail Indian Agency in Wyoming. But Camp Sheridan is in the process of relocating. They have no further information on his whereabouts."

"That does us precious little good."

"I know, I know. The Colonel promised to send word if they find him." He rested his elbow on the saddle. "I do have some good news. The hotel agreed to pack your things and send your trunk to the depot in Kiowa Crossing. I spoke with the station master and told him it was coming. He'll hold it for you. We can pick it up when we check back with the telegraph office."

"Good. I dislike wearing borrowed clothes."

Sam laughed and poked Hunter's chest through the gap in his shirt. "You could try something of mine, but you would have the same problem. Oh! I almost forgot. This came for you from the Marshal's office." Sam withdrew a folded telegram from his pocket.

"Thank you." Hunter tucked the folded missive into the inside pocket of his borrowed jacket.

"You're not going to read it?" Sam's eyebrow rose.

"Yes, of course. Later." Hunter turned to Bernard who waited near the water pump listening to their exchange. "Were you able to assist your nieces today?"

Bernard shook his head, casting a glance over his shoulder at Bayard and Amy who remained in the corral talking. "Not as much as I'd like. The girls can *twyne* if pressed by high emotion, but they should be able to twist their magic at will, as easily as shaking hands."

"Nichole and I were coming to offer our aid," Hunter said. "I'd like to see how she acts as a bridge between Amy and Alyse."

Bernard scooped water from the trough and rubbed it between his hands, then wiped the cool moisture on his face and the back of his neck. "Your help is always welcome, Mr. Hunter. However, it may be too soon to press them as hard as I did. Alyse is angry, and Amy frustrated." He flipped up the bowler and cooled his bald crown with a wet hand. "I'm no longer sure it's necessary. After all, they triggered the Prophecy by *twyning*, but the same Prophecy calls for two of their individual skills." Resetting his hat, he watched Amy and Bayard approach. "I may be channeling their focus onto the wrong thing."

"Are you done for the day?" Nichole asked. "If so, I'd like to head home."

"I thought we were staying here tonight?" Bayard stopped beside his brother. "And dine on the gracious gift of food your talented and thoughtful Cookie sent with us."

"Yes." Bernard nodded. "We've intruded on your hospitality far too much. Bay and I will investigate your town and procure supplies tomorrow morning."

"You are always welcome at our table," Nichole assured Bernard. "You're family."

"Speaking of family, where's Alyse?" Amy asked.

"She went in the house when Sam and Jim rode in." Nichole exchanged a significant glance with Amy.

Bayard looked puzzled at the two women. "What am I missing?"

Sam chuckled. "Jim asked where Alyse was as soon as we dismounted. Then followed her inside."

Bayard's eyes widened. "Oh."

"At least she's not upset anymore." A contented smile played across on Amy's lips, and a slight blush rose beneath closed lashes.

"You can sense what she feels?" Bernard's eyes narrowed. "Are you *twyned*?"

"No." Amy shook her head. "Not like you and Uncle Bay *twyne*, and yes I can sense her emotion."

"Can you hear what they're saying?" Bayard asked with an impish grin.

"That would be spying." Amy lifted her lashes and slanted a look at her uncle. "And no. I can't quite make out the details of their conversation." She matched his grin.

"I've got cool water and sugar cookies." Cat waved from the porch then went back inside. Her call drew everyone toward the house.

Hunter had listened to the exchange about *twyning* with interest, but dismay at the news about White Eagle sent his thoughts in another direction.

I can delay no longer. I must prepare. Time is limited, and I need to be at full strength before the demon arrives.

You'll not use Nichole's raw power? the voice queried.

Not unless I'm desperate, and by then it will be too late. The young one is willing, but she is untrained.

Cat, Jim, and Alyse joined the group on the porch.

Cat eased between Hunter and Sam and offered Hunter a cookie. "She did a good job with these sugar cookies, but I like my butter cookies better."

"You don't bake cookies," Sam interjected with a chuckle.

"You mean, I don't bake *you* cookies." Cat tossed her head and smiled at Hunter. "I could ask Cookie if she has the ingredients if you like."

Hunter fought the urge to touch Cat's soft cheek. "I would like that, *ma chère*. When there is time."

After refreshments, the men hitched up the wagon and horses and the group from The Highlands headed home. They arrived at the ranch near sunset.

Instead of dining with the Harris family, Hunter excused himself to Nichole and Cat. "Without White Eagle, the work of binding the demon will fall to me alone. I have much to prepare." He lifted Cat's hand and pressed a single kiss to her slender fingers.

"Would you have time to visit with me after dinner?" Cat asked, husky anticipation evident in her hushed voice.

Nichole grinned at them both. "If you'll excuse me, I'll peek in on Cookie and ask if she needs any help." She left them in the short, shadowed corridor between the kitchen and the dining room.

Hunter nodded to Nichole as she disappeared into the kitchen. His gaze slid back to Catherine. "Yes, *mon beau petit chaton*. We shall find time, perhaps later this evening or tomorrow. But for now, I must speak with *Madame* Cookie. There are essential items I need to gather, and she may be of help in this regard." He lifted her hand again, unable to pull his gaze from the raw emotion in her eyes. Had anyone ever looked at him with such tenderness?

My kitten's love shines for all to see.

She is young and innocent, in a way you never were, the voice reminded him. *I would not take that innocence from her.*

She will give it to you, child, as you already know. It is her destiny and your own.

As he straightened, Cat stepped into his arms, tucking herself beneath his borrowed jacket. Head tipped back, she wove her fingers into the hair at the nape of his neck and rose on her toes, pulling his mouth to hers.

At the touch of her lips, his arms tightened across her back, drawing her hard against his chest. His mouth slanted across hers as a small moan escaped her lips.

"... I think she's upstairs with Amy." Jason's voice reached them from the dining room.

"Probably fixing her hair." Sam's reply sounded just beyond the cove where they stood. His broad-shouldered tan jacket darkened the doorway.

As her brother's shadow passed over Cat's face, she opened her eyes and stepped back. "Until later," she whispered, patted her hair and moved from Hunter's embrace and into the dining room.

"*Seigneur Dieu!*" He shook his head to clear his lustful thoughts. Fist balled at his side, he headed in the other direction, away from Cat's distraction.

Cookie ladled garden vegetables into a large bowl, her round face dotted with perspiration from the oven's heat. Her smile welcomed Hunter to her domain. "Dinner is about ready, Mr. Hunter. I was fixin' to call Jeanne and Lawna in from out back to help serve."

"Unfortunately, I have an urgent task and must take my meal later."

"I'll set aside a plate for you." Cookie wiped her hands on her apron and studied the tall Cajun. "Is there anything I can help you with?"

"Actually," Hunter grinned, "I have a list of items I need to find."

"Go on." Cookie waved her hand for him to continue.

"I need a spool of thin black thread. All you can find. And a yard or two of old material or sackcloth." He hesitated, unsure how to make his next request. "I would also ask for a small, personal item of yours. Something of little value you wear or touch daily, like a button or a hairpin."

Cookie's eyes widened in surprise. Without hesitation, she felt along the back of her hair. "A hairpin, you say? Will this do?"

He took the bent metal pin and tucked it into his trouser pocket. "That is perfect, *madame*." He lowered his head in a small bow of thanks then crossed to the back exit. "Oh, and a basket, if you have one. Similar to something you would use to gather herbs from your garden."

The cook reached for a woven basket stored on a high shelf. She held out the basket handle to Hunter. "Anything else?" Her gaze dropped to the scar on his face, then jumped guiltily back to his eyes as her smile faltered.

"I'll need a bottle of good whiskey." He grinned at her expression.

Wide-eyed, Cookie nodded. "I'll ask Mr. Jason for the keys to the liquor cabinet."

"Thank you."

Outside, the dry evening air had cooled. Although the sun had disappeared behind the distant mountains, the sky held enough light to see. Several women chatted near a wooden table; most he had not met. He continued to be surprised at the number of people it took to run a cattle ranch.

Nichole spotted him and stepped away from the women to gather his arm. "Come. Meet the rest of the gang, err... staff." She indicated the teenager. "This is Katy, she helps in the garden and watches Hope-Anne." She indicated the older woman beside Katy. "Her mother, Henny, whom you've met. She's in charge of the garden. She used to work as the cook at my husband's ranch."

Hunter returned their nod of greeting. "*Bonjour.*"

"Jeanne Miller is my personal assistant." She grinned as Jeanne rolled her eyes.

"I'm her maid," Jeanne clarified.

"Jeanne came with me from Boston and is my oldest friend."

"Beside her is the newest addition to our ranch family, Lawna Caine, and her baby Hope-Anne. Her husband, Timothy, works with Tom and Lloyd. He's in Denver now on an errand. We expect him to return home at any time."

Lawna opened the locket that hung from her neck. "This is Timothy." She flicked open the clasp with her thumbnail. "I think Hope-Anne takes after her daddy."

Hunter's heart jumped with dread in recognition of the tiny face in Lawna's locket. The memory of a young man tossed brutally against the bricks of the Harris house in Denver bled across his mind.

I killed this woman's husband—this baby's father.

Not you, child. The demon killed her husband, the voice corrected.

Nichole continued speaking, "Everyone, this is the friend Marshal Kline and Cat had been expecting, Mr. Hunter."

Hunter swallowed the bitter taste in his throat and took the woman's coffee-colored hand. "I'm pleased to meet you." He forced a smile for the lighter skinned baby as she hid her beautiful tiny face against her mother's dark neck, only to peek back and smile at Hunter.

"Hope-Anne's flirtin' with you, Mr. Hunter," Lawna said, then handed the baby to Katy. "I'm off to set the table before Miss Cookie comes looking for me. You'll put the baby to bed for me?"

"Yes ma'am," Katy replied settling the toddler on her hip. She waved at the group and carried the baby toward one of the bunkhouses.

Henny followed close behind her daughter.

"I'll go with you, Lawna." Jeanne said. "A pleasure to meet you, Mr. Hunter."

"*Mesdames.*" Hunter nodded as the two friends departed.

"What's the basket for?" Nichole asked.

Hunter struggled to compose his thoughts. "To gather herbs and grasses, components for the spells I intend to call. One will secure your loved ones, and the other will bind the demon so the witches may complete their prophecy." He looked over her clothing and her long blonde hair. "I also need personal items from each member of your family and staff. Nothing expensive, but it will be most effective if worn on their person like a button or an earring." He pulled the hairpin from his pocket and held it for her to see. "This is a perfect item. A pin from Cookie's hair—small, personal, and worn close to her body." He returned the hairpin to his pocket. "A locket of hair—"

"You're making individual wards?"

"Yes. More or less." Hunter brows rose. "You're very perceptive."

"Bayard warded the ranch houses and outbuildings. You think we'll need more than that?"

"I felt Bayard's wards." Hunter nodded. "Good enough for those inside their boundary. But what of the ride between ranches? What of the trips to town? Besides, I fear *Monsieur* Bayard's wards may have a dangerous fault."

"What do you mean?" She studied the side of his face in the darkening twilight. "No one here was harmed by the demon."

Merril's and Jim's voices carried across the yard in the dry air as they returned to the house from the barn for supper.

"The demon never tried to enter I'd wager." Hunter lowered his voice. "I know the wards have a fault for I walked inside both buildings without issue."

Nichole scoffed. "Yeah, but you're not evil."

"Am I not, *fillette*?" He whispered as he walked toward the garden. A young man's terrified eyes played through Hunter's thoughts again. "Are you sure?"

He left before Merril and Jim reached the back yard, escaping through the garden. He paused to pluck several marigold heads and budding lavender stalks. Along the road, he gathered long blades of grass, their stalks feathered with seeds. When it grew too dark to see, Hunter went back to the house.

As promised, Cookie had left a dinner plate warming on the oven top. On the counter beside the stove, he found a bottle of bourbon and a drinking glass. He placed both on top of the greenery in the basket. A quick search of the pantry added a small parcel of cornmeal to his gathered items. Without interrupting the family evening, he slipped back into the night.

He'd never acted as a Voodoo priest or *houngan* to invoke one of the *loa*. To interact with the beings who resided in the space between *Bondye* and man was his mother's and grandmother's providence. A thing he had thought best to avoid.

As a young man, he'd watched his grandmother invoke the spirit while his mother acted as the *loa's chwal* or horse. He'd witnessed the *loa* take possession of his mother, and work through her, increasing her powers in exchange for services and gifts provided. Sometimes for only a taste of a life they could never have. Some *loa* desired dancing, while others requested fine clothing or liquor. Each *loa* had specific taste and requirements for their service.

On one occasion, he'd watched his grandmother attempt to save a woman whose *loa* refused to return to the spirit world. The poor woman had been brought to their house by her friends and followers, seeking the aid of the famed Priestess of New Orleans. Unfortunately, all of his grandmother's efforts failed to save the woman's life, and the spectacle had horrified him.

You were a traumatized child before your grandmother rescued you, the voice whispered. *You didn't understand.*

Hunter nodded. "*Oui.* That much is certainly true."

Years later, as a young adult, he refused to act as the *chwal* for his mother. Refused to allow an inhuman entity to possess his body. His defiance drove another wedge into their already painful relationship.

And now, after surviving Morago's possession, to act as a *chwal* was almost unbearable to even consider.

Except there is no other way.

He would need the *loa's* power to bind Morago.

He'd already decided on one of the *Petro loa*, a powerful spirit, *Carrefour*—Guardian of the Crossroads. He'd invoke Carrefour, ply him with food and liquor, and ask for his support and assistance. He had hoped the shaman friend of Merril's would have agreed to act as the *chwal*, but now Hunter would need to be both the sorcerer and the offering.

You plan to invoke a powerful being, unaided by a houngan or mambo?

I'm open to other suggestions.

Hunter found the road and walked south. When he reached a trail that crossed the main road, he dropped to his haunches and cleared the center section of rocks and debris. He built a small fire, stoking the flame with last year's dry undergrowth from the roadside, then spread the cornmeal on the ground and drew Carrefour's invocation rune.

He removed his shirt and jacket, folding the borrowed items carefully to the side, then poured a half glass of bourbon. He took a mouthful of the fiery liquor, relishing the taste as it burned down his throat. He set the glass beside the basket, then settled the plate of food beside the small flame. When he looked up, a spirit shimmered across the fire from him.

Her hair, bound in an elongated headwrap, lent stature to her thin frame. Ebony skin glistened in the firelight. She wore colorful shells about her neck, wrists, and ankles. Her gentle eyes, edged with crow's-feet, studied Hunter. She acknowledged him with a single slow nod.

Hunter shook his head. "Spirit, you are a long way from home and have chosen a poor time to come calling."

My home is where I choose. I call when and where I will. Her lips never moved though her chin rose a notch and her eyes twinkled. A voice he'd known since childhood spoke to his soul inside his mind. *But you already knew that.*

Hunter froze as his breath hitched. "Who are—who were you?"

Surely, I must seem familiar, more than simply the voice in your head.

"How should I name you?"

In life, I was known as Marguerite Darcentelin Saint-Dominique. Some called me Marguerite, but those closest to me called me Dessa.

Her image was distorted by the heat of the fire. The longer they spoke, the more corporeal she became. Were she to walk, Hunter knew she would leave footprints in the dusty soil.

"And Dessa, who are you to me?" Hunter crouched down to feed more dry grass to the small fire. He looked up at the elderly woman and saw the shadow of his mother's high cheekbones.

"I am your mother's *grand-mère*. Her magic, and her mother's magic, come from me. As does yours." She spoke now, from across the fire. "I will assist in your negotiations with Carrefour."

"I don't believe he will accept you as his *chwal*."

"Nor can I act as one. That is a burden you must bear, although we may be able to lessen the cost somewhat."

"How?"

"By offering him something far more desirable." She nodded to his preparations. "Call him."

Hunter inhaled deeply and let his eyes fall closed. Another deep breath and he spoke the incantation to call down the *loa*, Carrefour. Three times he called to Carrefour, indicating the delicious meal, the bourbon, and then he placed dust-covered hands on his chest, marking himself as the *chwal*.

Proud his voice remained steady, Hunter tossed back another mouthful of bourbon and hissed as the burn at the back of his throat caught him by surprise. When he opened watering eyes, another spirit stood beside Dessa, shimmering in the flame.

The man wore a red cape and held an ornate walking cane. He had a wide stance and carried a top hat by its brim. He stared hard at Hunter, and without breaking eye contact, placed the hat on his head, setting it with a tap of his gloved hand. "Who calls to serve?"

"I do," Hunter replied.

"We offer Carrefour a proposition," Dessa added.

"I've no use for the *Ghede loa*." Carrefour's lip curled at Dessa. "Be gone, wraith."

Dessa faded, then firmed again. "My most humble apologies." She bowed her head to the *Petro loa*. "The man who would serve you is a son from my granddaughter's loins. You know our family well, Dark One. I beg your indulgence to speak."

The loa glared at Dessa, then grinned. "Speak then, elderly apparition, while I enjoy my meal."

Carrefour moved toward Hunter.

A hot tingling spread from Hunter's scalp into his hands and feet. When he blinked again, he stared at the star-filled sky.

Are you back, child?

Hunter eased up to his elbows. He lay in the center of the crossroads, the clean plate and the empty bottle of whiskey by his side. His small fire had burned to ash. The cornmeal scattered as though stomped into the ground.

Or danced upon. Dessa's voice spoke inside his head.

Has Carrefour gone? Did he refuse your proposal?

Au contraire, my son. You serve as his chwal even now, yet by our bargain, you retain your consciousness. But make no mistake, Carrefour dwells inside you. The dark loa has accepted the terms of your service.

Which were?

Dessa remained silent.

A slow panic began to burn in his gut. Hunter surged to his feet, anxiety clawed hard and fast through his chest. His pulse raced. He spun in the crossroads, searching the empty darkness.

"What terms?" Hoarse from the liquor, his voice echoed in the night.

Chapter 9

Morago

—

Randolph Buckner threw down three of a kind—deuces—then pulled the small pot of coins across the table with a chuckle.

Morago had claimed the small room behind the ladies' parlor to discuss a special mission with his new gunmen and allow Buck to show him this game of chance.

A game of skill, Buckner insisted.

Morago bristled at his host's irreverent response but decided to let it go. To share the mind of a man, to witness his skills and learn human ways, challenged his meager patience.

Big Buck had no say in the matter, of course, and hastily acquiesced when shown the ugly and permanent alternative.

I have a keen sense of self-preservation.

You do, indeed.

Around the table, five men tossed down their losing hands.

Morago observed Big Buck shuffle the deck and deal five cards to each of the players seated at the table.

The gamblers studied their new hands as Buck leaned back and reviewed his cards.

Morago contemplated the men seated around the table. His gunmen.

Ten fighters should be enough if they catch the witches by surprise.

And they would be surprised.

"I asked you here to perform a particular job for me."

Five sets of eyes rose from their cards and met Buck's gaze.

"There's a family of ranchers east of Denver. They've displeased me. You boys are going to make them pay."

Murmurs of agreement passed around the table.

Buck picked up a cigar from the tray beside his elbow. "I want the men in this family killed. Massacred." He pulled a lick of flame across the room from the lamp and held it with his fingers as he lit the end of his cigar. He blew a cloud of smoke into the air, crushing the small flame in his fist. "These men are nothing to me. But the women—ah, the women—I need alive." He grinned at the men as he read their thoughts.

Wariness. Fear. Respect.

You're sending these men to their deaths. The woman prisoner in his mind taunted.

Mercenary gunmen, Morago had discovered, were easily purchased. Any fool could own a gun and pull the trigger.

This is a war of attrition I wage against your family, my dear. I find I have an unlimited supply of willing idiots. Can your granddaughters say the same?

One of the new gunmen tossed a coin onto the table. The stench of fear rolled across the table along with his coin. He cleared his throat twice before he could speak. "You—*ahem*—you talkin' about one of them two big ranches a hard day's ride east of town?"

"I am indeed. You're familiar with the area—Merv, is it?"

"Yes, sir. Merv. And I am, familiar that is." He ran his sleeve across the beads of sweat on his forehead. "I wrangled a bit this spring. Heard some rumors when I stopped off in Kiowa Crossing."

"Speak up, son. Tell us what you learned."

"Gossip mostly. I heard the younger Shilo killed his brother, then hitched up with the gal his brother aimed to marry. They say this Shilo's a madman. Might've even killed his own pa."

Buck nodded and considered his cards while Morago glanced through the eyes of Perry and Vince. Perry held three kings. Better than Morago's pair.

"I fold." Perry threw his cards down.

"Fold." Vince followed suit.

Buck stared down the remaining three players until they folded their hands. He pulled the small pile to his side of the table and set aside his cards.

"Well, Merv. Perhaps this time you'll be on the side of justice. If you run into the Shilo brother, put a slug in him for his murdered family." Buck rose from his seat.

"Avail yourself to the ladies tonight, gentlemen. Their fee is on the house." With a thought, he pushed one of his servants into each of the remaining men. "You'll need to be on the road by sunup, and I want each of you to bring along a friend. When you've finished your task at the ranch, return here. The rewards I'll shower on you will surpass your wildest dreams."

The demons that remained inside Morago twittered and screeched for their opportunity to prove their worth.

Silence, servile minions! It will soon be your turn to serve at my pleasure.

As the gunmen left the room, Buck spotted Violet, who waited by the door. He reached down and slipped the buttons on his trousers and grinned at the bare-chested woman. "Show me what you meant when you offered to suck Perry dry."

She dropped to her knees and freed his half erect penis.

As her mouth closed over Buck, Morago experienced his human host's physical pleasure, while at the same time, through his servant inside Violet, Morago delighted in Violet's disgust, degradation, and terror at Buck's possible displeasure.

She gagged when Buck's seed emptied into her mouth.

Morago chuckled as Buck shoved Violet away and buttoned his trousers.

This is the power I've always sought, as well as pleasure I've never known.

When I kill the witches and usurp their power, I shall be forced to return to the coil—The Prophecy fulfilled. Perhaps, if I possess the witches and hold them in thrall, I could remain in the human realm. How much sweeter would my ultimate victory be, a living being of magic and influence. A master of pleasure and pain.

***

Nichole Harris-Shilo

—

Nichole snuggled close to Merril, her head rested on his shoulder, her bare legs entwined with his. Making love with Merril was a joy that never disappointed. His hands were large, warm and thorough.

She smiled to herself as words to an old rock song flowed through her mind. *Merril certainly had an easy touch. Sure and strong. Slow.*

There were a number of things she'd taken for granted as Courtney Veau in her future life. Music, anytime and anywhere. Cell phones. Air travel. *Hot showers.*

But she didn't regret leaving those things behind to return here. The hardships weren't horrific. This life was the normal existence for Nichole, and the rewards left her serene and satisfied.

Merril pushed the hair from his eyes. Perspiration beaded his forehead and chest. He ran his hand down the indentation of her spine. "My love. My darlin'." He rested his other wrist against his forehead and spoke to the ceiling. "I'm not comfortable riding away and leaving you here alone."

Nichole pushed up on her elbow, drawing his emerald gaze to hers.

An oil lamp burned low on her dressing table, the flickering flame enough to highlight their lovemaking. The door of the balcony stood open. An occasional gust of night air blew chill across her damp flesh.

"I won't be alone. You're leaving more people here than you're taking." Her free hand caressed the side of his face. "My concern is for you. Things always happen when we're apart."

"I'll be safe. No need to worry about me." He pulled her head down to his and captured her mouth with his own. He inhaled slightly, locking their lips together. The warm palm of his other hand cradled her breast. His thumb brushed gently across her nipple.

She groaned as his touch elicited a responding pulse low in her belly. Their lips broke their seal as she arched her head back. "Merril, ah... I want to talk before you leave."

"We'll talk later. There's time." His lips fastened around her nipple as he raised her hips and brought her center down on his shaft.

Still wet from their previous intercourse, he slipped inside, filling her more and more with each thrust. She held his shoulders as he lifted and lowered her rump.

His mouth moved to her other breast as his rhythm changed from thrusting to circling. His fingers mirrored the circle on her already sensitive nub with a slow, steady pressure.

Round and round, he stretched her, as the drawing, tingling sensation grew tight inside her. She ground her hips down and pressed herself against his hand as her release came. Gooseflesh rose over her entire body as she climaxed. Her toes curled, and the long golden curls tickled her sensitized back, brushing across her hips. She arched her back one last time, then fell forward into Merril's strong warm hands.

He rolled with her in his arms, never pulling from her body. His mouth captured hers again as his hair curtained their faces and he thrust into her, possessing her as though fearful it might be the last time.

He held her tight, almost crushing her as he found his release. His gasp beside her ear close to a sob. "I love you, Nicki. I love you so very much."

He placed his forehead against hers, then shivered and laughed softly. "I'll be close for a few days while we round up the scattered Shilo stock. I might be able to see you again before we leave." He rolled to his side and pulled the cover over their damp cooling bodies. "Once we start on the trail, it will be a four- or five-day drive to Denver, barring rainstorms or mishaps." He kissed her forehead. "Two days in Denver to sell the stock, if we're lucky. If we have to drive to Cheyenne, I don't know. Maybe Jim can go on without me, and I'll come back here."

"Stay with Jim. He'll need your help. I'll be safe. The James family is staying here while you're gone. Amy's uncles will sleep in the bunkhouse with Hunter, and Alyse will share a room with Cat."

Merril exhaled a chuckle. "Hunter and the James twins. There's a combination for you. When did our life become so strange?"

"When I realized how much I loved you and knew I couldn't live without you." She leaned up and kissed the damp pulse along his neck. "And I agree. These skills are bizarre, but they've allowed me to come back to you. I'll live with all the weird magic as long as you're here."

***

Jimmy Leigh

—

Jim crossed the dining room and rapped his gloved knuckles against the closed office door.

"Come," Jason's voice sounded from within.

Jim opened the door and entered the small office. A dark mahogany desk practically filled the small room. Two guest chairs angled toward each other across from Jason. Along the back wall ran a narrow credenza stacked with ledgers and books. The window to Jim's left overlooked the side yard and corral. Left open, a whispering breeze carried rapidly warming air from the summer morning.

Jim pulled the work gloves from his hands and shoved the leather fingers into his back pocket. His gaze caught on the photographs and framed documents hung on the wall as if seeing them for the first time. They had been placed there by the original owner of The Highlands Ranch, Quincy Harris.

Quincy, Nichole's father, had left Boston with dreams of building a home elegant enough to impress his wife and young daughter. As chance would have it, Quincy had found Jim camped not far from where they would one day erect The Highlands' well-house. Nichole's father had come looking for a place to build his dream house and ranch, and Jim had come looking for *her*.

Jim had been camped on that prairie rise for twenty-five years before Quincy Harris appeared. Waiting. Drawn to that location by a curse he'd endured for nearly two millennia. He thought he'd find Agaria there, or rather, whoever she had been born in this lifetime.

Instead, he'd found only wind and prairie grass for as far as he could see. He remembered trading one of his rifles to a tribe of Arapahoe for an animal skin shelter the first summer he'd arrived. It had been a morning much like this.

Jim ran his hand through his hair, brushing remembrances aside. He slid into the guest chair as he eyed Jason. "I've hired six men and had to turn away three more. I don't want to spend more than two days rounding up the remains of The Shilo herd. After that, we'll be on our way."

Leaving Alyse behind to do his job was one of the hardest things he'd ever had to do. The fact that his role with her had always been one of protector played into his anxiety. Although in this life, Alyse commanded more power than he'd ever seen. She was even stronger than Nescato, the young enchantress who had cast the curse that controlled their lives.

But Alyse remains mortal. If Morago kills her body and traps her soul, will she be forever beyond my reach? Jim shivered, straightening his spine.

"How long will you be away from the ranch?" Jason seemed to read Jim's thoughts as he placed the pen in the crease of his ledger. His light blue eyes studied Jim.

"As short a time as possible. That's what I wanted to ask about." He leaned forward, elbows on thighs, and rubbed his palms together. "Say we drive the cattle to Denver and the yard isn't buying. It's another ten days, more or less, to Cheyenne. We'll need to pen the herd, broker the sale, and then ride back." His hands stilled, and he looked Jason in the eye. "That's just too damn long in my opinion. Anything could happen while we're gone. I know Merril would agree with me." He held up his hand to forestall Jason's comment. "What I'm trying to ask is what our minimum on price per head is? If I find a buyer who'll take the stock off my hands and drive them on to Cheyenne to sell, what do I need to get?"

Jason covered his mouth with the palm of his hand, eyes unfocused as he considered Jim's question "We don't know what the current market price is in Denver, but I could make a guess."

"The men I hired worked for Dale Green on his drive to Ellsworth. They said Dale got close to five dollars per hundredweight."

"That's more than you'll get in Denver." Jason shoved blond curls from his eyes and picked up the pen. "Whatever price you agree to will be up to you and Merril."

"I know, I know. But how much do I need to get to see us through the winter? For both ranches?"

Jason's pen scratched swiftly across the journal page. "Do you think we have a thousand head? Less?"

"Maybe a thousand. The Highlands had over eight hundred. There's no telling how many of the Shilo brand we'll find."

Jason nodded but continued his calculations. "Let's say a thousand head. If you get, say... thirty a piece, plus or minus a few dollars, we'll be fine."

"Understood." Jim rose to leave. "One more thing. Last night I forgot to mention it, but I ran into Cecil Cobb in town yesterday."

"Ah." Jason raised his eyebrows. "Jolly old Cecil. I know Merril still needs to sign paperwork on his inheritance, but I doubt he'll make it to town before you leave."

"I agree. But he was full of ugly rumors about Merril and eager to talk. Even so, I'd wager he still wants to be The Shilo attorney and move all of the Harris holdings into Merril's hands."

"That won't happen." Jason scoffed. "Merril never wanted the ranches, still doesn't, and Nicki isn't likely to let it go." His face grew thoughtful. "However, a married woman owning the property in her name might give Cecil an opening to raise an issue."

"Will you remain the Harris-Shilo's legal counsel?"

"Do you have an issue with that Jim?"

"I never had a problem with you, Jase." Jim grinned. "Well, now that's not entirely true, is it? However, my point is, Cecil won't let the Shilo account go without a fight or at least a few ugly words aimed at you and your cousin. He's already got a bit in his teeth about Merril."

"Words." Jason tossed the pen into the ledger. "The man is nothing if not wordy."

"And a gossip. A vindictive one. He may come calling while we're gone."

"I'll be safe enough from the old attorney." Jason leaned back in the chair. "The James family is staying at The Highlands while you're gone. A move I heartily endorsed."

From the stairs came the echo of feminine voices.

Jim walked to the front door as Nichole and Amy descended the stairs. Both greeted him with a smile.

The passion in his heart for Alyse hadn't changed how he felt about her sister, Amy, Jason's wife.

I love them both, yet Nescato's curse said I could love only one. Only Agaria.

"Jim, I'm glad I've caught you before you head out today. I doubt we will see you again before you return from Denver." Amy stepped from the stairs. Her hands reached to grasp his. "Please be safe." She leaned close and stretched to kiss his cheek.

Jim bent to allow her lips to reach his face. "I will. You'll keep your husband in line while we're gone, I trust."

"I heard that," Jason called through the open office door.

"I'd hoped to find Alyse before we left. Tell her—" Tell her what? Alyse's questions deserved answers, but there never seemed to be enough time for an eternity of explanations.

Amy's gentle smile and sparkling eyes added weight to his already heavy heart.

I'll always love Amy. I can't even try to stop. He glanced over his shoulder at Jason and found him watching from behind steepled fingers.

"Is Merril still outside?" Nichole asked.

Jim released Amy's hands and cleared his throat. "He should be. Merril was helping Henny get settled with the chuck wagon." He followed Nichole out the door, snatching his hat from the peg by the entry.

The sun had warmed the day considerably even in the short time he'd been indoors.

Merril stood beside the covered cook's wagon nodding to Henny as she spoke from the seat. She held the reins of the double team in her hands.

"Oh, Miss Nichole." Henny waved to the approaching group. "Please keep an eye on my Katy. Don't let her get underfoot."

"She's no bother, and you know it," Nichole replied.

Merril hugged Nichole's shoulders and kissed the top of her head. "I'll miss you."

Nichole wrapped her arms around her husband's waist. "I'm beginning to think I should go with you." She tipped her head back. "Bad things happen when we're apart."

He squeezed her to his side and glanced at Jim over her head. "Jim needs my help, and Amy needs yours. We'll be fine. I'll be home before you know it."

Nichole mumbled into his chest, and Merril laughed. "I find that highly improbable." He took the reins of the sorrel beside the chuck wagon in hand. "We'll be camped near The Highlands' branding site while we round up what remains of the Shilo herd, no more than a day or so. I'll sneak back for a visit if I can."

Chapter 10

Nichole Harris-Shilo

—

Lost in thought, Nichole tied a ribbon around her golden curls, picked up the straw sunbonnet from the foot of the bed, and studied the hat in her dressing table mirror.

Good enough.

Jeanne tapped on her door and handed Nichole a note. "This came for you."

Nichole opened the folded missive and glanced around Jeanne into the hall. "Came from who?"

"Bill brought it by the house. Is it bad news?"

Nichole shook her head. "No. Just disappointing." Merril's words were no substitute for his arms. The drive was underway, and he didn't want her to wait in vain. "He won't have the opportunity to visit again. They've already left for Denver."

"I'm sorry, Nicki."

"Not your fault." Nichole shoved the note into her pocket and followed Jeanne from the room. "He'll be back before I know it."

At the base of the stairs, Nichole stopped short.

Hunter sat near the head of the table, in Jim's usual chair, bits of grass, cloth, and thread scattered across the dark mahogany. At his elbow, a tall glass, half-full of Jason's finest bourbon, and a newly opened bottle across from him, in front of Nichole's chair.

"What are you doing?" She approached the far end of the table and stared down at the mess before Hunter.

He didn't acknowledge her. Eyes closed, he wrapped a square of cloth over a rounded wad of grass, marigold heads and lavender buds. He wound the black thread around the material and greenery, twisting the fabric into a bulbous bun on top of thicker blades of grass. Unfamiliar words formed a ritualistic mumble, as though he spoke a forgotten language to the item in his hands.

Finished with the thread, he picked up the tangle of blond tresses Nichole had given him from her brush. He straightened several strands, wrapped their ends around a straight pin, and plunged it into the doll's head. He repeated the process until the top of the figure's head was covered with golden ringlets.

He's making a doll. A fucking voodoo doll—of me.

"A voodoo doll, Xander? Really? I thought you'd do something useful to help us."

"This will help us." He plunged the last bit of hair into the cloth-covered head, took a deep gulp of bourbon from the glass, then held the doll before him, his chant became louder, more forceful.

Across his broad shoulders bled a translucent black flame. The phenomenon blurred the line of the fabric as though vapor rose from his back and down his arms. It flowed across his wrists to the doll, twisting around the small replica of herself.

"Holy shit, dude." Nichole bumped against the wall, unaware she'd backed away from Hunter and the dark flame.

Finished, Hunter set the doll aside and shifted his focus to her. "Why Xander?"

"What?"

"You called me Xander. I've never heard that form of my given name before. Why not Alexander or Alex or even Lex? Why not Hunter, as I prefer?"

"Alexander is too long and formal. Hunter is, well, technically it's your occupation, not your name." She returned to the table and studied his stack of little dolls. They were crude but recognizable representations of the people she knew.

"*Mon Dieu!* If I doubted your lineage before, I no longer have reason to do so. You've convinced me you are descended from Cat."

Nichole opened her mouth to argue—closed it—and pointed at the dolls. "Explain."

"These figures represent the people on your ranch, as well as those, like your husband and foreman, who drive your cattle to market."

"Yeah, I can see that. I know what a voodoo doll is. You stick pins in them to hurt people."

"You are a child who knows nothing of the *mystères*." Hunter slowly rose to his feet. His voice held a different tenor, foreign to his usual soft, smooth pitch. He rested his fists on the table and leaned forward. "You shouldn't speak of things you know nothing about." The dark, agitated vapor swirled around Hunter, giving him the appearance of motion, though he stood completely still.

Nichole's back bumped into the wall again. "What's wrong with you?"

Hunter clenched his jaw and lowered himself back into the chair. "Forgive me for my anger. I act as a *chwal* for Carrefour. He has agreed to increase the efficiency of my spells." The dark vapor lowered to just a hint of dark flame across his shoulders. "His passion, at times, overwhelms me."

Nichole slipped into her chair across from Hunter and moved the bottle of bourbon to one side. "Whose passion? Carrefour's? Who's he? What's a *chwal?*"

Hunter held up his hand to forestall her questions. "A *chwal* is a horse. A person who is ridden. In a traditional ceremony, they serve as a medium through which the *loa* speaks and acts. Carrefour is a powerful *Petro loa*, an entity who dwells in the realm between God and mortals. A *loa* may be petitioned and served, and may, in turn, choose to aid the petitioner."

Nichole shook her head and whispered, "What have you done?"

"Only what is necessary. You assume I act out of carelessness. I assure you, I do not." His thick lashes rose, and he pierced her with his haunted gaze. "As a young man in New Orleans, I watched my *grand-mère* make tiny replicas of the hated Union soldiers who occupied my city. I thought she meant them harm." He made an odd sound that could have been a laugh. "I was young and angry, but she shook her finger at me and told me to sit and calm my temper. 'I shield them,' she said, 'to protect angry young men like yourself.' And she was right. The soldiers would have swept through our city in provoked retribution should any harm have befallen them as they slept."

"How did she protect them?"

Hunter picked up one of the dolls with a small piece of Merril's silk scarf tied around its grassy neck. "She made these. Much better than I have done, I assure you. She dressed them in blue and laid them in small beds. Each night, *grand-mère* and *maman* would cover the sleeping figures with one of her large bowls. Together, they created a magical barrier to keep the soldiers safe from those who meant them harm."

"Is that one Merril?" Nichole pointed to the doll Hunter held in his hand.

"It is." Hunter gave her the small effigy.

Nichole's eyes fluttered closed as a warm sensation tingled her palm. "I can almost feel him."

Hunter plucked up the doll and returned it to his growing collection. "This is not a thing I would have a child of mine learn." His eyes narrowed. "This is more than divining a location of a lost child or conversing with spirits. There is darkness in this work which I would shield you from."

"Good morning, you two," Cat called as she and Alyse rounded the stairs. "Alexander, have you been sitting here all night?"

Down the stairs and into the dining room raced Alyse's two black cats. They puffed and arched their backs at Hunter, then slunk past the table and into the kitchen.

Hunter ignored the animals and rose to his feet as the women approached. He performed a slight bow. "I'm afraid I became engrossed in my labor." He pushed the errant strands of hair out of his face and smiled at Cat. "I trust you slept well?"

Color rose in Cat's cheeks, and she straightened her skirt. "For the most part. I had an unusual dream."

Nichole pressed her lips to stop a grin from spreading and shared a knowing look with Alyse. "I was going to check on breakfast." She stood and pushed her chair back into place beneath the table. "Would you care to join me?"

Alyse stepped around Cat's green satin skirt. "I would. And let's take our plate to the table outside. It looks lovely out there."

"Go on," Cat said. "I'll catch up."

Nichole moved into the servants' passage and whispered to Alyse, "Look at Hunter." She waited as Alyse gazed into the dining room.

Cat had rounded the table to stand beside the dark Cajun.

Hunter lifted her hand.

"What am I looking for?"

"You don't see it?" Nichole asked.

Licks of dark flame danced across his broad shoulders as he pressed his lips to Cat's fingers. When he lifted his head, his gaze slanted to Nichole's.

"Just Hunter and Cat. I think he's drinking already." Alyse moved toward the kitchen. "Maybe Cat will bring him a plate of breakfast if she can tear herself away from his side for long enough."

Nichole watched the dark flame tips ebb and flow in the air around Hunter, then shook her head and followed Alyse down the hall.

***

Hunter

—

"I would ask you to join me, but I've been seated for far too long." Hunter warmed Cat's hand between his palms. "Would you care for a walk before breakfast?"

"That would be delightful."

"You won't be cold, *mon petit chat?*" Hunter plucked his new flat-brimmed black hat from the peg.

"Did you buy that in town?" Cat waited as Hunter opened the door.

"Yes. And new boots." He closed the door behind them, and they strolled toward the road. "It's nice to have my own clothes again, although I do appreciate Merril's charity."

"Nichole said there was no word on Merril's shaman friend."

They walked west along the road. The morning sun at their back magnified the distant mountains through the dry air. The last of winter's snow dotted the highest peaks.

Cat held Hunter's arm. "What will you do?"

He measured his longer pace to her stride. "I shall proceed and make plans to help the James family as best I can."

"You're very noble to set yourself in harm's way to assist strangers."

"Not at all, or rather, I have my own motivation." He paused, choosing his words with care. He needed Cat to understand his reasons. "I know the fate those young women will suffer should they fall to the demon." He tipped his head and caught her gaze with his own. "But I must confess, it would be less than truthful to say I do not seek revenge against the monster, Morago."

After several paces, Cat's unusual silence caught Hunter's attention. He halted and turned toward the auburn-haired beauty on his arm. Her flushed face and tear-filled eyes tore at his heart. "Do not fear for me, *ma bien-aimée*." He ran his hands up and down the cold skin above her elbow. "We should return to the house. It is too early to be out without a shawl. You'll catch a chill."

"No, wait." Cat held her ground when he turned back toward the house. "I—I have something of yours." From the deep pocket in her skirt, she pulled a folded telegram and held it out to him. The letter trembled in her hand.

Sam had given him the message several days ago, after his first trip to Kiowa Crossing.

"Thank you, *mon beau chaton*. I must have left it in the borrowed jacket."

Cat's eyes brightened for a moment. Then she lowered her head. "No. You didn't." She swallowed and turned away as tears threatened to spill from her eyes. "I—um—took it from your pocket."

"You did?" Hunter looked from Cat's delicate hand holding telegram to her flaming face. "When? Why?"

"At The Shilo. Sam must have just given it to you. I didn't know what it was, or that it was important." She brushed at her tears. "Here. Take it. I'm ashamed, and I apologize for ever thinking myself so clever. Once I realized what it was, I couldn't find the right moment to return it to you."

Hunter took the folded paper from her hand. "What does it say?"

"You didn't read it?" Surprise lifted Cat's eyebrows.

"No." He gave a soft laugh. "I've had other things on my mind." Hunter opened the missive and read the words twice. The U.S. Marshal's office formally extended to him the opportunity for employment. There were several district openings that Hunter might find interest in. He was to contact Judge Anders at his earliest opportunity. He crumpled the offer and shoved it angrily into his pocket. "It doesn't matter now."

"I'm sorry I took it, and I'm sorry I read it, but don't let my foolish immaturity make you pass on such a wonderful opportunity."

"I applied for this position because of you, because of what I hoped our future could be like, together."

"And now I've ruined it."

"You?" Hunter shook his head. "A child's prank, even one so skillfully maneuvered, would never change my heart. Do not blame yourself. The fault lies with me."

Cat brushed a tear from her cheek and sniffed. "What do you mean the fault is yours?"

"I was recently reminded of my ancestry. My father, Phillippe Étienne Corriveau, is half *Chitimacha* Indian and half French. I was born out of wedlock and left on his doorstep not long after my birth. My first years were spent in his slave quarters, or in *Mémé* Corriveau's small house on his property. At least until my mother's mother learned of me. She came when I was five and took me away."

"How dreadful. Who's your mother?"

"No one I care to speak of. My *grand-mère* raised me until I left home." He shrugged then grasped both her hands. "I took the name Veau as my own. A portion of both my parents' names. It represents my heritage but rejects it as well." He kissed her hands and stared into her beautiful brown eyes. "Cat, nothing you've done can ever change the way I feel about you, *ma bien-aimée*, but you deserve better than a bastard mongrel *bokor*."

Cat stared at Hunter, wide-eyed. Her spiky lashes black against her pale skin. "I know your father, or my parents did. He was widowed without children."

"I was born before he married. So now you understand why a marriage between us could never be. Your brother would never allow it."

"I know nothing of the sort." Cat unbuttoned the single clasped button on his jacket and slipped inside, wrapping her arms around his waist. "You're so warm. I should have brought a shawl."

Surprised, Hunter pulled her close and kissed her head. The silent *loa* riding inside him stirred. "We should return to the house."

"Not before I tell you, and make you understand. I don't care who your parents are. My parents are dead, and Sam, well, I know he cares for me, but he doesn't know me. Not like you do." She stretched up and pressed her lips to his.

Unable to stop himself, he pulled Cat tight to his chest. He slanted his mouth across hers, caressing her tongue with his own.

A deep guttural chuckle whispered at the back of Hunter's mind.

Carrefour!

Hunter pushed Cat away and held her at arm's length. "My apologies, *mon beau chaton*. We should return to the house."

Cat blinked at Hunter, her lips puffy and swollen from his kiss. "What?"

He faced her toward the house, barely visible above the rise of the road, his arm wrapped around her shoulders. "The house will be warm. We can have breakfast and ask Cookie to heat water for tea."

"Hunter, I'm not that cold—" she began to protest, then paused, her steps stumbled to a stop.

Hunter slowed beside her and surveyed the two-wheeled carriage in the yard. "It appears we have a guest."

Chapter 11

Nichole Harris-Shilo

—

Nichole settled Hope-Anne on Katy's lap and gathered the breakfast dishes from the picnic table. "Why don't you take the baby to the blanket and play for a little while? She'll need her morning nap soon." Movement near the stable drew Nichole's attention, and she paused in her work.

Sam and Lloyd disappeared into the shadowy recesses of the barn as Jason waved farewell to the two men, then crossed the yard toward the house.

Nichole waited for Jason at the back door stoop. "You're out and about early. How's Lloyd doing with all the magic?"

Jason opened the door, and Nichole ducked underneath his arm and passed into the kitchen. "Fine, I think. He misses Tom and remains suspicious of Bernard and Bayard. Sam is working to convince him Amy's uncles are good men, even though they have an unusual skill set."

Cookie lifted the plates from Nichole's hands as she reached the sink. "Here now, you'll dirty your nice outfit."

"Thanks, Cookie." Nichole wiped her hands on a dish towel and followed Jason into the dining room.

Jason had stopped just past the opening and stared down at the table. Hunter's grass dolls, thread, and small personal items lay scattered over a good third of the table, not to mention an open bottle of Jason's best bourbon. "Is this mess necessary?" He held out his hand to the evidence and raised a brow at his cousin.

"I don't know." Nichole shrugged. "It's a different type of sorcery than Amy's."

"I'm not used to any of this—mumbo-jumbo. To be honest." He edged the basket half-full of grass stalks on the floor away from the office door with his toe. "I understand why Lloyd's uncomfortable."

The sound of a carriage turning into the yard carried through the front window.

"Are we expecting company?" Nichole questioned.

Jason reached into the office and pulled his revolver from the gun belt hung beside the door. "No." He quickly checked the load, then closed the chamber and nodded to Nichole. "Not that I know of."

She crossed the parlor and pushed the curtain to the side. "Cecil Cobb." She glanced back at Jason. "He doesn't look happy."

"Cecil has stomach problems," Jason quipped, returning the gun to its holster. "He never looks happy."

"Hmm." Nichole opened the front door before Attorney Cobb could knock. "Mr. Cobb. What a pleasant surprise. Do come in."

"Thank you." The heavyset man dipped his head to Nichole. "It's Mrs. Shilo now I understand. Congratulations on your nuptials." He spotted Jason in the office doorway and bobbed his head again, setting his double chins bouncing. He wore an expensive wool suit and polished boots. Considering the time of day, he must have set out from The Crossing at dawn. "Mr. Harris." He brushed past Nichole, handing her the top hat from his bald head. "It's good to see you again. Would Merril be available to meet with me now?"

Nichole tossed his hat onto the table and threw up her hands behind Cobb's back.

What the hell?

The misogynist attorney dismissed her as though she were irrelevant.

I'm not offering him any of Cookie's cakes.

"Unfortunately, Merril is away. Perhaps there's something I could assist you with?" A swift glance at Nichole froze the smile on Jason's face. He narrowed his eyes at her and gave a slight shake of his head as he gestured for the attorney to enter the office.

"Oh, my. This is most unfortunate." Cobb's chins waggled his displeasure. "I certainly hope he hasn't decided to liquidate any of the Shilo assets, and by that, I mean the Shilo cattle."

Nichole followed Cobb into the office.

Jason indicated the furthest guest chair to the attorney as he rounded the desk. "He's occupied with the Highlands-Shilo cattle drive along with our foreman, Jimmy Leigh." Jason took his seat. "I don't expect them to return for several more days."

"Are Shilo cattle included in this drive and sale?" Cobb leaned forward, resting one arm on the desk, showing his back to Nichole.

"What's left of them." Nichole seated herself and addressed the shiny spot on the back of the attorney's head. "There was an unfortunate stampede. Many of the Shilo cattle were killed or injured too severely to drive to the stockyard. Most of the head my husband will sell is Highlands' cattle."

Cobb's back stiffened when Nichole spoke. He sucked air between pursed lips as he peered at her over his shoulder. "Where might I view the remains of this so-called stampede? An estimate must be made for loss of inventory. Any proceeds from the sale of the Shilo cattle will be placed in probate until the matter and manner of Kevin's death can be ascertained."

Cobb looked Nichole up and down then lifted one eyebrow as though daring her to speak. His narrowed gaze switched to Jason. "As I'm sure you know, Merril has been sought for an attempt on his brother's life a few weeks ago." He cleared his throat and raised his voice. "Right before Kevin announced his engagement to your cousin at your yearly celebration. As far as I know, Merril hasn't been heard from since. Sheriff Wheeler will need to clear him of any wrongdoing before I can certify his inheritance."

"That is such bullshit!" Nichole slid forward to the edge of her seat.

"Mr. Cobb, I was one of the last people to speak with Kevin Shilo," Jason spoke over his cousin.

"Doc Johnson ruled Kevin's death a suicide," Nichole added. "Why are you doing this?"

"You may have been one of the last people to see Kevin alive, but the whereabouts of Merril Shilo after that time remains unknown. Several former employees of The Shilo Ranch have come forward to state their suspicion regarding Kevin's death, along with that of the father's mistress. Merril was not on good terms with her either, if I remember correctly."

"When I left Kevin, he was stinking drunk and angry," Jason argued. "Nichole had broken off their engagement in no uncertain terms. He hadn't been sober or slept for at least twenty-four hours. Merril and Tom Baker, our liveryman, caught up with me on their way to Denver."

"So you're unsure where Merril may have been before you met him on the road several hours after you left Kevin Shilo's company."

"He was with Tom Baker," Jason insisted.

"What's your point, Cobb?" Nichole's face and chest radiated heat. Despite her best attempt to modulate her voice, the words she spoke to the attorney trembled with hostility.

"You could be implicated as well, Mrs. Shilo." Cobb smiled, ever so slightly. "An investigation is in order."

"If this is true—" Jason's crystal blue eyes darkened to the color of steel and raised a single finger of caution at Nichole to still her protest.

"It is, I assure you." Cobb interrupted.

Jason cleared his throat and turned his angry glare on the attorney. "If what you say is true, then why hasn't Sheriff Wheeler served a warrant on Merril or Nichole?"

"No one knew where Merril Shilo had gone. Until I spoke with your foreman in town a few days ago, everyone assumed he had departed for parts unknown."

Nichole spoke through clenched her teeth, "Reverend Michael knew we were home."

"Excuse me?" Cobb turned and met her gaze. "Reverend Michael no longer resides in Kiowa Crossing. His testimony will be difficult for you to obtain."

The front door opened and Nichole turned in her chair and looked across the dining room to the entrance.

Hunter followed Catherine into the house and closed the door. He leaned against it, his gaze fixed on Cat as she stalked away.

Cat passed the table with short, sharp steps and disappeared into the passage to the kitchen.

Hunter removed his hat with slow deliberation, as though lost in thought. He stared at his gambler's hat for several moments before he hooked the black, flat-rimmed headpiece on a peg beside the door. The shadowy tips of dark flame pulled and danced across his broad shoulders.

Jason and Cecil Cobb continued to argue about the Highlands' property, the Harris family's possible collusion in Kevin's death and the cattle sale of both herds.

"Should Merril be found culpable in the murder of his brother, he would be ineligible to inherit Kevin's share of the ranch. What's more, the property he has gained by marriage to your cousin would be seized and sold at public auction."

"Now see here," Jason's voice rose with ire. "You're making a hell of a lot of unfounded accusations. Perhaps you should find your way to the door before I throw you out, Mr. Cobb."

Hunter glanced up as Amy and Jeanne descended the stairs, their arms full of bedding.

"Oh good," Amy called to Hunter. "I wanted to ask you about your, um ... craft project—"

The sharp crack of a gun echoed across the yard and in through the open office window.

All conversation ceased.

Nichole tore her gaze from Hunter's flames and asked Jason, "Was that a gunshot?"

Jason rose as two retorts sounded in rapid succession. Then everyone was in motion.

"Back upstairs," Hunter shouted and pointed toward the second floor.

Amy and Jeanne disappeared up the stairs without argument.

Jason opened the desk drawer and withdrew a pistol. "Are you armed?" he asked the visiting attorney.

Cecil Cobb's face had turned pasty white. His chins waggled as he vigorously shook his head.

"Of course not."

"Hunter, do you have your gun?" Jason called across the dining room.

"Only my knives. The guns are beneath my bunk."

Nichole peeked cautiously out the office window.

A man lay unmoving near the stable. The huge double doors were blocked open, but the interior remained shadowed.

"There's a man down between the barn and the corral," she called over her shoulder. The flash of gunfire sparked like firecrackers in the barn, and for a moment she could see faces. "Sam and Lloyd are pinned inside. Another gunman is behind the corral gate." A flash of movement between the bunkhouse and the barn caught her eye. "More are coming around the outbuildings."

Jason skirted past her and pulled his holster from the wall. "Hunter. Here." He slid the revolver across the table and freed his Colt from its holster, dropping the belt on the floor. "The shotgun over the mantel is loaded."

From the back of the house, the shouts and screams of women channeled down the hallway.

Cookie barreled into the dining room from the kitchen passage. "They're shooting at Lloyd!" she yelled and rested both hands on her heaving chest.

Behind her came Lawna with Hope-Anne in her arms.

"Stay in the hallway, Cookie," Jason directed. "Keep the children with you—"

A loud crack sounded at the front door as the latch absorbed a blow from outside.

Hunter's coat flared when he spun to face the door.

The flame tips which danced across his shoulders pulled away from Hunter, taking the form of a man and solidified.

Carrefour!

The specter wore a caped coat and top hat angled forward on his head. He captured his walking cane beneath one arm and rubbed his hands together in apparent anticipation.

Nichole blinked at the *loa*, but there wasn't time to question Hunter about his presence.

Another blow and the wood around the latch splintered, and the door swung wide. The gunman outside the opening held a pistol in each hand. A maniacal grin split his face while a bulging shade rode on his back near his neck.

The last time Nichole had seen something like this, the shadowy hump had been attached to the back of the Shilo cattle, directing the stampede. "He's possessed—"

The gunman stepped over the threshold, warded by Bayard's protective satchel above the door, and convulsed. Smoke spilled from burned-out eyes, and he sank to his knees. His stomach emptied on the floor as he toppled forward into the mess.

Stripped of its host, the minor demon leapt free.

In an instant, Carrefour's gloved hand snatched the entity from the air.

The demon's lumpy shape thrashed back and forth in an attempt to escape.

Carrefour rolled the gibbous shade between his hands like cookie dough, then popped the tiny devil in his mouth and swallowed. He threw his arms wide, cane in hand and laughed with delight.

Before the man on the floor ceased to convulse, a lanky, whiskered gunman, unencumbered by one of Morago's demon horde, rushed through the door, shooting wildly.

Hunter's boot knife took him in the throat, silencing his weapon. He toppled face first into the pool of vomit beside the dead man.

Shattered glass sprayed into the dining room as bullets flew through the windows from the side yard.

Jason shoved Nichole's head down and propelled her toward the servants' hallway. As soon as she was behind him, Jason backed into the cased opening and lowered to his haunches, gun held before him. "Stay down," he instructed unnecessarily.

"Can you see Hunter?" Nichole gasped.

"No." Jason edged out and viewed the front parlor. "He must have gone out the door."

Nichole glanced at the women in the hallway. "Where's Cat?"

Lawna held Hope-Anne, who wailed with fright while she hugged Katy close with her other arm.

"I don't know." Cookie shook her head, eyes round with terror. "She went outside before the shooting started."

Nichole edged past the women crouched in the hallway and looked toward the back door.

In the center of the kitchen, Alyse stared out the window. Red-hot flames, like gloves, licked from her fingertips to her wrists.

Nichole swallowed. Her ragged, panicked breath rasped in her ears, along with her heartbeat, drowning the sound of Hope-Anne's cries.

It's happening too fast.

Jason edged into the dining room and yelled at the ceiling. "Amy! Stay where you are. Don't come down."

"Run!" Alyse screamed. Her voice cracked.

Jolted by the desperation in Alyse's voice, Nichole's neck twisted back to view the kitchen.

Alyse edged toward the door, her posture rigid, her elbows bent as fire coalesced in her hands. "Run!"

Nichole climbed over Katy and Lawna's legs and crawled into the kitchen. "Is it Cat?"

A flurry of gunshots thundered outside the kitchen.

Nichole struggled to her feet, trembling and starting at each new explosion until she stood beside Alyse. Her horrified gaze pinned to the yard.

Bernard and Bayard, unable to reach the house, had tipped the wooden table on its side taking shelter from the barrage of bullets.

Two gunmen rounded the corner of the house, angling toward the table. Both wore the shadowy hump of demon possession on their neck.

"They're possessed," Nichole whispered to Alyse.

"Not if they're dead." Alyse shoved open the back door and stepped outside.

Nichole followed, close on her heels.

Alyse held out her hands, and a fountain of flames arched toward the two gunmen.

Bullets tore through the attackers' chests from behind. Their wide-eyed surprise visible for only seconds before fire engulfed their flesh.

Both demons sprang away from their dead hosts, only to be captured by an equally ominous entity.

Carrefour snatched both bulbous shadows in mid-leap.

Hunter rounded the corner a single pace behind the *loa*.

"Hunter!" Sam's shouted warning from across the compound made him turn, drop to his haunches, and fire at movement in the corral. Then he raced forward in a crouch toward the bunkhouse.

The *loa* remained beside the corner of the house, an angry shadowy monster in each hand. He pulled them into his chest, inhaling the tiny beasts before he turned and stepped into a vortex of swirling shadows and disappeared.

"He's—eating them," Nichole murmured.

"What?" Alyse turned with surprise to Nichole and their eyes locked. "Why are you out here? Go back inside."

"Cat's missing." Nichole scanned the yard then lifted her sight to search past the family bunkhouse and the garden.

Where could she be?

A dozen ugly scenarios flashed through her mind.

Would they take Cat hostage? Shoot her?

Near the dovecote, a flash of blue caught her attention. "There." Nichole pointed.

In the temporary absence of gunfire, the James brothers kept their heads low as they ran for the house. Bayard halted and turned, following the direction of Nichole's gesture. He immediately changed course and ran back for Cat.

"They're not *twyned*." Alyse hurried down the step to Bernard.

Gunfire, from Nichole's right, caused her to stumble backward and sit down beside the step.

Two men emerged from around the east side of the house. Ordinary gunmen, not controlled by demon-spawn. Nevertheless, their intentions were clear. They had come to kill.

Bernard faced the new threat, raised his arms, and the ground erupted between himself and the first gunman, throwing stones and dirt into the man's face. "Bay?" Bernard staggered, suddenly aware his brother was no longer by his side. "Bay!"

The second gunman had taken aim at Bayard as he moved toward Cat. Just as Bayard reached her, his back arched and both he and Cat tumbled to the ground.

"No. Please, no," Bernard shouted a litany of denial as he sprinted to his brother.

Nichole struggled to her feet. Her palms pressed to the back of the house for support.

Both of the gunmen continued to fire at the brothers.

Alyse screamed in rage. Tears streaked her face as the trespassers became immolated by the fire.

Nichole gagged as smoke from their burning flesh drifted across the yard.

As fast as the flame exploded, Alyse quelled the blaze. She took Nichole's arm and pushed her up the step and into the kitchen. "Get inside. Stay there."

Nichole stumbled through the kitchen to the window.

Bayard was on his feet between Cat and Bernard. Both men had lost their hats in the skirmish. Bayard's head hung down, but he remained on his feet, conscious although in obvious pain.

From around the family bunk, the two gunmen Nichole had spotted earlier stepped into the open. "Shit, shit, shit." She dashed to the backdoor and screamed, "Behind you! Run!"

Alyse paused in her race toward her uncles. She raised her arms and threw an orb of fire at the gunmen.

They dodged her fire, plunging in separate directions.

Bernard and Cat reached the back door with Bayard. Bernard took his brother's weight as Cat steadied him up the step from behind.

Alyse spun to race up the back step while gunfire pelted the house.

Nichole ducked as the kitchen window shattered, spinning glass across the room.

Blood from Bayard's wound stained the floor as both men and Cat dropped to their knees.

From upstairs, through the house, Amy's horrified scream reached the kitchen, "Alyse!"

The doorway stood empty.

"Oh no, oh no." Nichole scrambled on all fours to the door and peeked out.

In front of the family bunkhouse, Hunter fired both his weapons into the possessed men.

Carrefour easily plucked the spawn from the bodies as they fell, inhaling their essence before he faded with a flicker into the shadow behind Hunter.

And at the base of the steps, Alyse lay unmoving, face down in the grass.

Chapter 12

Jimmy Leigh

—

Dust swirled from the heels of Jim's boots as he crossed the open area of the Denver stockyard. He'd just finalized the sale of the combined Highlands-Shilo herd. Jason would have to be happy with what Jim negotiated with a rancher who planned to take the cattle north. A decent price and more than Jim would have received from the Denver slaughterhouses, had they been buying.

The rancher who purchased the H&S cattle had already instructed his drovers to move Jim's herd north of the stockyard, along with his own cattle. After they'd shaken hands on the deal, he'd confided to Jim he intended to make a tidy profit from the yard up north. He was as pleased as Punch to take them off Jim's hands.

Jim didn't care. He needed to return to Alyse—should have never left her side. Why hadn't he taken the time to explain their complicated history? Found time to convince her his heart was set, and his fantastic tale of ancient sorcery and immortal curses was indeed real. For the first time in their long history, she would have believed him, and he'd been at a loss for words.

As soon as I get home.

Now that the new hires had received their wages for their two-week effort, his next stop would be the bank to deposit the cattleman's note. After that, they would rest up at the Harris house on Pence Street and head home early the next morning.

Tom and Kelly had ridden ahead to take the horses to the livery stable near the house for the night.

Bill, Henny, and Merril waited with the wagon outside the open yard for Jim to complete his business.

Jim retrieved his leather gloves from his back pocket and pulled them on for the short ride to the house.

Henny waved to him, her face alight with both pride and satisfaction that she'd not only held her own as the chuck wagon cook but excelled at it.

Bill was also in high spirits. He danced forward, throwing playful jabs at Merril.

Merril stepped back, and with his long arm, slapped the front of Bill's hat with the back of his hand, flipping it over his head.

A chill twisted up Jim's spine. He slowed his pace as a sudden high-pitched whine swallowed the sound of the stockyard behind him.

Bill's boisterous shout grew distant and muted.

Dear God, not now. Not when I'm this far away—

Pain sliced through Jim's head and pushed outward, building pressure inside his skull as though the bone itself would burst.

Time slowed as ancient magic beckoned, binding him with its curse.

Bill's hat somersaulted up and over his head, then slowed to a stop, frozen in midair, halfway to the ground.

Merril's laughing jump back ceased in mid-step.

Henny's dark hand stilled above her head.

For a split second, less than a breath of time, the tableau held. In the next instant, time returned to its normal rhythm and movement.

Bill's hat slipped from his hand as he spun to catch it and landed on the dusty road.

A blade of agony sliced through the pressure in Jim's head, masking his vision behind a white glare. As the light and pain faded, and vision returned, a single point of pain remained above his left ear, like a hoof pick stabbed into his skull.

Only a mortal danger to Alyse could release a summons. A threat to her life bound him, called him to her side.

He lowered his head and rested his hands on his knees to catch his breath. Too many scenarios flashed through his mind.

Who could threaten Alyse and her family?

Had the demon returned already?

And the most crucial—*How fast can I reach her? Will I arrive in time?*

A pat on his shoulder roused Jim from his stupor. "Are you ill?" Merril asked.

Jim's spine popped as he straightened. He blinked at Merril.

How long have I stood here wasting precious time?

The stabbing pain in the side of his head, a needle shoved into his skull, pulled his attention from Merril. He turned his head to face the pain and felt it slice across his temple and forehead until it settled between his brows. He faced East. *The Highlands.*

"Jim?" Concern filled Merril's voice.

"I can't go to the house with you tonight."

"What do you mean? Wasn't the sale made? Tom and Kelly have already left with the extra horses."

"The sale is done." He pulled an envelope from his pocket. "The buyer's bank is in town. His note will transfer the money to you for the cattle. Be sure to get a deposit receipt for Jason." He held the bent paper to Merril. "You can take this over now, or in the morning before you head home."

"All right. I can do that. But what's wrong?" Merril took the envelope. "And don't tell me you're fine. You're pale, and your hand is shaking."

Jim clapped Merril on the back and turned him toward the horses. "I'm heading back to The Highlands. If I pace myself, I should be able to get there before sunrise."

Merril stopped walking. "What? Why?"

Jim faced Merril. The point of pain slid across his skull again, demanding his attention, pointing toward Alyse.

She needs me now. Explanations will take too long.

He'd move quicker alone.

"Take Henny and Bill to the house and meet Kelly and Tom. I'll see you at the ranch in a couple of days." Jim mounted his brown gelding, pulled the reins and rode to the east at a brisk canter. The blister of urgency burned between his brows.

***

Merril Shilo

—

Stunned by Jim's sudden change of plans, Merril followed him out of the stockyard and watched him ride away.

He never even looked back.

Had Jim ever behaved so peculiar? Merril peeked in the envelope, and an eyebrow rose. The money from the cattle sale would make Jason happy and pay the bills this winter. Not for the first time, he wished he'd had the chance to learn the ins and outs of ranching from his father.

He folded the envelope and slipped it into his back pocket. "Jim needed to return to the ranch," he told Henny and Bill. "Follow me over to the house, and you can get settled while I run to the bank."

He led the way back to Colfax Avenue and then west.

Bill rode beside Henny who handled the wagon to perfection on the city street.

As he passed a small boarding house, Merril caught sight of a familiar figure.

June McKay stood in the shade of the front porch. Her eyes narrowed with hate and anger. She lifted her chin and sneered as Merril rode past. She looked to have aged fifteen years since Timothy had taken her from the ranch, exiled from The Highlands for her vicious comments toward Nichole and Lawna.

Merril turned away, surprised at her vehemence. He looked back at Henny and Bill, but they didn't notice June. Of course, they had barely known her, having come from The Shilo after Kevin—

He stifled the direction of his thoughts and glanced again at June.

She'd moved to the edge of the street, her lips drawn back in a snarl. She lifted her arm and shook her finger. "I see you, Merril Shilo. You'll dine with Satan, you and your filthy wife." Her voice barely reached him across the increasing distance and traffic, but he heard her clear as a bell.

Henny and Bill continued their conversation, oblivious to the woman behind them in the street.

***

Morago

—

Morago sat alone in the gambling hall as he watched Buck's big hands shuffle and reshuffle a deck of fifty-two. No one approached him except Violet, who had accompanied him from the bordello.

She refilled his shot glass with whiskey then wandered away without saying a word. Violet knew to remain silent, or the demon inside her did.

Waiting for an update from demon-Perry had set Morago's nerves on edge and caused his temper to flare. He forced himself to remain still and cultivate what little patience he could find. While Buck shuffled, Morago reviewed his most recent communications with his gunman.

Demon-Perry had kept Morago abreast of the attackers' location, when they reached the nearby town of Kiowa Crossing, and again at the scattering of buildings where Morago had met his bitter defeat a few weeks ago. The witches were no longer there. The outbuildings had been abandoned, and the home, although recently inhabited, was also empty.

One of the gunmen suggested they pay a visit to the other big ranch in the area. The two families sometimes ran cattle together. Perhaps the individuals Buck sought would be found at the other spread.

Perry relayed this information to Morago and received the master's agreement to continue.

Perry's last contact had been when the gunmen reached the neighboring ranch. *These buildings are occupied. What is your desire, master?*

Enter the buildings. Kill as many of the men as you can. If the hosts are killed, return to me.

Then Morago withdrew and waited. Waited for his servants to return. Waited for Perry to whisper their progress into his mind. Waited for a count of how many men his demon-slaves had killed.

To hell with patience.

Morago sped down the silver thread that bound him to demon-Perry. But the thread was no longer attached to his servant. He tried the other four demon-gunmen, but his slaves were gone, as though they had never existed.

He rose to his feet and gripped the table before him with Buck's thick hands. Taking complete control in his fury, he flipped the table, frightening guests and interrupting the games. Morago didn't care. "Out! All of you, get out!"

He swept his hand across the nearby table, scattering coins and cards at the retreating men. All fled before his wrath, but it wasn't enough.

Buck's fists slammed into the wall, over and over until they were bruised and bloody. He panted with the exertion and threw back his head and bellowed his rage. "Where are my slaves?"

The demon horde at the back of his mind remained silent.

In a desperate attempt to calm himself, he reached out to the demon inside the small yellow finch.

Has June returned to her room?

No, my Lord. I've not seen her, or you would have been informed.

The only person remaining in the room stood near the door. Violet caught Buck's glance as he staggered to the nearest table.

You have her to divert your attention. Buck whispered to Morago. *She'll calm you. She knows how.*

"Violet," Buck sneered as he and Morago exchanged places. Buck unbuckled his belt. "On your knees."

Chapter 13

Nichole Harris-Shilo

—

Unsure if Hunter and Sam had dealt with all the attackers, Nichole scampered through the back door, down the steps and huddled beside Alyse. She pushed the hair from her friend's face. "Alyse?"

Alyse had fallen from the step, coming to rest on her stomach. A small blot of red spread from the bullet hole in her back.

Nichole checked her pulse and found one. Relief welled in her chest, and she sat down hard on the ground beside Alyse. Fast footsteps brought her head up.

Hunter ran toward her from across the back yard.

"Are there more of them?" she called to Hunter, then covered her mouth as a sob caught in her throat.

Sam and Lloyd, shotguns in hand, hurried from the barn.

Hunter gave a hand signal to Sam, turned and disappeared around the far side of the house.

Sam continued past Nichole and Alyse, toward the front.

Lloyd stopped beside Nichole. "Is she...?"

Nichole shook her head. "No. Alyse is alive." She brushed her hand across her face. "But she needs help."

"That's a bad place." He crouched down and pointed to the gunshot wound. "You say she's still breathing?"

Nichole nodded.

"Alyse!" Amy cried as she ran across the porch and side yard. She fell to her knees near her twin's head. "We *twyned* the instant Bayard and Cat fell." Amy closed her eyes and tears streamed down her cheeks. "She burned those men, and I quelled her flames." Amy opened her eyes, and whispered with sorrow, "I watched through her eyes as she ran up the step behind you." Amy's face crumpled as she turned to Nichole. "Then the *twyne* broke, and she was gone."

"You're gonna want to be careful when ya move her," Lloyd advised. "I don't see any blood under her. The bullet must be lodged inside." He made a *tsk* sound with his cheek. "The middle of the back is a mighty rough place to take a bullet."

"Shit. You're right." Nichole grasped Amy's forearm. "Can you look inside her? Find where the bullet is?"

Amy's mouth opened then closed. "Yes. Let me sit where you are." She shifted beside her twin as Nichole scooted back. She extended trembling hands above Alyse's back, and a warm orange glow filled the space between them.

From inside the kitchen, Bernard called for his nieces, "Amy! Alyse! We need you in here."

Lloyd rose to his feet and hollered at the back door, "One of your girls is shot." He lowered his voice and muttered, "Ya damned arrogant witch."

If Amy heard her uncle's call or Lloyd's comment, she ignored it. Her left hand moved down toward the small of Alyse's back while her right hand hovered above her twin's neck. Then both hands returned to the center, over the bullet hole. "It came in at an angle and lodged near the backbone." The glow from her hands increased, and beads of sweat dotted her forehead. "The tissue has begun to swell around the injury. Her lungs are clear." Her hand moved over her head. "She hit her head when she fell."

Movement at a window caught Nichole's attention, and she looked up.

Cecil Cobb stared down from the office window. His eyes bulged from their sockets.

"Jason!" Nichole called.

Cecil disappeared from the window.

Jason stepped onto the back stoop. "Bayard's been shot. Cookie's trying to stop the bleeding, have you seen my—" His words died in the back of his throat. He swallowed as he and Amy stared at each other. "Is she... how bad is it?"

"She's alive," Amy whispered.

Nichole tipped her head at the house. "Cecil's still inside."

Jason blanched. "Damn. I forgot about him."

"Get him out of here," Nichole called as Jason went back into the kitchen.

"Mm... uh," Alyse tried to speak, then coughed.

"Be still, my dear," Amy instructed in a calm voice, her hand pressed to her sister's shoulder. "The bullet in your back is in a delicate location. We don't want it to move."

Cat descended the back step and moved around Lloyd and the women. There was blood smeared across the side of her skirt and blouse. "Cookie has the bleeding about stopped on your uncle. The bullet passed through his side, beneath his arm." Her eyes opened wide when she saw the location of the bullet wound on Alyse's back. "Can you, um... can you heal her?"

Amy shook her head. "No. I don't think so." She raised her gaze to Nichole. "Even if we could *twyne*, Alyse does all the work. Her magic sparks the heart, stops the bleeding, and fills the lungs with air." She shook her head. "Perhaps we should send for Doc Johnson."

"No," Nichole answered promptly. "Medical science hasn't gotten around to this type of surgery. It would be better to deal with this ourselves."

"I have a salve that works well. It promotes healing."

"I remember." Nichole's legs had grown numb beneath her. She struggled to her feet with Lloyd's help. "Jeanne put it to my saddle sores."

"Cookie is using the ointment on Bayard right now," Cat supplied.

Nichole held on to Lloyd's arm as she counted dead bodies and considered their options.

Hunter and Sam led several horses from the front of the house to the corral. Three more followed behind the group, on their own.

The unmistakable sound of wheels on hard-packed dirt came from the front of the house, and she caught a glimpse of Attorney Cobb's carriage heading south.

Nichole narrowed her eyes as the black top of his vehicle disappeared over the first rise. "You can't stop the bleeding, but you can see the bullet, right?"

"Yes." Amy again held her hands above her sister's back and closed her eyes. "There is her backbone and a bundle of tiny membranes beside the bullet."

"Isn't metal from the earth?" She turned from the road and looked down at Amy.

Amy's palms rested on her thighs as she stared at Nichole. "It could be." She nodded and shoved her hair out of her eyes. Her traditional loose bun had slipped to the side of her head. Dark russet tendrils clung to her forehead and neck. "I've never tried to do anything with metal."

"Both *Earth* and *Fire* can manipulate metal." Bernard stepped down into the yard and joined the group gathered around Alyse. "What are you thinking?"

Nichole knelt near Alyse's head. Her gaze flicked from Bernard to Amy. "Can you move the bullet away from the nerves and spine?"

"Nerves?"

"The bundled membranes and the backbone. Guide the bullet out of her body along the same path it entered?"

"I—" Amy hesitated. "What if I cause her to bleed? I won't be able to stop it."

"Do it," Alyse said. She blinked tears from her eyes and glared at Amy. "You have to."

"Can you help her at all?" Nichole dabbed the tears from Alyse's eyes with the hem of her skirt. "Stop the bleeding?"

"I can try," Alyse said. Her words were distorted by her face pressing into the ground.

"You can't move, Alyse," Amy warned. "Don't move when the bullet appears to you."

"Now?" Nichole asked. When Amy nodded, she touched Amy's leg and Alyse's arm.

Amy held her palms face down above her sister's back. She remained silent for several moments. "I see the bullet," the sisters spoke in unison. "I'll try to move it."

The warm glow faded as both Amy and Alyse cried out in pain.

Amy fell back gasping. "The pain is too much—I can't. I can't."

Lloyd knelt beside Amy and supported her back. His eyes, wide and uncertain, looked at Nichole.

"Amy." Nichole gripped her wrists. "It's not your pain. Alyse is unconscious again. Move the bullet now."

Amy bent forward and caught her breath, her arms wrapped around her stomach. When she raised her head, determination burned in her dark eyes.

Lloyd moved back as Amy extended her arms again and closed her eyes.

Sam and Hunter whispered about the men who had attacked them as they watched Amy perform a miracle. Their voices were soft and respectful of her concentration.

Cookie stood on the back stoop with Lawna and Katy. Hope-Anne sucked her thumb as she rode her mother's hip.

Jason looked on from the side porch, his gaze glued to his wife, tears glittered in his eyes.

Bernard rested his hand on Amy's shoulder. "God and Goddess, extend your strength and wisdom to my niece. Guide her and protect her purpose with your divine might." Bernard's voice was quiet, his words soft enough that only Amy and Nichole could hear.

"I've got it," Amy murmured. "I'm moving the metal through the path of greatest damage toward her skin." She was silent for several moments. "There's bleeding near her backbone. Nichole, can you apply pressure? Only two fingers." She opened her eyes and pointed several inches above the bullet hole. "Here."

Nichole touched Alyse's dress where Amy had pointed. "Here?"

"Press harder, but not too hard. I don't see the pressure yet. Yes. Good. Closer to the wound. A bit more. There. Harder. Hold." The glow resumed beneath Amy's hands. Her neck glistened with sweat. "Cookie, I'll need the salve and a thick compress and bandages."

Cookie disappeared into the house.

"Lloyd, can you cut open her dress around the bullet hole?"

Lloyd shook his head and took a step back. "I can't. I mean, I don't think I should, well you know."

"I'll do it." Hunter knelt between Nichole and Amy, his knife already in hand. He gripped the material and cut it with the tip of his blade. He worked beneath Amy's hands, in the golden glow of magic. Once split, the dress tore. He pulled the material wide, then lifted her chemise and parted it the same way. When the wound lay exposed, he moved out of the way.

The movement of the bullet became visible underneath Alyse's skin. Blood gushed from the tiny hole in her back.

"You're just about there," Nichole said. "It's almost out."

Cookie ambled down the back step and around the crowd, bandages over her arms and the little pot of salve in her hand. "How can I help?"

"When the bullet exits the hole, apply pressure on the wound." Amy's eyes remained closed.

Cookie nodded and knelt where Hunter had been.

In less than a minute, the blood-coated tip of the smashed metal pellet surfaced.

Cookie grabbed it with a clean towel, then pressed a thick cloth compress down on Alyse's back.

Alyse hadn't roused.

"She'll need a tight bandage." Cookie said.

Amy sagged into her uncle's hands.

Bernard supported his niece. "You need to rest."

Jason hurried to his wife and gathered her in his arms, helping her to her feet.

"Give her something to eat, and let her sleep," Bernard advised.

"I'll take care of her," Jason replied as he assisted Amy onto the side porch. They disappeared inside.

"Alyse needs to be carried to her room so she can be undressed and bandaged properly." Cookie looked up at Cat. "Is she sleeping with you?"

Cat nodded. "We shared a bed last night."

"We'll have to find another place for you tonight."

"I can carry her," Hunter offered.

"Wait a moment. Let me get the camp bed." Lloyd looked at Nichole. "The one we used when Tom broke his leg. You don't want to jostle her more than ya have to." Lloyd took off toward the stable. His brisk pace slowed halfway to the barn.

"Good idea." Sam winked at Hunter. "I'll bring the bed back, and we'll both carry her." He ran to catch up with Lloyd.

"Should I let go?" Nichole asked Cookie.

"Yes. I think it'll be alright." She peeked beneath the blotter. "The bleeding is already slowing."

Nichole stood and stretched her back. Not for the first time, she wished Merril was home.

Near the back of the house lay several dead men. "What should we do with the dead guys?"

"Sink them." Bernard frowned at the corpses.

"No," Hunter replied. "We'll take them to the sheriff in Kiowa Crossing. Someone will miss these men and will know they were here." He ground his teeth and looked Nichole in the eye. "Someone besides Morago. There's no crime in defending ourselves."

Movement caught Nichole's attention and she peered at the office window. Two black cats stared solemnly down at Alyse.

Chapter 14

Morago

—

Buck slept.

The frail human vessels required a great deal of this useless deathlike trance to continue to function properly. Morago could have jumped to another host while Buckner slumbered, but he did not. Instead, he contemplated the inconceivable.

His questions, heavy as stones around his neck, could not be answered. Still, Morago pondered. How had the threadlike shackle broken? Were their hosts slain, his slaves would be forced to return to him. Enthralled to serve for eternity, they had no will of their own—only what Morago allowed.

I should have watched through demon-Perry's eyes the entire time. Then I would know what severed the bond.

In his impotent rage, he had almost injured his host, had nearly snapped the neck of his trusted lieutenant who resided inside Violet.

The singular female voice inside his mind whispered. *You're pathetic. Once again, my children have defeated your—"*

He quelled the old woman's mocking words, choking them off. Her short cry of agony set the horde of demons atwitter with delight.

Silence!

In the quiet that followed, he reached out to the demon-finch. *Has June returned to her room?*

Just this moment, my Lord.

Without hesitation, a portion of Morago's consciousness sped down the silver thread to the finch. The caustic bite of June's siren call was far too powerful for Morago to resist, especially after such a loss.

His view through the cord was less than perfect. Spherical and stretched, he peered through the bird's eyes at June. Her voice, beyond the window, likewise distorted, but the hateful twist to her lips and the bitter rancor of her voice succored him.

"How dare Merril Shilo tip his hat to me? *To me!* He was only one of many who chased after that little bitch in heat." She paced her small room, from the dresser to the headboard and back, twisting her fingers with agitation.

"Because of Nichole, and her spiteful jealousy, my sweet Amy and I were banished from the ranch. Because of her, that black whore, Lawna, has taken my place. Oh!" She threw her hairbrush to the floor, then covered her mouth as the handle shattered from the head. "Now look what she made me do," she whined.

June picked up the broken brush and held the two ends together. "Merril with his coal-black nanny driving a wagon down my street. *Right down my street!* Why would they be here?" Her voice became wistful. "I wonder if Amy is nearby?"

Morago could hear her words but was unable to read her thoughts or feel her emotions. The thread had its limits. Still, he knew who Merril Shilo was, knew the man's connection to the witches.

Buck stirred in his sleep as Morago slammed back into his host. With unbridled excitement, he reached out to another of his hosted demons and whispered fervent instructions.

***

Merril Shilo

—

Tom and Kelly waited on the new front porch when Merril, Bill, and Henny reined to a stop in front of the house.

Tom hurried to help Henny from the wagon. "Can we leave the chuck wagon on the street overnight?" he asked Merril.

"It should be fine." Merril found the front door key hidden beside the porch and unlocked the door. "Leave my horse saddled. I still need to ride over to the bank."

"I thought Jim would do that." Kelly helped Tom free the draft horses from the yoke. He looked around, then called out to Merril. "Where is Jim?"

"Make yourself at home." Merril ushered Henny into the house, then returned to his gelding to remove his saddlebags. "Jim headed back to the ranch."

"What for?" Kelly raised one brow at Merril.

"He didn't say," Merril replied with a grin. "And I didn't ask." He carried his bags to the room he and Nichole had shared before their wedding. Without changing, he headed back downstairs. Hat tossed on the kitchen table, he took a towel to the backyard water pump. A full bath was what he needed to wash the dust from his hide, but that would have to wait. He'd indulge himself with that luxury when he got home to Nichole.

It's funny how The Highlands seems like home, and The Shilo never did.

He washed his face, neck, and hands in the cold well water. Wetting his hair, he pushed it back from his forehead and sprinkled droplets on his shoulders. He slipped his hat back on as he passed through the house and hung the towel back on its peg to dry.

In the front yard, Tom had Bill's horse and the draft horses by the leads. "I'll take these over to the livery stable." He spoke to Kelly but nodded at Merril.

"All right," Kelly called over his shoulder as he hefted a box of goods from the back of the wagon. "Henny said she wanted these in the house."

"Howdy neighbor." Albert Fielding crossed the hard-packed dirt street. Thumbs hooked around his suspenders, he looked over the wagon, then smiled at Merril. "I don't suppose you've heard. It appears you just got into town."

"Hello, Albert." Merril took his neighbor's outstretched hand. "Heard what?"

"Well, you know I hate to be the bearer of bad news, but someone has to tell ya." He hung his head for a moment. "Two men and a horse were found dead in your yard a couple of weeks back." Albert pointed toward the side yard. "I told Chief McCallin that the Harris house sits empty most of the time, ever since Miss Amy returned to live at Quincy's ranch with her husband. I keep an eye on it, and help you out with repairs, as you know."

"And it's much appreciated, Albert." Merril glanced at Kelly and Tom. "Does the chief know who they were?"

Kelly and Tom had stopped working and listened to Merril's conversation with the neighbor.

"Not as far as I know," Albert replied. "Chief McCallin wanted me to ask whoever showed up to stop by the police station. The corpses were buried, of course, but McCallin has their personal effects at his office. He'd like for you to take a look to see if you can identify either man."

"Of course, I will. Though I doubt I'll be much help." Merril ran his hand over his face. "How did they die?"

"Well, that's the strange thing," Albert kicked his toe at a stone on the road, then squinted one eye at Merril. "The man and his horse in your back yard died from lack of water and exposure—like they just didn't take the time to drink. Fella even had a half-full canteen strapped to his saddle." He pointed again at the side of the house. "Now, the poor cuss they found alongside the building, he'd been murdered." Albert tugged on his ear. "Had his head smashed so hard against your bricks his skull caved in."

Merril winced and cast a backward glance at the side of the house. "Damn."

Albert stepped back. "Don't want to interrupt. I can see you're busy as bees." The neighbor waved his hand at the group as he retreated across the street to his house. "Let the chief know I delivered his message."

"Thanks again, Albert," Merril called, then spoke to Tom and Kelly as he mounted. "Let Henny and Bill know I might be gone a bit longer than anticipated."

"Sure thing." Tom removed his gloves. "Are we still heading home in the morning?"

"Yes. We leave at first light."

Merril stopped at the bank and deposited the draw note for the cattle sale into The Highlands' bank account. At first, it appeared the bank might refuse to accept the deposit since he wasn't on the account. But after explaining the circumstances to three separate people, and then again to the bank manager, he was allowed to deposit the note. No withdrawal would be allowed, however.

Once the deposit was made, he stopped at the police station. He introduced himself to Police Chief McCallin. The chief escorted him to a back room with a small table and three chairs. Before long, a uniformed officer brought two envelopes in and set them on the table.

"John Doe one and two. We'll hold the saddle and bags from the horse for 60 days to be claimed. If you want to see those, I'll take you over to our storage building."

"I doubt I knew these men. I can't imagine—" From the first envelope slid a small, stitched sampler, frayed around the edge, with the name Hope-Anne embroidered into the center. "Damn." Merril dropped into the chair beside the table.

"Did you know him?" The officer asked.

Merril nodded. "Was this the man with the horse?"

"No, sir. John Doe number one was the murder victim." The officer removed a pencil from his jacket pocket. "His name, please."

"Timothy Caine."

"How do you know the deceased?"

"He worked for me, um, for my wife."

The officer gave Merril a questioning look. "Your wife, sir?"

"For us. We are newlyweds." He shook his head. "I was the one who sent Timothy on an errand to Denver. But I've been away from the ranch on a cattle drive. I just assumed he'd returned home."

"And the other individual?"

Merril looked through the effects—a billfold with two dollar bills, a packet of chewing tobacco, and a worn religious medal on a broken chain. Merril returned the items to the envelope. "No. This man I can't identify. Is he the man who killed Timothy?"

"We don't think so, sir. The deceased with the horse was in bad shape. I doubt he would have had the strength to strike the younger man such a devastating blow." He picked up the envelope and stepped to the door. "It's more likely there was a third individual in the yard that night." He exited the room, then looked back. "The personal effects of Timothy Caine are yours. Do you know if you will want to move the body to a different burial location?"

Merril slipped the few items, including a tarnished wedding ring, back into the envelope. "Can I discuss that with his wife? I don't know what his family will want to do."

"Certainly, sir." The officer shrugged. "He's not going anywhere."

Merril signed for the envelope at the front desk.

Timothy Caine! Who would have done such a thing?

Merril bumped into a large man near the hitching rail where his horse waited. "Excuse me," he murmured.

The man grinned, and a sudden chill swept across Merril's skin. Before he could take a second breath, he'd become an observer inside his own body.

"Take good care of this one," the big man instructed. "I want to find out what happened to the others. If you see one of the witches, give her a kiss for me."

"I will." Merril heard himself agree. He watched his hand reach for the saddle horn. "I'll let you know what I find."

"Be discreet. His companions remain at the red house. Return to them. Can you read his thoughts?"

Merril looked down from the saddle and nodded. "They plan to return to their ranch in the morning."

"Good." The man slapped the rump of the sorrel as Merril rode away.

Chapter 15

Jimmy Leigh

—

The last golden clouds above the mountains had faded to black hours ago. A sliver of the waxing new moon rode high in the night sky, shedding a little light on the prairie.

Jim reined his tired gelding along The Highlands ranch road to the house. Lloyd would be asleep, and his horse needed care. However, the undeniable call persisted.

I have to get to Alyse.

Obligation warred with desire inside his chest as he rode past the main house. Salvaged wood from Nichole's overturned carriage and several old horse blankets covered the downstairs windows.

What happened here?

His compulsion to leave the tired horse to his own devices and run into the house pressed on him. Duty lay in one direction, his heart in another.

His equine companion pulled at the bit and strained toward the stable. He knew the long ride home was almost over. Food and rest awaited him.

Jim acquiesced to his horse's needs. After all, Rascal had carried him a long way home to Alyse. He deserved to be cared for first and allowed to take his rest in comfort. The compass point of pain which had rested between his eyebrows on the trail home shifted to the side of his head as he passed the house.

Alyse is inside.

In front of the stable, he looked back at the second-floor window as he dismounted. A warm light from Jason and Amy's bedroom beckoned him even as the dot of pain pierced the spot above his nose. Amy would be awake. Caring for her sister, perhaps?

Where is the danger?

He turned his head and led his exhausted gelding into the stable.

Lloyd had just put a flame to the wick as Jim walked in. "I heard a horse come up the road." He blew out the match and tossed it into a metal tray near the lamp. "You alone?"

"I am. Merril and the rest stayed in Denver. You'll most likely see them late tomorrow or early the next day." He handed the reins to Lloyd. "What happened here?"

"You didn't stop at the house then." Lloyd clicked his tongue and shook his head. He led the tired horse to an empty stable, unbuckled the cinch, and then paused to raise a brow at Jim. "Gunmen attacked the ranch. Amy's family took the worst of it, what with her sister and uncle getting shot—"

Lloyd's voice faded behind him as Jim spun and raced for the house. He leaped onto the porch and rushed through the front door.

Hunter, seated at the end of the long dining table, came to his feet and stared at Jim. His gaze lifted to the stairs as Nichole hurried down clutching her night robe.

"I heard a horse outside—" She stopped and locked eyes with Jim. "Is everything all right? Is Merril with you?" She pressed against the rail on the narrow staircase as Jim brushed past her, two steps at a time.

"Merril's fine," he stated, barely glancing at Nichole. "He stayed in town." The sting on his forehead pointed to the far door on the left, the east-facing bedroom beside Nichole's. He raced across the corridor and shoved the door open. He barely noticed Cat's curious face peek out from across the hall.

In the soft glow of a shuttered lantern, Amy dozed in a chair beside Alyse's bed, holding her sister's hand.

Two identical black cats curled together on the bedcover near Alyse's feet.

When he saw Alyse, the urgent pain pinned against his skull dissolved. He closed the door behind him and moved forward.

Amy lifted red-rimmed eyes to his and blinked.

He halted at the foot of the bed, his heart in his throat. "Is she? No, she can't be. I would have known."

"She's not dead." Amy shook her head. "But she is in a deep sleep. A result of the poultice's healing properties." Amy's usual loose bun had been brushed out and braided. A few of her dark russet tresses had escaped and hung long over her shoulder. She pushed an errant strand from her eyes and sniffed. "However, she should have awakened by now."

Jim rounded the bed and sank to his knees. He lifted Alyse's hand and felt her pulse beneath his fingertips. "How bad?" He lowered her hand but kept it cradled between his palms.

"Bad enough. Had that bullet struck anyone else..." Amy clutched her handkerchief to her nose, her voice tight with emotion. "Alyse could have healed them."

"She can't heal herself?"

"She tried." Amy shook her head. "But the pain was too great, and the concentration required to repair the wound was impossible for her to maintain." Amy dabbed her eyes. "She fainted from the pain. Sam and Hunter carried her upstairs. Cookie and I bandaged her and applied my salve, but she hasn't awakened."

"But your poultice will heal her?"

"I don't know." A tear slid down her cheek. "It hasn't so far."

"No." Panic seized Jim's heart, and it fluttered against his chest. "Your salve will work. It has to." He laid his hand on the side of Alyse's face. Her skin felt cool against his palm. She didn't stir. He rose from his knees and eyed her mirror image. "How can you tell it's not working if she's asleep?"

Amy stood and pulled one of the darning needles from a basket at her feet. The cats jumped from the bed as she threw back the bedcover, exposing Alyse's foot. She looked up at Jim, pressed her lips, then stroked her sister's foot from heel to toes with the blunted tip of the needle. The white line turned red, with no reaction from Alyse. "There's no feeling below the bullet wound in her back."

"But she's unconscious."

"Asleep or awake, her toes would react to the sensation on her foot. A reflex. And they don't." Amy shook her head and stabbed the needle back into the yarn. "When I look inside her, at the wound, I see swelling where the bullet had lodged against her backbone. I removed the bullet, but the injury remains. The tissue has expanded against the membranes in her back."

"I still don't understand."

"Without feeling in her legs and feet, she won't be able to stand or walk." Amy balled the handkerchief into her fist and swallowed. "I can't say yet if this is a temporary or permanent condition."

"But she's alive."

"Yes. Alyse is alive." Amy paused as she scrubbed a hand across her eyes. "But we can't say she's out of danger until she wakes."

"Who did this to her?" As his fear eased, Jim's chest filled with powerless fury.

Who must I slay?

"I don't know who they were. There were ten gunmen—now dead and stacked behind the stable. Both Nichole and Hunter saw demons guiding several of them."

"Not the devil monster that held Hunter?"

"No, but these men were his tools. The Prophecy has not ended." Amy lowered her gaze. "Bayard saved Cat during the attack. He suffered a bullet wound as well, though nothing like hers." Amy pulled the cover over Alyse's foot.

They were silent for several moments, listening to Alyse's even breathing.

Amy covered a yawn and then used the same hand to cover her heart. "If you intend to stay with her, I'll find my bed."

"I'll be right here."

"Cat's taken Sam's room across the hall. Sam's in the bunkhouse."

Jim nodded as Amy slipped from the room. He removed his hat and made use of the ewer of water on the dresser. A bath would wait until morning when Amy returned to sit with Alyse. He relaxed into the chair Amy had vacated and lifted Alyse's limp hand. "Ah, my girl. Ours has been such a long road."

He kissed her fingers, then rested his head against the wall, closing his eyes. "I owe you an explanation, I know." His voice thick and soft, a rumble of a whisper, meant only for her sleeping ears. "I know I do."

He remained silent for several minutes before he spoke, choosing his words. "I fell in love with you, God, what's it been? Almost two thousand years ago, on the other side of the world. Our lives were different then, of course. There weren't as many people. We didn't build houses or farm. We lived a nomadic life in tribes. Our clans were larger than families—smaller than towns. The women made our clothes from animal hide and wove fabric and made tunics for important occasions. I think you'd understand when I say; the world has changed a great deal since the day we first met.

"My father was a northern clan leader. He was big. Imposing. I suppose I've grown to look much like him. Sometimes, when I see myself in the mirror, I remember him—Jor, leader of the Langobarden clan." He opened his eyes and watched Alyse slumber. "For the sake of our tribe, he made an agreement with the Baraci clan. I was old enough to wed, and their druid, a young woman, would be my bride. It would bind the tribes and make them our allies against the Roman invaders.

"We traveled weeks it seemed to reach their camp. Farther south than I'd ever been. They welcomed us with ceremony, a feast of union and celebration. My future wife remained hidden until the final ceremony, to be revealed only as our lives were bound to one another.

"Seated beside my father, I looked across the fire and saw you. I can't explain the emotion that filled my chest. I hoped and prayed to our Gods that you were the druid I would wed. I knew it had to be true. Even then, I realized there could be no one for me except you.

"Later, after the meal finished and the revelry began, I sought you out, confident you were my intended bride. Who else could provoke such unbridled emotion within my soul?"

"I followed you away from the fire. I was a youth of fourteen summers, so sure the world evolved around only me and my desires. Around us. I remember how your eyes reflected the summer moon, and your shy smile as you took my hand. You didn't know I was the intended groom for your clan druid. You only knew, as I did, that the bond between us stirred deep in our blood and took root in our souls.

"Eventually we were found, naked and entwined in each other's arms, oblivious to the dishonor we had cast upon our clans. My intended bride, dressed in her wedding finery, enraged beyond care or reason, cast a binding curse upon us. Upon me."

Jim opened his eyes, but instead of the bedroom ceiling, the memory of Nescato's angry, pain-filled eyes had surfaced.

Her hateful glare had pinned his young self to the ground as Agaria trembled in fear for her life in his arms. Nescato's words—Nescato's curse—scored forever into his mind.

"*For this deceit, I curse you to love only her for all eternity—in whatever form she is reborn. You will watch her die a thousand times, knowing your life goes on. Bound to her call, you will never rest in the slumber of death's arms. Your torment shall be everlasting.*"

Jim had to clear his throat before he could continue. "They drove us from their combined camps. Reviled. Dishonored. Alone. We made our way west and eventually found acceptance with another clan."

He took a deep breath. "I aged with you until we reached maturity, and then my aging stopped. Nescato's curse bound me to life, and along with my love, the curse bound me to you. As you grew old, I provided for you. A gift I've been lucky enough to give many times over the course of this long, strange life.

"Eventually, as all mortals do, you passed into the world beyond. I wandered alone, seeking companionship only to find my never changing appearance to be thought demonic. I learned to move on before fear of the unexplained could cause trouble. And although I've sustained many injuries, I cannot receive a killing blow. Chance, it seems, favors me beyond all measure, making my isolation complete.

"When the first magical summons came, all movement around me ceased, as though time itself had frozen. Once life stirred again, a strike upon my brow brought a searing pain and blinding light. I thought my end had finally come. I didn't understand at first, but the agony gave direction—a painful compass and compulsion to locate the essence of whatever drew me forward. And now, of course, I know my pain is also my utmost desire, for it brings me to you. Always you.

"My princess. My warrior. My beautiful sorceress. This life of mine is yours as surely as this curse, which, for the moment, is a blessing in my eyes. For through them, I'm allowed to hold your hand once again." Jim lifted her fingers and kissed the back of her hand. A tear dropped onto her pale flesh. He brushed the dampness away with his thumb.

"And that, my only love, is why I seem familiar. You do know me and have known me for centuries." He cleared his throat and rubbed the moisture from his eyes. "I love you, Alyse, with every fiber of my being." He counted back the lives they'd shared, and like counting blessings, it eased his exhausted mind to sleep.

The soft sound of the door easing open woke him.

Amy poked her head into the room, then withdrew, leaving the door slightly ajar.

Jim blinked and sat forward in his chair. He still held Alyse's hand in his. With tender care, he returned her limp arm to the bed.

Alyse remained still and pale, lost in a profound healing sleep, or so he hoped.

Damn.

He rose from the chair and pressed his palms to the ceiling, stretching the stiff muscles in his back. Daylight filtered through the thin curtain. He must have had at least a few hours' sleep.

With a last regretful glance at Alyse, he retrieved his hat from the dresser and slipped from the bedroom. As much as he wanted to remain by her side, he needed a change of clothes and as close to a bath as he could manage. The rumble in his stomach reminded him of something else he needed to remedy.

The four bedroom doors on the second floor stood open. The rooms were empty and tidied.

Downstairs, in the dining room, Hunter was still in the same chair he'd occupied when Jim came in last night. A tall glass of bourbon at his elbow.

Jim paused at the table across from Hunter. "You been up all night?" Bits of dried grass, clipped edges of sackcloth, and black thread littered the tabletop. On the serving table beside the office door, a straw basket held several small dolls each decorated with a small personal item. "Is this your plan to defeat the demon? Drink all Jason's whiskey and play with toys?"

"Easy, *mon ami.*" Hunter's piercing gaze lifted to Jim's face as he tied a knot and then bit the thread. "These puppets are simply a way I can help protect innocent lives."

"Well, they damn well didn't protect Alyse and her family yesterday, did they?" Impotent fury filled Jim's chest. He balled his hands into fists at his side, fighting the urge to throttle the dark-haired Cajun and his useless, magical dolls.

Hunter's chair scraped back as he came to his feet. Though tall, the top of his head would only have reached the bridge of Jim's nose had the table not separated them. With his thick black hair tied with a leather string at the nape of his neck, and wearing a finely tailored jacket, Hunter stood apart from Jim and the ranch hands, whether by choice or upbringing, remained uncertain.

The man had the look of a gambler. A knife-wielding gunman who dabbled with voodoo, and not the least bit intimidated by Jim's physical superiority.

Only a slight flush on his skin, which highlighted the white scar along his cheek showed his temper. "She stepped outside to defend her uncle, *monsieur*. Without her bravery, more would have been harmed."

"And you were here?" Jim bit out between clenched teeth. "With your dolls?"

"He saved me, Mr. Leigh." Cat stood in the kitchen passage, wringing her hands. "He risked his life to save all of us when he ran outside to stop the gunmen." She stepped toward Jim, eyes flashing. "But you wouldn't know what *actually* happened, would you? You weren't here."

"There's no need to defend me, *mon beau petit chaton*." The flush on Hunter's face faded. He placed the doll he'd finished in the basket with his growing collection of figurines and gifted Cat with a weary half-smile that didn't reach his eyes. "A woman he cares for lies gravely injured upstairs. If that were you, and I did not know how such a thing could have happened, I would be angry with anyone who failed to prevent such tragedy as well."

Jim lifted his hat and ran his hand through his hair. "That and I haven't eaten in twenty-four hours." His stomach grumbled to punctuate his statement. He resettled his hat and tipped the brim to Cat. "I apologize for my rudeness, Miss Catherine, Mr. Hunter. Now, if you'll pardon me, I'll see if Cookie can find me a bite to eat." He stepped around Cat and came to an abrupt halt.

Amy, tray in hand, looked up at him from the shadow of the kitchen passage. "I thought to bring you breakfast." The platter held coffee, eggs, bacon, and griddle cakes.

His stomach growled again at the delicious scent of the food, and his heart clenched at the tender look in Amy's eyes.

Her hair, coiled into a soft bun atop her head, matched the color of her brown day dress. Narrow white lace trailed from neckline to waist and outlined her slender figure.

Jim swallowed back a burst of emotion that his continuing affection and gratitude for Amy thrust into him.

I loved Amy first—before I knew Alyse. I love her still. How can that be?

"Thank you, Amy." He managed to say as he lifted the tray from her hands. He cleared his throat. "I'll eat out back, if that's all right. I'm not fit for polite company this morning." He glanced over his shoulder at Hunter and Cat. "I apologize again if I spoke out of turn."

Chapter 16

Merril Shilo

—

Merril couldn't remember the ride from the police station back to his wife's house on Pence Street. His last clear memory was talking to a police officer about the bodies found on the property. Timothy Caine's envelope remained a lump in his back pocket. Merril knew he should tell the others what he'd discovered about Timothy, but the words wouldn't form.

He sat in the kitchen with Kelly, Tom, and Bill, while Henny moved around the table serving the last of her camp rations in a hearty beef stew.

"Don't you boys worry. I've set aside enough for supper tomorrow night," Henny assured the men. "One more day and I'll see my darlin' little Katy. I bet that child has grown an inch since we've been gone." She dished herself a serving and took it to the counter to eat. "My baby is in a growth spurt, Miss Amy said so."

Merril held a piece of fresh baked bread in one hand and his spoon in the other. He stared at the meal in his bowl while the others dug in.

What's wrong with me? Have I taken ill?

Tom and Kelly teased Bill about something that happened on the trail drive.

Merril didn't catch what they were saying. Their conversation didn't concern him. He looked back at the stew and realized he'd taken a bite and chewed slowly. He tasted nothing.

Bill leaned over and slapped Merril's shoulder with the back of his hand and laughed. "You're gonna let them get away with that?"

Merril shook his head. "I didn't hear what they said."

"It doesn't bear repeating," Kelly smirked.

"I heard ya clean over here, Kelly Doane, and you're a darned fool. I'd hoped Tom Baker would at least have a lick more sense." Henny piped up from across the kitchen. "Anyone will tell ya, Shilo folks know their way around a barn dance better than any of them Highlands' boys. Two-steppin' with cow patties, my foot." Henny chuckled and winked at Merril. "Mmm hmm. I remember one time not long after your pa left Georgia…" Henny continued to talk and bob her head, but the words became garbled nonsense.

"She wouldn't say that if Jimmy Leigh were here," Tom whispered, and the men around the table erupted in laughter.

Except for Merril.

He stared at the happy faces but wasn't a part of them.

You've never been a part of them.

Even though Bill and Henny came from The Shilo, their loyalty would always be to his father and brother.

Never to you.

Why, he hardly knew Kelly Doane, a wrangler from The Highlands. He'd known Tom Baker longer, of course, but not by much.

You're the outsider.

As Tom implied, they all belonged to Jimmy Leigh.

You'd best be careful.

"What did the police chief say about the bodies they found in your yard?" Kelly asked.

Gooseflesh spread up his arms as a thought whispered from the back of his mind.

Keep your mouth shut and your head down until you get to the ranch. It's better this way.

Merril looked down to find his bowl empty. His hand released the spoon, and it clattered against the porcelain dish.

Around the table, the natural banter fell silent. All eyes focused on him.

Tom chewed and swallowed. "You feelin' all right, Merril?"

Merril surged to his feet and stepped back, knocking his chair over. He leaned forward to grip the edge of the table as his vision blurred. Tom's narrowed eyes swam in-and-out of focus. "I'm just tired," Merril murmured. His voice sounded weak and distant inside his skull.

He turned away from their counterfeit concern and navigated the narrow stairs to the second floor bumping against the wall with his shoulder. Down the hall to the room above the kitchen. He sat on the edge of the bed and stared at the closed door.

What's wrong with me?

Boot and clothes on, he stretched out on the bed and closed his eyes.

***

Merril blinked as the chuck wagon swayed. The heavy cart moved back and forth as the wheels turned from the road. Dust blew past his face, and his eyes were scratchy and dry. Nausea coiled in his stomach as he looked over his shoulder at the long stretch of mountains, blue and distant beneath the late afternoon sun. The shock sent a shard of terror through his core.

What's happening?

His horse followed Henny's wagon off the worn path and toward the dry riverbed under the shady cottonwoods at their usual midpoint stop between Denver and the ranches.

Bill and Kelly had already dismounted.

Tom tied off a line for the remuda then ran to help Henny guide the wagon down to the camp area. He walked the wagon team to a halt, then began to unbuckle their harnesses.

No one looked at Merril. The conversation between wranglers was sparse, turned solely to getting their animals comfortable and their camp set up for the night.

Sensation rushed over him. He needed to dismount, but his legs had cramped, and his arms tingled.

Have I been in the saddle all day?

His full bladder pained him, as though it would burst. He licked his dry, split lips with a swollen tongue. "Bill," he called. His voice cracked.

Bill glanced over his shoulder as he loosened the cinch strap. "Yup?" He froze, his eyes going wide. Without hesitation, he left his horse half unsaddled and hurried to Merril. "You're white as a sheet."

"Help me..." Merril's voice failed. He cleared his throat. "Help me get down." The joints of his hands had seized around the reins. One by one, he forced his fingers to release. He gripped the saddle horn and kicked one foot free of the stirrup, then groaned as he stepped over the leather seat.

Bill held him steady as he dismounted. "Can I get you anything?"

Merril shook his head, and half-chuckled. "I need to piss and stretch."

"Your horse needs care," Bill reminded him. "You refused to change horses. Hell, you refused to speak to anyone." His voice lowered. "Tom's furious with you."

Merril nodded as he pulled his gloves from his hands and massaged his fingers. "I don't remember leaving the house."

"What?"

"This morning. The last thing I remember is sitting at the table last night."

"You're pullin' my leg." Bill ran his hand over his face and scrubbed at his chin. "Are you sick?"

Merril shook his head. "I don't know." He pushed away from his horse and stretched his back. "There's something wrong. Maybe I am sick. I don't know." He walked stiff-legged a few paces from camp and struggled with the buttons on his denim trousers. Finally, he relieved himself, and the pain in his bladder subsided.

Bill returned to his horse, finished removing the saddle, and then carried it to the fire pit. He set his gear on the ground not far from Tom's saddle and bags, then returned to help Merril. "I'll see to your horse. Talk to Henny. She might have something for your gut."

Merril's stomach was nauseous, now that Bill mentioned it. As he staggered toward the wagon, a soft chuckle sounded behind him, and he turned to see who laughed at his expense.

Bill lifted the saddle from Merril's mount and set it beside his at the fire pit.

Across the camp, Tom and Kelly fed and watered the horses tied to the line.

With an arm full of kindling, Henny crossed to the circle of stones that marked the pit. Without a glance at Merril, she bent to start their evening fire.

None of his group lingered near the wagon. He turned and looked back the way they had come.

That's it. Spin around again. There's no one near you.

Merril felt bile rise in his throat. He gasped for air as pain shot across his chest and down his arms.

Stand still and calm yourself, or you'll be pushed aside.

Merril struggled to speak, to shout a warning to the others, but his jaws clamped shut.

Enough. As amusing as it is to taunt your inferior intelligence, the presence of my demon-slave must remain our secret for a while longer.

A high-pitched giggle escaped Merril's throat as his consciousness was thrust backward. Control of his body, his voice, even his thoughts were taken from him.

This time, I'll instruct my servant to only allow you to watch.

***

Alyse James

—

Soft voices came and went marked by long periods of silence and darkness. Bits of conversation hovered above her head, dropping down to incorporate themselves into her dreams.

Amy and Cookie spoke quietly while they kneaded bread on her back. Their words faded in-and-out. More seasoning would be needed.

Amy cried softly nearby, cuddling a kitten. Amy's thoughts brushed hers several times, filled with anxiety and sorry. *Was the kitten dying?*

The tight grip of a giant restrained Alyse's limbs and pulled her dream away from her sister, down into the night.

She floated in silence without dreams.

A familiar voice whispered to her. The mere sound of Jim's voice warmed and comforted her. His low rumble rose and fell as his words tangled her in a dream.

He told her the story of Jor-danis and Agaria. His tone, soft and even, but at times, it would fill with emotion. He narrated a dream of love with depth unimaginable, its lure, undeniable, of mistaken identity and a broken vow.

The lovers were discovered. Words were spoken in anger. The curse, raw and powerful, flowed around them.

For this deceit... to watch her die... your life goes on.

When his voice stopped, Alyse struggled against the healing current to reach consciousness but failed. Forgetfulness pressed her down into the darkness of sleep.

Dreams came and went. Forgotten imagery, part fantasy, part memory, part horror, danced across her mind.

After a while, her sister whispered her name from far away. A mirror appeared beside her. She saw herself smile and extend a hand. Alyse reached for her sister and grasped her fingers.

Alyse? Thank the Goddess. Can you hear me?

Yes. Where are you? Where am I?

We're at The Highlands. You were injured. My healing salve put you in a deep sleep, but you've slept too long. You must awaken.

How did we twyne?

Nichole is here. She acts as our bridge.

The image in the mirror turned and spoke briefly over her shoulder. Her words lost to the shadows.

I told her we are twyned. She doesn't share our communication.

The grip on her hand grew stronger.

Alyse, you need to wake up.

I've tried. I don't know which way will take me out of these dreams.

Amy's brow knit, then her eyes opened wide.

Look up.

Above them, the gloom swirled and changed. Flecks of sunlight reflected off the top of the water. When Alyse looked back at the mirror, Amy's hair and nightdress floated around her body in the underwater current.

Come. Amy urged as the mirror fell away.

Pulled by their clasped hands, Alyse ascended through the clear liquid.

The surface rippled far above her head and appeared to recede each time she drew close.

Stop holding your breath, Amy commanded.

Was I? How do you know?

I'm looking right at you. Amy laughed. *We're about there. When we breach the water, open your eyes.*

The film between sleep and consciousness slid over her face. Alyse opened her eyes—blinked—and closed them again.

"That's it," Nichole said. "Try to keep them open."

Through the water, she could see Nichole. "What—?" *Was that croaking sound her voice?*

"There you are." Nichole dabbed a handkerchief to the corner of her eye and her vision cleared. "You had everyone worried."

"I've never seen anyone sleep so deeply from the healing salve," Amy said.

Alyse turned her head with effort. Her neck muscles were tight and sore.

"I'm glad you're finally awake." Amy sat beside the bed still holding her hand. "Jim has been impossible."

"Jim's back?" The scratchiness in her throat made her cough.

"He came back the night before last." Nichole brought a glass of water. "I expect Merril and the rest to return sometime today."

Alyse sipped the water while Amy held her head up and Nichole tipped the glass.

"Better?" Amy lowered her head back to the pillow.

"Are you hungry?" Nichole asked.

"I don't know." She tried to sit forward, but her body felt like a lead weight. "I need to sit up."

Amy lifted her shoulders while Nichole stuffed pillows behind her.

"How long was I asleep?"

Amy and Nichole exchanged worried glances.

"Two and a half days," her sister said. "What do you remember?"

"By the Goddess! Two days?" Alyse shook her head. Her neck moved a bit easier now. "We were outside by the table." She scrunched her eyes closed and rubbed her temple. "Lawna sat Hope-Anne on the blanket. Something happened..." She gasped as memory rushed back. Eyes wide, she looked at Amy. "We heard gunfire near the stable." She turned to Nichole. "Is everyone all right?" She brought up her hand before Nichole could answer. "No— Bayard went to help Cat." Fire sparked from her fingertips for a moment, then it sputtered and extinguished.

Amy grasped her hand. "He's all right. He was shot, but the injury wasn't as serious as yours. Please, be calm."

Alyse stilled. "My injury—" her voice faded. Eyes closed, she took stock of her body. Her head had a slight ache. Stiffness from sleeping plagued her neck and arms. Bandages wrapped her midriff, and the knitting skin pulled taut in the center of her back. Her hips, her legs—did not exist to her senses. "I can't feel my legs." Panic lunged into her chest. She reached down and grasped her thigh in confusion. "Why?" Her gaze rose to Nichole then flew to Amy. "What's wrong with my legs?"

"The bullet injured your back." Amy moved from the chair to the bed and captured both her hands. "The bleeding has stopped, but there's swelling—inflammation near your backbone."

"I want to see." She lifted her hand to Nichole.

Nichole glanced at Amy, then took Alyse's hand and touched Amy's shoulder.

The twins *twyned* with ease through Nichole.

Here. Amy directed her sight. *I flushed the blood from the bullet cavity, but I can't calm the swelling. That's the problem. It's pressing against your spine causing paralysis.*

Alyse pushed her healing flame through Amy's vision—and the view of her injury disappeared. She blinked and looked at her sister.

Amy's back pressed against the wall across the room. "If you try to heal it now, you'll do more harm than good. You need to regain your strength, both physical and magical."

"Amy, please. I can't stay like this."

"The inflammation will go down on its own." Nichole rounded the bed and reached for the door. "We should work your legs manually until the feeling comes all the way back."

"How do you know this?" Alyse asked in a soft voice.

"Human Anatomy 101." Nichole opened the door. "I thought I wanted to be a physical therapist when I was in high school, and I watched a lot of medical dramas." Nichole looked back and dimpled her cheek. "Also, your feet moved a bit while you were *twyned* with Amy."

"What?" Alyse blinked. "They did?"

"I didn't notice." Amy clapped her hands as she laughed. "That's wonderful. You must have been trying to swim."

"Can I come in?" Jim ducked through the doorway. His grin widened as he looked around the room. "This looks like good news."

"It is, Jim." Amy touched his arm as she followed Nichole out the door. "And what's even better is Nichole and I were just leaving."

Alyse wondered how she looked. Shot in the back. Asleep for two days. Her hand rose automatically to her hair. It had been braided and hung over her shoulder. She wore a nightgown, as Amy had in the mirror. *How odd.*

Then Jim smiled at her.

The last time they spoke had been at The Shilo. He'd tried to be honest, but to share a secret he'd held in his heart for so very long hadn't been easy.

Jim eased himself into the chair beside the bed. His tall frame made it seem like a child's chair. "You had me worried."

"I know. I'm sorry."

"Amy thinks you may have trouble walking until your back heals some more."

"She's undoubtedly right. Nichole said she saw my feet move, but I can't feel them." She ran her hand down the covering along her thigh to the knee and back. "It's like they're not there."

"I want to ask your forgiveness."

"My what? Whatever for?"

"For not being here when you needed me. For not telling you the truth about how you know me the first time you asked, hell—even the second time."

"Jim." Alyse laid her hand on his arm and squeezed.

The eyes which lifted to hers were sad and filled with regret.

"Let me ask you something first."

"Anything."

"Tell me everything you remember about Agaria."

Chapter 17

Nichole Harris-Shilo

—

Nichole paused in the doorway to Alyse's room but hesitated to speak.

Jim sat perched at the edge of the bedside chair, bent toward the dark-haired beauty who reclined in bed. His large, callused hands had captured and held her delicate ones between his palms.

His voice didn't reach the doorway, but Nichole could tell by the sparkle in Alyse's eyes and the blush on her cheeks that she was totally into whatever Jim was telling her. It seemed a shame to interrupt, but everything was ready downstairs. She watched for a few seconds longer, unable to keep the grin off her face. A happy ending in the making, despite Alyse's injury.

Jeanne and Amy had helped Alyse dress earlier.

Alyse covered part of her dark blue divided skirt with an edge of the bedsheet. The white lace trimmed blouse Amy had given her brought out the color in her cheeks as she lay propped against the pillows. Her hair, swept to the side in a braid, hung over her shoulder, and her toes wiggled inside white stockings decorated with cornflowers up the calves.

Between Amy's poultice and the short healing sessions each day with her sister, Alyse could now stand, but walking still eluded her. Her right leg didn't respond as well as her left, and the strength in her hips and lower back remained a problem.

None of those issues were evident by the expression on her face when she gazed at Jim. The scene between Jim and Alyse reminded Nichole of herself and Merril. A thrill shot through her as she imagined his homecoming celebration between the two of them tonight.

She rapped her knuckles on the doorframe and brought both sets of eyes to hers. "The parlor is set up if you want to come downstairs."

Jim released Alyse's hands and leaned back in the chair. "We'll be right down." He shared a smile with Alyse. "If you're ready."

"I am."

Jim scooped Alyse up in his arms and held her to his chest. His height combined with such broad shoulders made Alyse appear the size of a child in his arms.

"Are they coming down?" Amy's voice echoed up from below.

"Right now." Nichole hurried to the stairs, then waited for Jim and Alyse.

Jim eased Alyse through the door and ducked his head beneath the frame.

Alyse had wrapped her arm around his neck and tucked her head against his shoulder.

"You two are too cute." Nichole held up her hands to form a small square and made a click sound with the side of her cheek. "Captured." She laughed at the puzzled looks on their faces and hurried down the steps.

Amy and Jeanne had rearranged the front parlor, shoving the small table and embroidered chairs against the wall. The sofa now faced the open entryway and dining room table. Beside the couch stood a contraption Bernard and Bayard had fashioned according to Nichole's instructions.

A medical walker, similar to the one Courtney's Grandma Curtis had used, only made out of carved wood, smoothed and polished. The separate pieces bound together with leather straps, the grip and feet covered in soft leather. The brothers must have worked all night.

Jim placed Alyse in the center of the couch and stood back.

Alyse stared at the wood and leather appliance. "How do I use it?"

"Like this." Nichole demonstrated, placing herself between the four legs of the walker, she put her weight on the leather grips. "Keep in mind, you won't need this for long, but it will help you get around right now." She slid the device forward on its leather feet and took a step. "See? It's easy."

"Easy, you say." Alyse gave Nichole a look filled with trepidation. "I'll give it a try."

Nichole spun the walker around and placed it before Alyse. "Getting to your feet might be a challenge, but you'll build a ton of upper body strength." She pointed to Alyse's sturdy shoes she had placed beside the sofa. "Let's get these on your feet first."

While Nichole and Alyse secured the shoes, Jim bent over the back of the couch and carefully placed his hands around Alyse's waist, avoiding the injury on her back. "I'll help her stand. Let me know when you're ready."

Alyse gripped the top of the device and nodded.

Jim lifted Alyse to her feet, then kept his hands on her waist.

"Now what?" Alyse asked.

Nichole backed up two steps. "Take a step. Slide the walker forward. Take another step. Carry your weight with your arms until your feet are steady. See if you can get to me."

Jason came out of his office and rested his shoulder against the doorframe, arms crossed.

Hunter sat in his usual place, a glass of bourbon at his elbow.

Cat occupied the chair beside him.

Bernard and Bayard were seated at their end of the table directly across from the parlor. They'd turned their chairs to watch Alyse.

Amy hurried across the room and kissed first Bayard and then Bernard on the cheek. "Thank you."

"It wasn't difficult," Bernard replied.

Bayard nodded. His attention focused on Alyse. "It would have been easier with our tools, although Lloyd has quite a few. Enough to get the job accomplished."

The windows were boarded over with temporary repairs. Any panes of glass still intact were shuttered by curtains to shield rooms from the heat of the day.

The James family's easy banter and boisterous encouragement to Alyse kept them from hearing the horses outside.

***

Merril Shilo

—

Only two choices remained. Merril could witness the abomination inside his mind interact with the world around him, or he could sink inside himself—abandon all hope of taking back his life—and that, he would never do.

The thing inside him broke camp with the others at dawn. No one commented on Merril's silence.

Once they were on the road to The Highlands, Bill dropped behind the wagon where Merril rode. After several moments Bill asked, "Are ya feeling any better?"

Merril felt himself nod. "Yep."

Bill narrowed his eyes as he stared at Merril. "If you don't mind me saying so, you still ain't right."

Merril's shoulders rose and fell. "Say what you like."

Bill studied him for several moments, then shook his reins and returned to ride point with Kelly. Tom and the remuda brought up the rear.

At least Bill knows something's wrong with me.

They stopped to change horses at noon. Everyone, including Merril, ate jerky from their saddlebags. They were only a couple of hours away from home, and there was nothing he could do. He thought his mind would break from his impotent fury and helplessness.

It would be so much easier if he didn't have to bear this burden, to slip over the edge of sanity and disappear forever in the darkness.

Stop tempting me to give up. This is my body. My life. And I'm not done yet.

Nichole had never given up on him, even when she returned to a different time. A different life. Could he do less? He would watch and wait. Try to find a way to warn Bill or Nichole about the horror that lurked behind his familiar face.

They topped the last rise and the smoke from The Highlands' cook fire rose straight into the still afternoon air. The horses picked up speed, knowing rest and care lay ahead.

The demon-spawn inside him must have realized their destination as well. With a shake of the reins and a sharp kick to the flank of his mount, Merril shot ahead of the wagon.

Tom yelled, but from behind, his words weren't clear. His concern would have been for the horse Merril rode.

Merril passed Kelly and Bill down the small incline and crossed the little bridge over the now dry creek. As he climbed the hill to the house, desperation gripped Merril's mind. Would Nichole recognize a monster controlled him? Would she see the demon on him the same way she had on the animals?

Unless what she sees is different with people.

He couldn't take that chance. He had to find some way to warn them.

Emotion built in his throat and stung his eyes.

I can't lose Nichole like this. Not now.

A tear escaped and rolled down his cheek, unnoticed by the demon. A message of sorrow and apology Merril hoped she would see and understand.

For the first time in two days, he heard the high-pitched giggle of the demon as he kicked free of the stirrups, slid from the saddle, and mounted the step of the front porch. Too preoccupied with his destination to notice the tears.

Merril could hear laughter and shouts inside. He watched his hand reach out and grip the door handle.

***

Nichole Harris-Shilo

—

Nichole clapped her hands then covered her wide grin with her fingers. "Wow." She sniffed and clapped again, laughing with tears in her eyes. "You're doing fantastic!"

Alyse's right foot turned inward as she pulled it across the floor, but her left foot had gained a lot of strength already. She was able to step and stand steady on it. Crossing the entry from the sofa to the table, she made an awkward hop to turn the walker and then smiled brightly at Jim. "This is exhausting."

"You'll get your strength back," he assured her, and held out his arms. "Come back and have a seat. We can do this again tomorrow, and every day until you don't need it anymore."

"I think we could make a few improvements on the device," Bayard said. "Perhaps a wider base for more stability."

"Then it would be heavier," Bernard replied. "She's already tired from lifting it."

Alyse had almost made it back to Jim when the front door opened and Merril stepped inside.

"Merril!" Nichole called with delight as he entered the room. Her breath caught in horror and she went still with shock at the sight of her husband.

Merril's clothes were filthy and covered in trail dust. His hair had come unbound and hung in oily strings from his scalp. He grinned at Alyse who stood only an arm's reach from the door. Silt from the road had dried on his teeth. A tear rolled slowly down his grime covered cheek.

He took another step forward.

When he moved, Nichole saw the shadowed hump of a demon on his back.

Merril reached for Alyse.

Jim intervened between the two and gripped Merril's arm. "Hold up, Merril. She's a bit unsteady on her feet."

Merril jerked his arm free and glared at Jim. Tears streamed down Merril's face.

"Is Tom with you?" Jim grabbed and held Merril as he tried to step around him. "Let's go outside, and I'll help you take care of your horse."

Nichole's eyes rose to the satchel above the door. It was missing. Knocked from its nail during the gun battle and swept up with the broken glass. They'd never thought to replace it. "Watch out, Jim." The words caught in her throat, but she forced them out, "Merril's possessed."

Wild laughter burst from Merril's stiff grin at her words as he shoved Jim away and lunged for Alyse.

Everyone surged into motion.

Jim knocked Merril back against the wall, plucked Alyse from her walker, and moved her to a chair along the parlor's back wall. He pivoted to defend her.

Both Bayard and Bernard stood and looked at Nichole. "I sense no magic in him," Bayard remarked.

Bernard pulled Amy back before she could rush to defend her sister. "Stay beside us."

Movement behind Nichole caused her to turn.

Hunter picked up Merril's voodoo doll and murmured an incantation. He downed the tall, half-filled glass of bourbon in two gulps, flipped it over, and covered the miniature of Merril. With his hand firmly pressed to the bottom of the glass, Hunter continued his chant. A red seam of light shot between the rim of the glass and the table.

From a swirl of shadows behind Hunter, Carrefour stepped forward.

What have you done, chwal?

"I've caught him," Hunter stated.

Nichole spun back to Merril.

Near the door, sealed like a bug in a jar, Merril pushed his hands against an invisible wall. His face locked in a silent scream. He slipped down the barrier to his knees, slapped the obstruction twice, and then the demon separated from his back.

Merril twisted as he vomited on the floor.

The monster thrust itself against Hunter's impediment as it sought a means of escape.

"It's trapped." Nichole turned to Hunter. "The devil-thing has separated from Merril."

Hunter nodded but continued to chant.

Bayard glanced between Merril and Hunter. "Is he doing that?"

Carrefour strode forward and faced the invisible barrier.

Release the demon. It is beyond my reach and dying. It will be of no use to me.

Hunter shook his head. "My friends shall remain guarded until the demon is gone."

Carrefour whirled to glare at Hunter.

Release your spell this instant. I require all of the demons, as promised.

"I promised you nothing," Hunter replied.

"Promised who?" Bayard raised a brow at Hunter.

Nichole knelt on the floor beside Merril's convulsing body. "He's sick and needs care, now, Hunter."

Inside the trap, the shadow-demon had become frantic, bouncing from side to side, throwing itself against the invisible obstruction, its hellish face distorted as though pressed against glass.

Jim hurried to aid Merril but rebounded against Hunter's unseen trap. He ran his hands in disbelief against the curved invisible wall, unable to see the demon inside. "Let him out."

Carrefour paced the edge of the invisible confinement; his walking cane whipped in a fury against the impediment. *Yes, let him out.*

"I am sorry, *mon ami*. That, I cannot do." Hunter stared at the frantic shadow. "There is an angry demon trapped inside with Merril."

"A demon?" Bayard shook his head. "It wouldn't get past ..." He pointed at the empty nail above the door. "Where's my satchel?"

"It was destroyed during the gun battle. I was going to tell you," Amy said as she crossed the room to her sister.

"I wish you had. That would have stopped the demon," Bayard replied.

"From what I saw, your satchel of protection would have killed Merril as well," Nichole retorted.

Bayard rubbed his chin. "Well, there is that."

The shadow at the top of the trap ceased to move. It floated downward, dissipating like a dark fog, and was gone before it reached Merril.

Carrefour bellowed and stalked toward Hunter. He slapped his red cane down on the table.

The sharp crack of wood on wood made Nichole jump, but no one else appeared startled by the loud noise.

I demand what I was promised.

"And what was that?" Hunter shouted. "In return for what? You have done nothing but drink Jason's whiskey and berate my skill since I summoned you."

"Who—are—you—talking to?" Jason looked askance at Hunter.

Carrefour scowled at the Cajun then walked into a vortex of shadows and vanished.

Hunter lifted the glass from the table.

Merril slid from the side of the rising barrier and rolled like a rag doll onto the floor.

Chapter 18

Nichole Harris-Shilo

—

The odd exchange between Hunter and Carrefour fled her mind as Nichole gathered Merril in her arms. She tugged his shoulders across her lap, pushing the befouled hair from his face. "Merril?" Relief washed over her when she found his pulse. She gently slapped his cheek. "Merril?"

"Do you want the smelling salts," Amy asked.

Nichole shook her head when Merril's eyelids fluttered. "Not yet." Her throat was so tight with fear, she could barely understand her own words. She looked up at Jim and Amy and cleared the emotion from her throat. "A wet cloth to wash his face will be enough for now. Please hurry."

The door opened, threatening to bump Nichole.

Jim stopped the door's swing with his long reach.

Bill poked his head inside. His eyes bugged at Merril and Nichole on the floor. "I reckoned he was sick."

"You knew?" Nichole lifted her attention to the wrangler.

"Yeah. Merril acted mighty peculiar." Bill shuffled sideways through the door, shaking his head.

"When did you first notice his odd behavior?" Hunter approached and lowered to his haunches beside Nichole. He placed his palm across Merril's brow and closed his eyes.

"Right after he came back from talking with the police chief."

"The police chief?" Nichole asked. "Why did Merril speak with him?"

"I guess you wouldn't know 'bout all that." Bill shut the front door, and the sound of the wagon, pulling into the yard, cut off. "When we first got to your house in Denver, one of the neighbors came over. He told us two men were found dead in your yard."

Bill scrubbed his chin with his hand and nervously scanned the silent room. He shuffled his feet as his face colored. "Since Merril had to go to the bank, he said he'd stop and talk with the chief on his way home. He was fine when he left the house, but when he came back..."

Nichole turned from Bill and stared up at Jim. "Don't you usually handle the banking in Denver?"

"I do." Jim's jaw tightened, and he glanced at Alyse. "And I would have that day as well except—"

"Except he knew my life was in danger, so he came back to The Highlands instead," Alyse whispered. Her lashes lifted, and she looked at Jim.

Jim nodded and faced Nichole. "I gave Merril the bill of sale and a draft to draw on the buyer's bank while we were still at the stockyard. I left straight from there and came home."

"So it might have been you the demon took instead," Amy handed Nichole a damp washcloth, "if Merril became possessed near the bank."

"I don't think a demon can seize me," Jim replied. "My life would be in mortal danger, and that could never happen."

Hunter's eyes opened wide, and he rose to stare at Jim. "That's a bold statement, *mon ami*. Take it from one who knows of such things. You would be as open to possession as Merril, or myself."

Jim's mouth twitched, and he shook his head. "I don't think so."

"Why? Because of your size? Your strength?" Hunter chuckled and looked around the room. "What sets you apart from the rest of us?"

Nichole washed the tear stains from Merril's cheeks then folded the cloth and placed it on her husband's brow. She raised her face to watch the two men who stood over her.

Jim glanced over his shoulder at Alyse.

She nodded. "You should tell them."

Jim narrowed his eyes at Hunter. "Alyse and her family have not been my first brush with magic. In fact, now that I consider it, my initial encounter was most likely with a spell caster of your kind."

"My kind?"

"A shaman of spirits. A young woman with far too much power for her youth." His mouth twisted. "I live with the result of her—displeasure." He indicated Alyse. "We both do."

Hunter's brows drew together as he studied Jimmy Leigh. "You live under a charm from this sorceress?"

"A curse."

"*Mon Dieu!*" Hunter breathed. He raised his palm toward Jim's forehead, then paused. "May I?"

Jim nodded. "You can't hurt me."

Hunter chuckled and placed his palm on Jim's brow. He stood motionless for several seconds. Eyes closed. The smile slowly faded from his face. He lowered his hand as his somber gaze met and locked with the foreman's. He bowed his head to Jim. "Forgive me, Jimmy Leigh. I could not have known the depth of your knowledge or the length of your suffering."

"Can you help him?" Alyse called from the sofa. "Help us?"

Hunter shook his head at Alyse. "No, I'm sorry. Not with this. Your—affliction far exceeds anything I've encountered. I wouldn't know where to begin." He faced Jim. "You should speak to my *grand-mère*. She may be able to offer suggestions. She's more knowledgeable in the dark arts than I will ever be."

"It's true then?" Bayard asked. "He can't be possessed?"

"There's no doubt." Hunter's gaze moved around the room. "I know of nothing that could harm him."

"But I've seen you injured." Amy left her sister's side and approached Jim. "I've bandaged your wounds."

"The injuries were never life-threatening. Especially under your care."

Merril coughed and struck out with a cry.

Both Hunter and Jim crouched to restrain Merril.

"Easy, *mon ami*, the demon has gone."

"Shh, Merril, shh. You're all right," Nichole soothed.

Bill, his eyes as large as saucers, edged back to the door. "I'm jus' gonna... help Tom see to the horses." He opened the door and slipped outside.

"We've scared the crap out of Bill," Nichole chuckled. Relief that Merril was home and now safe made her giddy.

"Yep," Jim stood. "I'll go talk with him. The last thing we need is him swapping tales with Lloyd."

Merril had calmed down, no longer fighting against Hunter's restraints. "You don't know," he begged Hunter. "It's tricked me before. It can hide inside me, waiting to take over. Then I'll disappear into blackness again. I don't know what I might do."

The sympathy in Hunter's eyes caused Nichole to choke up. *He understands the horror Merril feels.*

"Rest easy, Merril. We watched the demon die. More than that, I checked your soul for signs of possession. You are free, *mon ami.*"

Nichole blinked tears from her eyes. When she looked up, Lawna had taken Jim's place beside her. She held out a glass of water. "Miss Cat said I should bring Mr. Merril something to drink."

Nichole smiled her appreciation at Cat, who remained near the table, and took the glass. "Thanks, Lawna."

Hunter eased Merril forward until he sat on his own.

Merril nodded, then took the water from Nichole. "Thank you." His gaze rose to Lawna's face. He blanched and looked away, taking small sips of the water.

"How did you learn to kill the demon?" Merril whispered to Hunter.

Hunter straightened and gave a small chuckle. "I did not intend to kill it. I only meant to separate you from those the demon might do harm."

"I felt it panic." Merril held out his hand to Hunter.

Hunter gripped Merrill's outstretched palm and pulled him to his feet. "How so?"

Merril gave the empty glass to Lawna, then helped Nichole to stand beside him. "There were two of those bastards. The servant inside my mind, and its master, Morago. Morago would speak to me sometimes. Taunt me, but his servant never did.

"I saw—" Merril paused and addressed Alyse. "I saw myself come into the house, felt the demon's excitement when he spotted you within arm's reach." He looked at Hunter as he hugged Nichole to his side. "Morago urged him on, watching through my eyes, when suddenly his master was gone."

"The barrier must have severed your possessor's tie to Morago."

"As soon as I felt his panic, I lost consciousness."

"He must have tried to find his master." Hunter rounded the table. He picked up the small voodoo doll of Merril. "And when he could no longer feel Morago, he abandoned you to seek his master. But if he could not reach Morago, why not return to you?"

He could not. A minor demon such as this would not have the power of possession. Released, he would have been mine—as promised.

Carrefour's angry stride took him from the shadows to stand beside Hunter.

"Perhaps because I was unconscious," Merril suggested.

Nichole wrapped her arms around her husband and hugged him close. "He's gone, and you're here." She tipped her head back. "Bad things happen when we're apart, Merril Shilo. Never again, do you hear me?"

Merril nodded and tucked her head to his shoulder, kissing her forehead. "Then maybe you can help me with a bath."

***

Morago

—

Morago watched through Merril's eyes as his demon-spawn opened the door and stepped inside the witch's house. Both twins were there. One stood close enough for his minion to grasp. Just one more step. Merril's hand reached out and—the tiny silver thread between Morago and his servant severed.

Big Buck's eyes flew open. He sat alone in his personal room at the brothel. Morago searched in alarm, desperate to find the thin silver thread which shackled his demon-spawn, but it was gone.

No slave remained at the end of the thread.

The witch no longer stood within grasp.

"Ah!" He jumped to his feet, picked up the lantern on the side table, and smashed it with fury against the wall. "What have they done? What magic do they use against me?

Violet opened the door and peeked inside the room. She ducked out as the porcelain pitcher smashed against the door, followed by the basin.

"Must I go myself? Are all of you incompetent failures?"

A chorus of denials filled his thoughts from his remaining demonic slaves.

A lone female chortled at the back of his mind.

He followed a silver thread to the demon-finch. It waited in the treetop near June's room. He fluttered to the sill and peered through the finch's eyes between the gap in the closed curtains.

June knelt beside the bed in prayer.

Back and down a different thread to demon-Albert.

Albert was on his hands and knees, gardening beside his wife. He sat back on his heels at the touch of Morago's mind.

Master?

Morago pulled back without responding.

At least I have two. Faithful and diligent.

It seemed as though his servants had been released or destroyed when they approached the witches.

How is that possible?

Morago touched the sensation of moisture on his face. His fingertips glistened red. He turned to the mirror and stared at the image of his host. Twin trails of blood flowed from his nostrils. He cleaned Buck's face with a handkerchief as angry eyes glared back at himself.

Furious, he tossed the bloody cloth into the corner.

How were they releasing his servants?

I may need to go there myself and find out.

Chapter 19

Hunter

—

The James brothers and Sam offered to help Tom settle the horses from the cattle drive while Amy and Jeanne went along to help Henny unload the chuck wagon. Jim carried an exhausted Alyse upstairs and had yet to come back down.

Only a small group remained at the dining room table—Cat, Merril, Nichole, Jason, and Hunter.

Lawna returned occasionally to fill Merril's water glass, then disappeared down the kitchen passage.

Dark circles underscored Merril's eyes. He drank glass after glass of water and flinched away from Nichole's touch.

Hunter remembered that befouled sensation. Always wondering if somewhere, in the back of your mind, some part of the demon who dominated you remained. Terrified it would appear at any moment to seize control of your body and endanger the ones you loved.

"It is gone, *mon ami*. Your wife and I, we saw it die."

"I know." Merril shoved the long hair out of his face. "I just... I don't know. I feel unclean."

"I can fill the tub for you," Nichole offered, halting her hand at the last moment before she caressed her husband's arm.

Merril pulled away from her touch offering a sad, one-sided smile in apology. "I'm filthy, Nicki. You know I love you."

Jason leaned forward and looked past Nichole to Merril. "Before you bathe, could I have the receipt from the bank? I assume Jim had paid the new hires before he released them." He sniffed and cleared his throat. "I wrote out the draws for the temporary wranglers and gave them to Jim before you left."

Merril drank the last of his water. "I'm sure he did. They were gone when he returned from the buyer with the sales receipt and a check drawn from a Denver bank."

"How much did we get?"

Merril pulled two envelopes from his back pocket and tossed them onto the table. "He didn't tell you?"

"He hasn't left Alyse's room, much less taken the time to speak to me about a little thing like having enough cash to make it through the winter." Jason reached for the bank envelope. "He only said you'd be here soon enough with the sale and deposit receipts."

"I have both, and they're the same. The bank would only allow me to deposit into the Harris account, me being a Shilo and not on the accounts."

Jason read both receipts. "Better than I'd hoped."

"Our people still need to be paid for the drive."

Jason nodded. "I'll take care of that."

"Make sure Henny receives the same pay you'd have given a new hire for the cook position." Nichole dimpled a sarcastic smile at her cousin.

"Is that necessary?" Jason replied.

"You planned to cheat her?" Nichole shook her head. "Consider my full review mandatory." Nichole relaxed back in her seat and crossed her arm.

"But she's a woman," Jason argued.

"Don't even go there with me, Jason." Nichole's face darkened. "You will not win."

"And colored," Jason spoke at the same time.

"What?" Nichole twisted in her chair to face her cousin. "God! You piss me off." She glowered at her cousin. "If you like, we can review my thoughts on inequality right now. I'll use smaller words this time."

Jason stared at Nichole, his lips tight with annoyance. "That won't be necessary."

"Good. So you know how important this is to me, I fully intend to compare Henny's pay with the ledgers from last year. Just to keep you honest." Nichole rolled her eyes in the face of Jason's anger. "I need to review those ledgers anyway," she muttered.

Hunter closed his gaping mouth after the cousins finished their argument. He cocked a brow at Nichole. "Where do these concerns come from, *fillette*? Your Boston upbringing?"

"Not at all." Jason snorted. "Her aggressive, manly behavior came about after her head injury." He pointed at his temple and twirled his finger. "Along with a whole host of other strange ideas."

Nichole narrowed her eyes at Jason, flipped her hair over her shoulder, and smiled at Hunter. "Things were different where Courtney grew up. Or should I say when." She shrugged and pointed to the other envelope. "What's this?" She opened the flap and several items spilled onto the table. A tarnished wedding ring, a small buck knife, and a stitched sampler.

Lawna set the water ewer on the table. "Those are... those are Timothy's things." Her large eyes stared at the items beside the envelope. "Why would you have his ring?" Then understanding dawned, and she covered her mouth with thin trembling fingers. Tears filled her eyes and streamed down her dark face. A sob escaped as she lifted the sampler and felt the thread with her thumb. Her haunted gaze lifted to Merril. Her lips quivered, and she cleared her throat before she spoke, "What happened?"

"The police aren't sure."

Hunter cleared his throat. "Timothy—the man whose image you carry in your locket?"

Lawna nodded, crushing the sampler with Hope-Anne's name in her fist.

Hunter shifted his attention to Merril. "And the second man in your yard was found with a horse?"

"How do you know this?" Merril asked.

"Do their spirits speak to you?" Nichole whispered.

"No." Hunter gave a self-depreciating scoff. "Nothing like that." He glanced around the table, caught Lawna's teary gaze, then stared down at his hand on the table. "I used my pendulum that morning to track the witches. The arrowhead said I'd find an individual from The Prophecy at your house." Hunter sighed and shook his head. "I misunderstood. I thought it would be one of the witches." He shrugged and looked at Nichole. "I ignored the voice in my head. I believed I knew best. When I stepped into your back yard, there was a cowboy on his horse, staring up at your second-floor window." Hunter leaned forward and faced Merril. "Morago was in possession of the cowboy. With a single glance, he was inside my mind. In control."

Cat shivered, and Hunter took her hand.

"I watched the man and horse fall, an observer. My purpose—my will—ripped from me. The cowboy and his horse had been bitterly used and discarded. When I turned—" Hunter cleared his throat and glanced up at Lawna. "When Morago turned my eyes, I noticed a young man along the side of the house." Hunter rubbed his forehead, then held out his hand in supplication. "He must have followed me from the street." His fingers closed into fist. "Your husband was killed by the demon using my hand. I am filled with remorse, *madame*."

"My God," Merril murmured. "You saw Timothy murdered."

"I was powerless to stop it."

"What happened to him—to his body?" Lawna's voice was raw. She stepped back, still gripping the small sampler with her daughter's name. "Where is my Timothy now?"

Both Merril and Hunter came slowly to their feet.

"The police buried him in the Denver cemetery." Merril took the distraught young woman in his arms. "I'm sorry, Lawna."

"What's happened?" Cookie asked from the doorway.

Lawna pushed from Merril and threw herself into Cookie's arms. "Hope-Anne's daddy is gone. My Timothy is dead. Murdered."

"Murdered?" Cookie patted Lawna's back and gazed wide-eyed at Merril. "Did you find that out in town?"

Merril nodded. "Yes. The police chief hoped I could identify the personal effects from two men found dead near our house." He placed the small knife and ring back in the envelope. "Unfortunately, I recognized Lawna's sampler."

Lawna held out the sampler to Cookie. "I made it for him when she was born."

"Oh, my child. I'm so sorry." Cookie guided Lawna down the servants' hallway. "I'll get you something warm to drink, and we'll pray for Timothy. My lands, I never dreamed of such things."

Hunter watched Lawna until she disappeared down the hall, then resumed his seat. "I couldn't stop him."

Merril's hand dropped to his side. He went limp as he nodded at Hunter. "I'm afraid I'm acquainted with just how that feels." He tried to give his wife a smile as he helped her from the chair. "You promised to draw me a bath."

"I did, and I will. You need it." Nichole led Merril solemnly toward the kitchen.

"And I've paperwork and checks to write." Jason stood, rounded the table, and withdrew to his office.

Hunter acknowledged Jason with a slight nod. With pressed lips, he kept his sight on his long, slender fingers, pushing down on the polished wood until his nails turned white.

If he had the means, he could bind Morago to his host. But without this powerful magic, the demon would take flight, and possess another, leaving Amy and Alyse no chance to defeat him. And if he were successful, Morago's host had to die.

It must be me. I'm the only one with a chance to hold him.

Impossible. Carrefour emerged from the shadows and paced behind the table, swinging his walking stick. *You already carry the weight of another, my chwal, or have you forgotten?*

"I forget nothing," Hunter murmured between clenched teeth. He eyed Carrefour as he crossed to the front door.

"Really?" Cat chuckled.

Hunter blinked and focused his attention on Cat.

"I could have sworn you forgot I was even sitting here."

"Forgive me, my love. Merril's trial has raised the horror of my own. In many ways, I am still a man possessed." Ignoring the *loa*, he took Cat's hand. "My work, my thoughts, and even my dreams are filled with how I might defeat the monster."

Cat's face flushed slightly at his touch. "I thought Amy and Alyse were to defeat him. You take too much on yourself."

"Perhaps you are right, *mon beau chaton.*" He rose, drawing her to her feet. "I have been inside too long. A breath of fresh air, with a lovely companion, will help reorder my thinking."

He ignored Carrefour as they passed. Hunter handed Cat a parasol and plucked his hat from the peg. As he closed the door, he narrowed his eyes at the loa. "We shall talk."

Yes, we shall. Carrefour bowed over his leg as the door shut.

Outside, the afternoon had warmed significantly. The weather had gone from daily showers and moderate temperatures to desert heat.

"There's shade on this side of the house." Cat led the way around the corner to the tall cottonwood near Nichole's balcony. "Only one, but with plenty of leaves." She closed her parasol and strolled beneath the tree.

Hunter followed, drawn forward by Cat's beauty, and the affection in her eyes. "Its taproot must be as deep as the well." He looked up through the green leaves at the dark blue sky.

"I could not have imagined a land without trees." She smiled at the tall cottonwood and shrugged. "For the most part."

"I've mapped many places. This ocean of grass was strange to me as well, the first time I came west from New Orleans."

Cat relaxed against the trunk and tipped her head back. The tiny tip of her tongue moistened her lips. "Sam wants to continue to Denver when he takes the bodies of the gunmen to Kiowa Crossing. He intends to take me home."

"He told me." He lifted his hand and brushed his knuckles along her soft cheek.

"I don't want to go." She leaned into his touch, closing her eyes with a sigh.

He lifted her chin and brushed his mouth against hers. "It's best you return with your brother. Leaving this place would be safer for you both."

She pursued his lips as he straightened. Gripping his jacket, she pressed her open mouth to his.

Hunter could not withstand her passion nor deny his pleasure. He pushed her back against the tree, holding her with his body while his lips sucked first her top lip, then bit and tugged gently on her bottom one. He trailed a line of feathery kisses to her ear.

Cat gasped and arched her neck. "Where is my home now?" she whispered. "Sam stays at the boarding house, and I lived at a school I no longer attend." She plucked the tie from his hair and ran her nails up through his scalp, directing his lips back to hers. "I want my home to be with you, Alexander."

Her words sent a thrill of desire through his chest and to his loins. He wanted that as well. A life with Cat. A home. A future. His mouth slanted across hers and he drew her into his arms, tightening his grip. His soft groan was more than sexual. He wanted all the things Catherine Kline represented. Respectability. Decency. Everything he could never have because of who he was.

He broke the kiss and pulled away from her swollen lips.

Her mouth found his neck, and she kissed down to the notch of his collar bone. "I love you."

"I love you too, *ma belle* Cat." He held her from his chest at arm's length then watched as her eyes fluttered open. "When this is over, and I return home to New Orleans, then you and I—"

Would what? Talk about the reasons she could never marry a man like me?

Would he confess his past, his family, and watch the love light fade from her eyes? Could he bear it?

Kiss the girl again, or better yet, take her someplace private. Carrefour lounged against the side of the house, studying his nails. *She won't put up a fight. She wants you; can't you tell? Besides, you owe me a demon. I would play the voyeur in recompense.*

Cat stared up at Hunter as though he could do no wrong. "Tell Sam to let me stay, that you want me to stay with you." Trust glistened in her eyes. "Let's not wait until you return to home. We can be together now." She licked her lips and inhaled, lifting her chest. "Please."

You see? What did I say? Carrefour laughed. *Take the girl inside and be done with it.*

"No." Hunter shook his head. "You need to leave with Sam."

"What?" Cat pulled from his arms and stepped back. "You don't want me to stay?"

"I can't keep you secure and fight like I must. I want you far away from this conflict, and safe with your brother."

Cat backed away. In the sunlight, tears sparkled on her cheeks. She covered her mouth with her hand and ran to the back yard.

Hunter watched until she disappeared around the back of the house. The sound of Katy laughing with Hope-Anne floated to him on a slight breeze. At counterpoint to the child's laughter, the cries of her bereaved mother rang softly from the kitchen window.

Before Hunter could return home to New Orleans, and to Cat, he would make Morago pay for the damage he had done to these lives. His gaze shifted to the *loa*.

Carrefour shook his head and twirled his walking staff at Hunter's perusal. *You must have many opportunities with lovely young women to spurn one such as she. Remember, I am owed.* He tapped his top hat with his hand and disappeared into a swirl of shadows.

Hunter needed to discover what agreement *arrière-grand-mère* made with the powerful *loa*, but he hadn't heard Dessa's voice since he woke in the crossroad.

Chapter 20

Nichole Harris-Shilo

—

"Take her bag to the wagon." Nichole directed Kelly, pointing at the carpet bag beside the door. "Be sure to put it on or under the seat." Her voice lowered. "Just not in the back with the bodies."

Lloyd had used most of the ranch's oiled sackcloth in the back of the wagon. The heaviest cloth covered Sam and Cat's trunks, separating their belongings from the bodies. The rest concealed the ten dead gunmen.

Kelly nodded and lifted the bag. His gaze darted from Nichole to Cat's stiff back where she stood before the bedroom window. "Anything to help."

"Thanks." Nichole closed the door and shifted her attention to the distraught young woman clutching a handkerchief. Roughly the same age Courtney had been when she had closed her eyes and followed Merril's voice into her past life, Catherine Kline could have been Courtney's twin. Physically, the resemblance still startled Nichole. Emotionally, the auburn-haired young woman had some serious growing up to do.

"Dry your eyes." Nichole wrung water from the washcloth into the basin and handed it to Cat. "And wash your face. You don't want Hunter to see you cry."

"Why not?" Cat took the cloth from Nichole. "He has to know how much I love him. How much I want to stay here."

"No, he doesn't." Nichole snatched the cloth back and brusquely wiped the tears from Cat's cheeks. "All Hunter needs to know is you're safe." She lifted an eyebrow at Cat's stubborn glare. "Do you want his last impression of you to be one of a puff-eyed, petulant child?" She pushed Cat toward the mirror on the bureau. "Smile at him. Wave goodbye." Their gazes met in the mirror. "Toss your hair over your shoulder and look away if you feel the tears start. Cry yourself sick all the way home if you like, but don't give Hunter one more thing to worry about."

Cat took back the cloth and dabbed at her swollen eyes. "You're right, of course." Her lips trembled, and she shook her head. "I thought I'd lost him to the demon when he walked into the yard at The Shilo, and then again when Jim shot him." She pressed her lips and looked at Nichole from the corner of her eye. A chuckle escaped along with another tear. "I know it's wrong, but I hoped once he received acceptance into the Marshals service, he would ask me..."

"To marry you?"

Cat covered her eyes with the cloth and nodded.

"You'll be with Hunter—Alexander Veau. You'll have a child. A son together." Nichole gripped Cat's arm. "Hunter will come home safe to you in New Orleans." She shook the taller woman a bit, then walked to the door. "But for God's sake, give him a lovely smile with a sparkle in your eye as an incentive to get there in one piece."

Downstairs, Kelly had left the front door open. Dust and flies from the animals in the yard ventured into the house. Nichole rushed onto the porch and pulled the door shut.

The wagon Sam and Cat had arrived in days ago stood hitched to the livery's horses. In the back of the cart, the dead men were stacked like cut logs. Their saddles and bags were piled on top of the cover. They drew more flies than the horse manure. Nichole covered her nose and rounded the corner on the porch.

Tom tied the dead men's horses in two lines from the back of the wagon. His mount stood several paces away, saddled and ready to ride.

Merril, Sam, and Hunter watched Tom work from the porch.

"Is she ready yet?" Sam asked Nichole.

"Just about." She shaded her eyes and looked up at the tall men. "She should be down any moment."

Sam spoke to Merril, "I'll talk to the sheriff as soon as we get to town and turn over the bodies of the attackers and their belongings. I'll give a written statement as an eyewitness, and also file it with the Marshal's office." The two men shook hands, then Sam pulled Merril close and pounded him on the back. "Don't be a stranger." He released Merril and his gaze switched to Hunter. "If there are any messages about White Eagle, I'll send them back with Tom."

Hunter tipped his head. "I don't hold out much hope."

"He'll be almost impossible to find," Merril agreed. "But we had to try."

Cat opened the front door, rolled her eyes at the stench, and covered most of her face with a handkerchief. "Dear me," she muttered.

Sam and Hunter exchanged a look, and Sam stepped from the porch and walked past his sister.

Nichole tucked herself under her husband's arm and wrapped her arms around his waist.

Cat strode toward Hunter and smiled. She reached up and touched his face with her hand. "You'll be careful."

"*Oui, mon beau chaton.*" He kissed her palm and then turned her hand to kiss her fingers. "I will be home as soon as I can."

As soon as Hunter released her hand, Cat trod past him and hugged Nichole. "Thank you."

"You and your brother are welcome to visit anytime," Merril said when Cat stepped back.

Cat smiled at Merril, glanced at Hunter, then tossed her hair over her shoulder and walked to her brother with the handkerchief over her nose and mouth.

"Good girl," Nichole murmured.

"Hmm?" Merril asked.

Nichole shook her head.

Sam assisted Cat onto the bench, then settled beside her and took up the reins.

Cat waved at the porch with one hand, holding the white cloth over her face. When the wagon turned onto the road, she spun around and didn't look back.

***

Morago

—

With his other gunmen inexplicably gone, Morago sent Violet to fetch the man who guarded Buck's property. He waited impatiently in the small gambling room at the bordello.

The front door swung open. Vasquez crossed the lady's room and approached Buck's tiny office. His flamboyant red shirt and shiny, pointed toe boots caused a grunt of amusement to escape from Buck's throat. Vasquez pulled his wide-brimmed hat from his head when he reached the back room. "You sent for me, *señor*?" He grinned and rolled the tip of his black drooping mustache.

Buck smirked. "That I did." He turned and handed the thin gunman a drink. "As it happens, I have a position available that I want you to fill."

Vasquez reached for the glass, a wary look in his eye. "Me?"

As the glass left Morago's hand, he sent one of his demon-slaves into Vasquez.

The Mexican blinked several times, then focused on Buck. "Anything you need, señor."

"Splendid." Morago poured himself a drink. "First, we will need to recruit more men, twenty, if we can find them."

"Twenty?" Vasquez scoffed. "I know of maybe five or six *hombres* who could use the work." He downed the rest of his whiskey and set the glass on the table. "But it's a start. *Si*?"

Buck stared at Vasquez for several moments. The invisible silver thread to the demon-slave inside the Mexican remained intact despite the brazen behavior displayed by Vasquez. "Soon," Buck replied.

Master.

The sibilant whisper of demon-Albert diverted Morago's attention from Vasquez.

In less than a heartbeat, Morago was with his servant inside Albert Fielding's mind. He gazed across the dirt street toward the rebuilt porch and the red "H" on the front door.

A thin, dark-haired man wearing a tailored suit attempted to peek through the parlor window of the witch's house.

Find out who has come calling, Morago whispered.

Albert picked up his hat from the side table and walked outside.

"Where are you going, Al?" his wife called.

Albert ignored her question and crossed the street to the Harris house.

"Jason?" The handsomely dressed man pounded his fist against the door. "You can't hide from me."

"Hello, stranger," Albert called as he paused several feet from the porch steps. "Sounds like you're looking for Mr. Harris."

Startled, the dark-haired man spun around, grabbing at his top hat which had wobbled off his head. "Who might you be, sir?"

Albert indicated the nearest house across the street. "Albert Fielding. I'm a neighbor of the Harris family. I watch their house while they're away."

The summer wind blew the stranger's light-weight jacket open to display wide shoulders and black slacks. His blue and yellow silk tie knotted around his collarless shirt had been tucked into a yellow silk vest. His dark, thick mustache matched the color on his head. Clear hazel eyes looked Albert up and down. After a moment, he stepped from the porch and held out his hands to Albert. "Otis Pierce, an associate of Jason's from Boston."

Albert shook the man's hand. "Jason and the missus live at the ranch now." He stood back and thumbed his hat to the back of his head. "You do know about the cattle ranch?"

"His Uncle Quincy's ranch, if I remember correctly." The well-dressed man sniffed derisively.

Albert grinned. "Yup. Right up until poor Quince bought the farm. His daughter owns the ranch now. That's her house too." He pointed at the red H on the door.

"You don't say?" Otis glanced at the house. "Nichole, wasn't it? Quite a fetching little thing, as I recall." He winked at Albert. "Does she abide at the ranch as well?"

"Yup." Albert rocked back on his heels. "With her cousin and her new husband."

"Well, that is a shame." Otis chuckled.

Ask him if he intends to visit the ranch. Morago prompted. *Send him to me.*

"Their ranch is a long day's ride due east." Albert glanced over his shoulder.

His wife had come onto their porch, hands on her hips as she stared in his direction.

"Might you pay them a visit?" Albert smiled at Otis. "If so, tell them I said hello."

"Albert, was it?" Otis brushed at a speck of dust on his jacket. "Perhaps I will venture out and visit with my old friend. I've come all this way, after all."

"You're staying in town?" At the man's nod, Albert produced a card from his trouser pocket. "Be sure to look up Randolph Buckner. He's the man to know in town. Owns a number of fine establishments."

"Thank you." Otis took the card with two fingers and read the name. "I may do that. I have a room at the Union Hotel near the station." He slipped the card into his vest pocket and climbed into his carriage. "Good day to you, Mr. Fielding."

Albert waved and moved from the dust kicked up by the carriage. "To you too, Mr. Pierce."

Morago sped back along the silver thread and blinked Vasquez into focus.

The swarthy Mexican sat at a nearby table, boots crossed on the tabletop, a full glass of Buck's best whiskey beside his elbow.

"What the hell are you doing?" Anger moved Buck forward. Otis Pierce was momentarily forgotten.

Vasquez came to his feet in a single smooth motion. "I saw you were called away." He picked up the glass and held it out to Buck. "I poured this for your return." He bowed his head, looking at the floor until Buck took the glass from his hand. "Is everything good, *señor*?"

Buck took a large drink, and Morago relished the smokey flavor of the whiskey as it burned down Buck's throat. He wiped his lips with the back of his hand and gave Vasquez a nod. "Yes." He finished the whiskey in a large gulp and swallowed, hissing at the heat on the back of his tongue. "Round up the new men. Bring them here to me." He dropped the glass onto the table. "Twenty. Gunmen. *Comprender*?"

"Twenty will take time, *señor*, but I can have eight, perhaps nine, here this evening."

Buck nodded. "Twenty by the end of the week, but no less than eight here by tonight. Violet?" He bellowed toward the door.

From the reception room, the dark-skinned beauty stepped into Buck's private room. "Master?"

"I expect a guest. I want you to care for his needs personally." Morago chuckled, and Buck laughed out loud. "Anything he wants, do you understand me?"

"Yes, sir." Violet nodded.

"Vasquez, bring me those men." Buck gestured him away with annoyance. The henchman nodded and slipped out the door.

"Wash up and remain chaste until he arrives." Morago's vision centered on Violet. "I need you to show Otis Pierce the benefits of my friendship."

Chapter 21

Merril Shilo

—

Merril hitched his belt then paused on his way out of the bedroom to glance back at Nichole.

She lay naked on her stomach, diagonally across the bed, tangled in their bedsheets. Her thick blonde curls scattered across her back and around her face. Eyes closed, she resembled nothing more than a young angel fallen from heaven.

Merril's one-sided grin ticked up. She left him astounded at every turn. His chest tightened as he eased out the door and headed downstairs. Nothing mattered as much as her safety. And now that Sam had taken his sister home to New Orleans, there was one less protector between Nichole and the demon that threatened them all.

Thank God Sam was here when Morago's gunmen arrived.

And Hunter, for when I returned.

The dining room table gleamed with new polish. The bits of grass and sackcloth that cluttered his end of the table were gone, along with the straw basket of handmade dolls.

Voodoo dolls.

A tickle of disquiet crawled up Merril's spine. He'd spent some time in New Orleans and heard the talk in the bars on the west bank. Still, Hunter had saved him. Nichole believed he was Courtney's direct ancestor, but what spoke most in the Cajun's favor was Sam's good opinion. Sam trusted Hunter, and because of all those things, Merril intended to put his uneasiness aside.

Tom Baker's return from Kiowa Crossing, late last night, brought unwelcome news.

The officials at Camp Sheridan were unable to locate the elderly native man in question. They again sent their regrets, but the camp's relocation to the west fork of Beaver Creek took precedence. White Eagle must have left the Spotted Tail Indian Agency not long after he arrived. They would not respond to further inquiries on this matter.

Outside, thick clouds covered the usually blue and sunny Colorado sky. Scattered raindrops left dark spots in the hard dirt yard.

Merril quickened his step to the bunkhouse.

Lamps lit the long dormitory, and the beds had been pushed aside to make room for one of the large outdoor wooden tables.

Hunter, Jim, and the James brothers, Bernard and Bayard, questioned Tom about the gunmen he and Sam had turned over to the Kiowa Crossing sheriff.

"You're positive they'd been in Kiowa Crossing before they attacked us?" Bernard asked.

Tom shrugged. "Yep. Sheriff Wheeler asked the waitress from The Thirsty Mule to come to his office and look at the faces of the dead men." He raised an eyebrow at Bernard. "She wasn't happy 'bout it, but she recognized four of the ten—said they'd had food and drink at The Mule the day before they showed up here."

"Why would that matter?" Merril stepped to the table and looked down.

On a scrap of tanned hide, someone had sketched a rough outline of The Highlands and the road to The Shilo Ranch that continued to Kiowa Crossing.

Hunter looked up from the map. "If the attack originated from Kiowa Crossing, Morago may be closer than I thought."

"You believed he escaped to Denver." Merril met Hunter's gaze.

"Yes. I could sense the demon for a short time after I revived. He fled west."

"Can't you use your Voodoo to find him?" Merril asked.

Around the table, all eyes rose to Merril, then shifted to Hunter, awaiting his reply.

Hunter shook his head. "Not easily, *mon ami*." His black hair gleamed in the light hung above the map. "I no longer have a connection with the demon."

"What kind of connection did you have when you tracked our nieces?" Bayard asked.

"The blood of a prophet who died to deliver The Prophecy." Hunter ran a hand over his face. "But the blood had been tainted. Even had it not, there is no more."

"Assume the worst." Jim tapped his finger on the penciled outline of the train station in The Crossing. "Revise the plan as we learn more."

"Fine. What is your plan?" Merril demanded.

"Isolate the demon away from anyone or anything he can possess," Bernard responded.

"Trap him long enough for Amy and Alyse to finish him," Bayard added.

"And you know how to accomplish those things?" Merril looked at the faces around the table, but no one responded.

***

Nichole Harris-Shilo

—

Nichole pulled on her boots then rose and tossed the bedcover over the mattress. She pressed her fingertips to her lips, and ever so lightly, traced them down her chin and neck. Eyes closed, she allowed the feathery touch to remind her of her husband's late-night passion. The tingling sensations still fresh in her mind.

Downstairs, she paused to marvel at the clean dining room table. "Huh," she muttered to herself. "Where's Hunter's craft project?"

He moved the puppets to his sleeping quarters. Under his bed, I believe.

Nichole spun on her heel and stared at Carrefour.

The crossroads *loa* lounged against the parlor wall, dressed in a cutaway dove gray riding jacket and trousers that accentuated the silver at his temples. He raised his chin and smiled at her with light gray eyes.

At this moment, he attends a planning session with little or no plan in mind. Why am I not surprised?

"How did you?" she sputtered, glancing over her shoulder to make sure they were alone.

I don't read minds if that is what you're wondering.

He pushed away from the wall and swung his walking stick in a circle as he stepped forward.

Everything you think flutters across your face. Perhaps it's your big blue eyes. You should learn to guard your thoughts.

"How are you here when Hunter's not?" She lowered her voice. "What do you want?"

You know extraordinarily little. Carrefour smirked. *I go wherever I choose, within a reasonable distance of my chwal.*

He caught the cane beneath his arm then studied his nails.

As to why I'm here—

He raised an eyebrow and trapped her with his gray gaze.

This is where the excitement is.

"What excitement?" Nichole listened to the everyday morning sounds inside her house. Cookie in the kitchen busy assembling breakfast. From the floor above, footsteps in Amy and Jason's room.

She closed her eyes and threw her senses wider.

Jeanne and Katy chatted on the third floor as they dressed. Across the back yard, in the family bunkhouse, Lawna and Hope-Anne slept. Henny had already risen and walked the garden pulling weeds.

She pushed further than she had ever tried and knew the pulse of Merril's heartbeat. Surprised, she heard him discuss strategy, as Carrefour had said, in the bunkhouse with the other men.

Lloyd, Kelly, and Bill worked their morning chores, cleaning the stalls, feeding and watering the animals.

She opened her eyes and shook her head. "I think you're full of shit, Casper."

His grin widened. *Perhaps you failed to search far enough.* He saluted Nichole with his cane, performed a precise about-face, then passed through the front door.

Without hesitation, she threw open the door and followed him outside. "Wait!" The wind caught her hair as a gust blew both dust and rain across the porch.

Carrefour strolled down the hard-packed drive, swinging his cane, untouched by either the wind or rain. He turned his head and winked at her when he reached the road then continued west.

The summer squall would be short-lived. The sky had already cleared in the west. The darkest part of the storm now passed overhead.

She grabbed the raincoat from a peg on the porch and pulled it on over her skirt and blouse as she pursued Carrefour down the drive.

Rivulets of water ran from the house toward the road. The streamlets splashed over her boots, found the stitched seams, and drenched her stockings.

"Oh, great." Each step she took squished between her toes. Merril would be furious if he knew she followed Hunter's *loa* into the storm.

When she reached the road, both she and the water turned west. The water raced ahead of her toward the dry creek.

Carrefour stood at the edge of the bridge.

Lloyd and Tom had to rebuild the small span each season after the spring thaw and rains flooded the little creek. A dry gully yesterday, the brook gurgled and ran swift with rainwater now.

"Well, this is exciting," Nichole said as she stomped to a halt beside Carrefour. "You've ruined my boots."

I've done no such thing. He glanced down then shook his head. *You could have waited on the porch and let them come to you.*

"Let who come to me?"

Beyond the bridge, a quarter-mile in the distance, three figures crested the rise as they traversed the road in the rain.

"Who is it?" Nichole asked. Receiving no answer, she turned. Then spun in a circle. Carrefour had disappeared.

"What the hell? Carrefour, you dick."

She waited as the people narrowed their distance from her. Indecision held her planted beside the bridge but prepared to run. The last group to show up at The Highlands had wanted blood.

The rain had slowed to a scattering of drops blown in the outflow from the receding clouds. Beyond the figures, the clouds gave way to blue skies.

Backlit by the bright sky behind them, Nichole couldn't make out the faces until they were almost to the span. When recognition settled in her brain, her breath hitched, and she shoved the rain hood from her head.

White Eagle crossed over the creek first. Covered head to toe in brown oilcloth, he leaned heavily on his feathered staff. He spoke and tipped his head to Nichole in greeting.

"Grandfather says he is pleased to see Lost Wind again," the middle-aged Indian woman, also covered in a raincoat, called from the bridge. She pulled a small two-wheeled cart behind her. Her deep-set black eyes and dusky skin tone highlighted the streaks of silver in her hair. "My name is Waynoka," she added. "The Wolf Spirit told grandfather a guide would be sent to take us to you. We have come at her request."

Nichole nodded, unable to speak or breathe, her attention beyond Waynoka.

Waynoka leaned forward to set the cart in motion. She followed White Eagle up the shallow incline toward the turn-off to the house.

The last figure topped the bridge and paused. The woman's gaze locked with Nichole's. Her clothes were different. The last time Nichole had seen her, she'd worn a flowered day dress.

No—scratch that.

Nichole had never set eyes on this woman, but Courtney had. In another life. In Denver.

Her thin frame and large dark eyes were the same, but instead of a lightweight housedress, the elderly woman on the span wore a black and lavender robe with a matching head wrap. She had walked through the storm without rain cover, and yet not a drop of rain had touched her ebony skin.

Granddaughter, she bowed her head and spoke with a familiar voice, spiced with an island accent. *My name is Dessa.*

Nichole took an involuntary step back and blinked in disbelief. "Holy shit."

Chapter 22

Morago

—

Despite sending Vasquez to the Union Hotel, Morago had been unable to locate Otis Pierce. The desk clerk had informed Vasquez there was no Otis Pierce currently registered at their establishment. The impertinent receptionist refused to confirm if Pierce had ever been at the hotel at all, stating the manager held all his guests' information in the strictest of confidence.

Had Morago been there instead of watching through the silver thread, he could have read the bastard's thoughts—known the truth the hotel employee refused to share. Even burned the Union Hotel to the ground, had he so desired.

Demon-Vasquez, however, could only swear at the man and leave before the desk clerk sent for the police.

The demon-finch pecked at crumbs tossed on the window ledge by June—the leavings from last night's boarding house supper. June continued her tirade against Nichole Harris and the awful Merril Shilo.

Her anger. Her hate. Her endless suffering of the unbearable defeat by the witch's friends would have soothed his annoyance at misplacing one Otis Pierce.

Instead, Morago was forced to experience the bitter, resentful twist of June's soul as a voyeur. It left him ungratified.

Information gained through the silver thread could only impart dry and unsatisfactory details.

And I am capable of so much more.

Morago downed the remains of Randolph Buckner's drink and studied the women waiting in the welcome room at the bordello.

Boots and heels resonated on the staircase as a patron followed one of the girls up the stairs. Probably the light-haired young whore, who remained a popular choice for most visitors.

Two men looked over the available stock before making their decision about which pleasure doll would serve them tonight.

In the corner, the former house madam slumped in a winged armchair, arms and legs crossed, a pout on her painted lips. No longer in charge, her resentment at being forced into the role of the old whore, while young demon-Violet ran his henhouse amused Morago.

Still, her dismay is not as satisfying as June's.

"I'll be back," Buck spoke to the room as he slid his empty glass to the bartender.

Advise me should Otis Pierce arrive.

Yes, master. Violet grinned and directed one of the new gentlemen toward the former madam.

The afternoon stayed cool after the morning rain had passed. Scattered clouds chased the departing storm leaving the day pleasantly mild. Along the avenue, shops were busy with women carrying parasols and packages, and jacketed men who tipped their hats when they passed the ladies.

Buck tipped his curled-brim hat to a group of matronly women who chatted in front of the mercantile. He grinned as they gasped in outrage and turned away. They apparently knew of Randolph Buckner, whoremonger, and gaming house owner.

Power. Notoriety. Fear.

In fact, Morago no longer thought of himself as separate from Randolph Buckner. The serpent demon, desperate for power, merged nicely with the big power-savvy property owner. The change had happened gradually, grafting the knowledge and personality of Big Buck onto his own. The integration benefited them both. Buckner continued to pursue new ventures with thoughts and feelings separate from Morago. He even advised the demon on how best to use other humans to obtain Morago's desires.

They had formed a partnership of sorts—comfortable and profitable for both the demon and the man. Although each knew Morago held all the cards in the final hand.

For the first time, Morago thought it might be possible to remain in the human world by keeping the women alive and in the thrall of his demons.

Could it be done?

He already had elemental power. And with Buckner's aid, he had worldly influence and wealth. Were The Prophecy of the Twins never fulfilled, he could remain forever in the human world.

He swaggered the several blocks between Buck's bordello and June's boarding house, more aware of the world and his surroundings than ever before. His plans were coming together to possess the young women, hobble their power but keep them alive, while he enjoyed the use of their grandmother's elemental skill.

Demon-Vasquez continued recruiting gunmen and bringing them to Buckner to be infused with one of Morago's servants.

His multitude of servants had thinned considerably with the loss of demon-Perry and his crew. Then there was the loss of Merril's demon. Next time Morago faced the witches, he would be there in person to finish the task.

I'll be able to use my power to combat whatever tricks they used to destroy my minions.

When he looked up, he stood across the avenue from June's boarding house.

Fewer people recognized him this far from his neighborhood. Both men and women brushed past wishing him a good day. Their thoughts were light and pleasant.

I could crush them all with a thought—burn them to ash and rend their souls.

Across the street, a disturbance caught Morago's attention.

June emerged from the residence, her handbag over one forearm and a closed parasol clasped tight in her hand.

Several men reclined in porch chairs. Their legs stretched across her path.

She swatted one man's knee with her parasol. "Move those sticks. This isn't your house. Where are your manners?"

"Why, yes ma'am." The man pulled his long legs back. "Wouldn't do for you to be pleasant on such a fine afternoon."

"Don't sass me, you young fool." June opened her umbrella and put her nose in the air.

Morago extended his senses toward the hate-filled woman as she made her way down the steps. A slow smile spread across Buckner's face and his eyes closed. Such a delicious stew of resentment, self-pity, and anger.

Her thoughts were on an upcoming interview as a housekeeper for a young family not far from the boarding house. Lips pinched, she marched up the avenue like a general going to war.

Morago followed her with his senses from across the thoroughfare. He clenched his fists and fought the urge to pursue the old woman, drink up all of her rage.

Master? demon-Violet inquired.

What is it?

Otis Pierce has arrived.

Pleasure him. Keep him entertained and keep him there. I'm on my way back.

Morago watched June's parasol become one of many along the side street. When her broken and bitter view of the world faded from his senses, he strode back up the avenue to the bordello.

***

Nichole Harris-Shilo

—

Nichole's world tilted wildly off-center. She stumbled backward into the grass along the side of the road. Her knees wobbled then failed, and she sat down hard on her rump.

This isn't possible.

Sparks shot across her eyesight. Her vision swam between the future and present as she stared at Courtney's landlady. The old woman had given her a silver key to the apartment in Denver. She'd opened the attic door and led Courtney to the trunk holding the photograph of the Shilo brothers and Nichole.

Concern rounded Dessa's eyes, and she shuffled to stand above Nichole. "Now you've muddied your pretty outfit." She held out her hand. "I didn't mean to surprise you, child. Let me help you up—"

Dessa continued to talk, but her voice floated further and further away. Nichole's vision collapsed to a pinpoint around Dessa's face. "You can't be here," Nichole whispered. Then the pinhole spun to blue sky and winked out.

"Nichole!"

The panicked edge of Merril's voice cut through Nichole's darkness. She blinked open her eyes. "Merril." Dampness seeped through her skirt and chilled her skin. "What am I..."

"Are you injured?" Her husband sank to his knees in the grass beside her. "Did you hit your head?"

"No. I don't think so..." Memory descended like a punch to her gut. Bile edged up the back of her throat. She swallowed hard and pushed her shoulders from the ground. "Where did she go?"

Merril supported her back and helped her sit upright. "Who?"

Beyond her husband, White Eagle and Waynoka looked on in concern.

Nichole scanned the road in both directions.

Kelly and Bill, both with rifles in hand, bookended the group—Kelly on the other side of the bridge and Bill near the turn-off to the house.

Dessa had disappeared.

"Who are you looking for?" Merril asked again.

"I—" She hesitated, then lowered her voice. "An old woman was here. Someone I knew from Courtney's life. When she spoke to me, I—I guess I fainted."

"I didn't see anyone else." Merril helped her to her feet. He brushed at her skirt and straightened her raincoat. "I could carry you to the house."

"No." Nichole chuckled despite her unease. "As much as I know you would like that, I don't think it's necessary. I'm fine. Really." Nichole wiped her hands dry on her thighs and touched the wet cloth on her backside. "I need to change, though."

Merril wrapped his arm around her shoulder, supporting her as she stepped into the road.

Hunter, Jim, Tom, and the James brothers watched from near the corral.

"How did you find me?"

"I asked Kelly and Bill to keep an eye on the roads while the rest of us met in the bunkhouse this morning. I don't want to be taken by surprise again. When Kelly spotted White Eagle, instead of signaling with the rifle, he ran back to alert us." Merril paused and spoke briefly to White Eagle and his granddaughter in their language.

White Eagle nodded, then he and Waynoka retraced their path toward the house.

"I cut through the yard to meet White Eagle on the road when I saw you sit down by the bridge." He felt the back of her head and brushed grass from her raincoat. "Who did you see again?"

White Eagle replied to Merril as they all moved up the road.

"What did he say?"

"He said you spoke to your spirit guide, then fainted."

White Eagle nodded at Nichole, then looked ahead.

"I'll help with the cart," Bill said and handed Merril his rifle. "Where do you want me to take it?"

"To the cottonwood. They can set their camp away from the animals and dust in the yard."

A brief discussion ensued between Waynoka and Bill. Finally, Bill hefted the handles and Waynoka followed close behind.

White Eagle chuckled and spoke.

Merril nodded and laughed.

"What?" Nichole asked.

"He said she complained about having to pull the cart for miles, yet let someone else pull it, and she moans even louder."

Nichole smiled as they took the Highland Drive.

Dessa was a spirit? How is this possible? She called me granddaughter.

Merril left her at the front door. "If you're sure you're well, I want to see White Eagle settled. I doubt he'll be comfortable in the house, but we could serve a welcome meal in the back yard."

"I'll check with Cookie." She stretched on her toes and gave her husband a quick kiss on the lips. "Thank you for coming to my rescue."

"You were already coming around." Merril ran his hands up and down her arms. "I just wish I knew why you fainted." He kissed her forehead. "Ask Amy to have a look at you and keep Jeanne with you in case you fall."

"I'm good. Go." She pushed playfully on his arm then took off the raincoat. "See to our guests."

Upstairs in her room, Nichole changed out of her wet clothes and into one of the divided skirts Jeanne had altered for her. She brushed last fall's dead grass from her hair and bound it with a ribbon. When she turned to leave, she pulled up short.

Carrefour lounged against the closed door. *Madam.* He bowed his head, eyes somber. *I owe you an apology. I did not realize seeing Dessa would bring on vapors.*

"Do you know Dessa?"

Why, yes. Her name was Marguerite Darcentelin Saint Dominique.

Carrefour paced away from the door as he adjusted his cuffs.

Nichole sank onto the dressing table bench. "Who is she? How can she be here?"

Ah, well. I'm not sure it is my place to lecture you on family business. I sincerely thought you knew who she was.

"She called me granddaughter."

Both you and Hunter are her direct descendants. A family line, strong with the gifts of Voodoo.

"She must have been a spirit in Courtney's life too. She seemed freakin' real, yet she was a ghost."

She is more than a shade. She is a Ghede loa. By choice. Carrefour sniffed. *One of the few Ghede I find tolerable.*

"By choice. What does that mean?"

Carrefour rolled his eyes. *Spirit-walkers, and those gifted with your particular nature, can choose to be born again or to remain in the spirit world. Dessa decided to continue her journey as a spirit and ascend as a Ghede loa.* He turned and twirled his cane. *Most human souls have no choice in the matter. They are reborn until they reach ascension.*

"And if Dessa had chosen to be reborn?"

She would have lost her power or most of it. Although magic resides in the soul, it is either a gift of birth or stripped at birth. I have known few who once they were reborn retained even an inkling of their former skill. Untrained and unknowing, the gift fades before they reach maturity.

"And I still have Courtney's magic because I wasn't reborn. I spirit-walked to this life, to Nichole's life."

I don't know why this wasn't explained to you as a child. Those born with your skill—

"My family was killed when I was very young."

Carrefour ceased pacing and stared at Nichole. *Before you were trained?*

Nichole nodded. "I was a little kid when their plane crashed. Years after my father's death, I used to watch him on tape. He was a medium."

Carrefour tipped his head and his brow furrowed. *A medium what?*

"He communicated with spirits. They would appear to him. He had a show on television." Nichole grinned at the *loa*. "It doesn't matter. No, I never received training."

Well, that explains your vapors I suppose.

"Will I see her again?"

Carrefour stepped back into a swirl of shadows.

I wouldn't be surprised.

After the *loa* had gone, sounds from outside captured her attention. White Eagle's camp would be beneath her balcony. She peeked out the door, but the tepee had been erected on the far side of the cottonwood tree. Fully leafed, she could only catch glimpses of Bill's boots and the sound of Waynoka's slowly spoken directions. Closer at hand, but out of sight, she heard her husband speaking with White Eagle.

"Oh lunch!" she exclaimed and hastened downstairs to find Cookie. Her short talk with Carrefour had driven all else from her mind.

Chapter 23

Morago

—

Morago rested his chin in the palm of his hand, his elbow on the arm of the cushioned chair.

Across the room, Otis Pierce and Violet slept naked, entwined together in the whore's bed.

Eyes closed, Morago pilfered through the young man's thoughts and dreams. A slow smile spread across Randolph Buckner's broad face.

Otis Pierce required money. He needed funds quite urgently, in fact. Visions of a substantial sum loaned to Jason Harris filtered through his dreams.

Otis hopes to call in his debt.

Morago found Pierce's actual memories more troubling, for reasons all his own.

Otis dreamed of wide, paved streets in a town much larger than Denver. Booming financial markets and leaders with worldly reach. Compared to Boston, the prairie village of Denver appeared sadly provincial.

Morago had run through the city of Boston as a canine, hot on the scent of the witches. Unaware of the power to be procured, the influence traded by human officials. Bankers. Senators.

Should I leave Buck and possess Otis? Seize more power in a larger town?

Temptation ground like grit in his gut, but he couldn't afford to make long-term plans. He was bound to a path set forth by The Prophecy. Unless he could cheat fate—win or lose—he'd return to his tangle in hell.

My thoughts run in circles.

He clenched Buck's teeth and brought a spark of flame to his fingers. He held them up before his eyes. "Power." He crushed the fire in his fist. Inside his mind, the old woman whose magic he'd stolen remained silent.

Perhaps I'll find a way back to the human realm—a seam in the vault, once I command supreme elemental power.

He reached out to demon-Violet. *Wake him.*

Violet's hand slid down the sleeping man's chest and continued beneath the covers. "Wake up, Otis," she whispered as her hand stroked, moving under the blankets.

Use your mouth.

Morago rose and stood at the end of the bed, grinning as Violet's head disappeared under the spread.

Otis gasped and opened his eyes. They widened further as they focused on Buck.

"Don't let me interrupt your pleasure." His lips twisted in a sarcastic smile. "Sometimes visitors request an audience for their... performance." Buck snickered. "While there are others who will pay to observe certain carnal acts." He jerked the cover off the bed and watched Violet's lips and tongue work their magic on Otis.

"Violet enjoys giving pleasure with her mouth. Such a talent."

Otis's eyes rolled back as Violet's pace increased. He groaned and reached down to hold her head, thrusting hard.

Buck chuckled as he opened the door, then paused. "When you've finished, bring him downstairs to me. He and I have a business transaction to discuss."

In the chamber behind the welcome area, Buckner poured himself a drink. The whiskey burned and he hissed with pleasure. The man upstairs with East Coast banking ties would legitimize his plan. He swirled the whiskey and took another sip.

Moments later, the echo of boot heels stumbling down the front stairs gave Morago a grin.

The door opened, and Violet stepped aside to let Otis Pierce into the room.

"Have a seat." Morago pointed to a chair and poured a second drink. He sauntered to the table and set one whiskey beside Otis. "Drink up. I have a proposition to make." He sat across from the younger man and watched over the rim as he took another sip.

Otis tasted the whiskey and returned the glass to the table. "Were you in Violet's bedroom earlier? Was that you?"

"Guilty." Morago nodded. A slight smirk twisted his lips. "It's a good idea to check in on my girls now and then. Make sure my customers are completely satisfied." He paused and stared at Otis. "And were you? Completely satisfied?"

"I apologize for being a bit muddled." Otis cleared his throat and sat forward. "Are you the owner of this establishment?"

"I am."

Otis picked up the glass and checked its cleanliness. He took another sip, made a face, and set the glass back on the table. "I appreciate your... um... Violet. But I need to let you know I won't be able to pay you for... um."

"Her time and skills were gratis, Mr. Pierce."

"Good. That's good." He took another sip and sniffed. "I worried that might be the business transaction you mentioned earlier." More confident now that he was fully dressed, he downed the remainder of his whiskey and put the glass on the table. "I must say, however, that you should check with your clients before surprising them in such a compromising position. Not that I minded, of course."

"Of course."

"If that's all then I should be off."

"Sit down, Mr. Pierce. I haven't finished with you quite yet."

"Now see here—" Otis shook his finger in phony outrage.

With a wave of Morago's hand, the door to the office slammed shut. His lips twisted in a smile when Otis jumped in surprise. "Sit and listen. We can help each other."

"Besides being the proprietor of this establishment, you are?"

"Randolph Buckner, among other—things."

"And Randolph Buckner, how can you be of any use to me?"

His superior tone irked Morago. "First, let me tell you what I know about you. Your name is Otis Pierce, a former employee at Peabody and Pierce, your father's firm in Boston. It seems you borrowed a substantial sum of money from the company coffers, then lent it to your friend, Jason Harris. He made several dubious investments based on your personal recommendations and lost every red cent, as your father put it. Now you've come west hoping to collect on that old debt. Does that cover everything?"

Otis eased back down in his chair. "How could you possibly know any of that?" he whispered, his eyes bulging.

Morago smiled. "I know every thought in that tiny human skull of yours. I could own you if I so desired. But I don't. Instead, I would propose a partnership."

Otis swallowed. "Go on."

"Bring your complaint of this unpaid debt to the authorities. In return, I'll provide the muscle to enforce the collection efforts."

"What if they don't see the situation the same way we do?"

"That would be my concern."

"Why would you do this for me? It seems I'll be the only beneficiary of our agreement."

"And that makes you wary?"

"It does indeed, sir."

Morago nodded. "You know Jason's wife?"

"Amy Prescott?" Otis nodded. "I knew her in Boston."

"My interest is with her and her sister. Once her husband and those protecting them are out of the way, you'll get what you want, and my reward will be Amy and her twin."

"I wasn't aware Amy had a sister, and a twin at that." Otis shrugged. "I'm sure twins would provide quite an unusual addition to your—collection of ladies." He leered as he tipped his head toward the front room. "Amy was always a bit strange to my mind, but attractive enough for what you intend. You, sir, have a deal."

***

Nichole Harris-Shilo

—

Cookie served dinner that afternoon in the back yard. The residents and visitors at the ranch dined on her hearty vegetable beef stew served from

Henny's chuck wagon cooking pot. Blankets were strewn across the damp grass for a picnic-style celebration.

Nichole sat with Merril, Hunter, and White Eagle. The enormity of those three men, and what they meant in her life, made her thoughtful. Each man, in their individual way, had a hand in determining her past, her present, and her future life. The only one missing, the primary manipulator, was Dessa.

She'll show up soon, according to Carrefour.

White Eagle did not know the whereabouts of Gray Wolf. He knew only that his grandson continued north seeking allies in their struggle against the encroaching white man's army.

Nichole remained silent on what she knew about the eventual outcome of the conflict between the Native Americans and the American government. She did learn Waynoka and Gray Wolf were cousins, and that Waynoka was widowed five years prior.

Waynoka took advantage of Merril's language skills and left White Eagle in his care. She shared dinner on a nearby blanket with Amy, Jason, Alyse, and Jim. Their laughter and easy conversation centered around twins, and when Amy and Jason might have twins of their own.

Alyse had progressed to using a cane, and although Jim would have preferred she allow him to carry her, she refused. She leaned her head against his shoulder as they enjoyed the evening meal and chatted with Waynoka and Amy.

The uncles had begged off from the dinner festivities and volunteered to stand guard while the others ate.

"It's no trouble at all," Bayard had insisted. "We want to perform experiments with distance and our ability to *twyne*."

"Amy and Alyse *twyned* involuntarily across the country. Certainly, we should be able to manage a *twyne* at shouting distance." Bernard called back as he departed with his brother.

That Amy and Alyse could rarely *twyne* without assistance from Nichole didn't lessen the fact their nieces had done something the brothers could not.

After dinner, Tom and Lloyd relieved the brothers from guard duty, and Jim brought the planning map from the bunkhouse to spread over the cleared table.

Everyone not involved with the strategy session against the demon found a moment to view the crude map.

Bill and Kelly excused themselves to settle the animals for the night for Tom and Lloyd.

Lawna and Katy disappeared into the family bunkhouse to put Hope-Anne to bed for the night.

Henny, Cookie, and Jeanne folded blankets and carried the remaining dishes and baskets into the house.

Eventually, the only ones remaining had experienced the demon battle at The Shilo. Everyone except White Eagle and Waynoka.

Nichole looked over the pencil drawing sketched on a large piece of Lloyd's tanned leather hide. The men had made a darned good rendering considering they didn't have survey equipment or a satellite mapping program.

The building layout for The Highlands Ranch was easy to recognize, as were pencil squares depicting the structures at The Shilo Ranch.

They had only drawn the two main cross streets of Kiowa Crossing, calling out the rail station, The Thirsty Mule, and the post office. Additional squares took the place of random houses and businesses.

"The biggest problem," Hunter stated, "is we don't know where the demon is right now. We only know he headed west, toward Denver after the encounter at The Shilo."

"That's true," Merril added. "But the gunmen were in Kiowa Crossing before they attacked here. At roughly the same time, I was ..." He hesitated as though searching for the right word.

"Compromised," Nichole supplied.

Merril's gifted her with his lopsided smile. "When I became compromised in Denver."

Nichole fought a sudden burning in her eyes and tightness in her chest.

I almost lost him.

Hunter pointed to the town on the map. "Then let's assume any attack will come from Kiowa Crossing, or that we'll need to draw our adversaries away from there."

Jim nodded. "Too many innocent lives would be jeopardized in town."

"And too many potential hosts for Morago to populate with his demons." Hunter tapped his finger on an empty area. "We need an isolated location. One we can prepare beforehand to spring our surprise."

"I have a small hunting cabin about here." Merril pointed to a place on the map. "But there isn't room for more than a couple of men inside."

"Is there a good place to stage an ambush around your cabin? Anywhere to hide?" Jason asked.

"May I?" Merril took the pencil from Jim and sketched a small square to represent the cabin. He continued to add details as he talked. "There's a road, actually more of a wagon trail, which branches from the main road about here. The path passes about fifty yards west of the cabin. However, the tracks wash out because of the creek." He added a wiggly line that ran behind the cabin, then intersected the road. "This time of year, there will be high grass along the creek as well as brush here and here."

"When were you last there?" Hunter asked.

"Less than a month ago." He looked over at Nichole. "The night after your carriage accident and my father's death."

Nichole blinked and shook her head in wonder. It didn't seem possible so much had happened in such a short span of time.

"There would be cover." Hunter ran a hand over his mouth as he studied the map.

"Probably. It depends on what you have in mind."

Waynoka hadn't been translating for her grandfather. He followed the conversation, asking her a question now and then.

White Eagle must understand English but doesn't speak it.

"My plan, what there is so far, is to draw the demon to an isolated location. We would have gunmen waiting, hidden in the brush." He pointed to a few places. "Here and here." Hunter glanced around the table. "It must be a place of our choosing." He pointed to Merril's lodge and the surrounding area. "Because once I cast the ward, and set the bowl over the boundary, the trap will be sprung."

"How's that?" Jason asked.

"The demon trap will accomplish three things." He counted the points on his fingers. "First, it will cut Morago off from his possessed men. We saw this happen with Merril. Second, it will prevent the demon from fleeing. The invisible barrier will make him an easier target. And third, once our gunman kills Morago's current host, the demon will be forced to take me."

"What?" Nichole stepped forward. "That's a terrible plan."

Hunter ignored her comment. "With the demon inside me, I will hold him from escaping while Amy and Alyse finish him off."

"Finish you off, you mean." Amy looked over Nichole's shoulder. "You need to come up with a better plan."

"The demon needs to be isolated. We must drive Morago into someone able to hold him." Hunter captured Nichole's gaze. "You and I are the only ones with the ability to bind a soul to a body. Between the two of us, I have the most experience, *fillette*."

"Absolutely not." Nichole pointed at Hunter. "You would break Cat's heart, not to mention end the Veau family line before it even gets started."

A chorus of voices broke out around the table. Everyone wanted to share their opinion.

Finally, Bernard held up his hands to gain attention. When all eyes focused on him, he looked at Hunter. "You've been possessed by this demon before. Could you have held him then?"

"No," Hunter admitted. "But I hope to have the assistance of *Maître* Carrefour."

"Carrefour?" Nichole shook her head, aghast and amused. "Unless it was part of some original agreement he talks about, I wouldn't count on him."

"Who is Carrefour?" Merril asked

"*Maître Carrefour* is one of the *mystères* or *loas* that dwell between man and our *Bon Dieu*. The *loa* may be served, and in that way, be called upon to grant requests." Hunter spoke reluctantly. "However, like Nichole, I have come to doubt this *loa's* true intentions."

White Eagle spoke in the silence that followed Hunter's statement.

"Grandfather says he has more experience with the spirit world than either of you."

White Eagle continued to speak while Waynoka translated.

"He likes your plan, but he wants to see how the bowl trap will work. A... demonstration." She smiled shyly at Hunter. "He reminds you that you cannot be both the trapper and the trapped." Her eyes widened as she listened to her grandfather. She shook her head. "No, please. There must be another way."

White Eagle tapped her arm, pointed at the people around the table, then spoke again.

She turned to Merril and Hunter with resignation in her eyes. "Grandfather says *he* must be the one to take in and hold this demon. He says that he will be your sacrifice."

Everyone remained silent for several moments, then Jason asked, "How are you going to draw him to the cabin in the first place? According to The Prophecy, he only wants Amy and Alyse."

Hunter stared at Jim and Jason over the table. "Then Amy and Alyse will be the ones who lure him to White Eagle."

Chapter 24

Nichole Harris-Shilo

—

The next morning the entire group set out for Merril's hunting shack. Because of the feeble road, traveling would have been easier if everyone could ride mounts. But that wasn't possible.

"Alyse can't sit a horse, yet." Jim's lowered voice reached only to Merril, Tom, and Nichole. They gathered between the barn and the corral with everyone else. Tom and Lloyd had been saddling horses since daybreak, turning them loose into the corral to await their riders.

"You're right. White Eagle won't ride either." Merril addressed Tom, "Looks like you'll need to hitch a wagon."

Tom nodded, turned on his heel, and headed through the stable as he called Lloyd and Bill to help him get one of the carts ready.

On the other side of the corral, Amy and Jason helped Alyse from the house. Their progress was slow, with Alyse pausing every few feet to rest.

Nichole left Merril and Jim to meet them part way. "You could have waited on the porch. Tom is hitching a wagon."

"Is he?" Alyse let out a sigh. "That's a relief. With this leg, I don't know if I could stay on a horse."

"We could go back to the house and wait for them to bring the wagon." Jason hesitated, looking to each of the women for confirmation.

"I've come this far." Alyse took another step. "Might as well go the rest of the way."

They stopped at the edge of the corral. Alyse leaned against the split rail fence muttering with disgust at her physical condition. "Why aren't I getting better?"

"You are!" her sister exclaimed. "You're much better."

"Give it time," Nichole advised. "You're super lucky to walk at all."

"She knows it." Amy raised her brows and addressed Nichole. "We do have some exciting news to share. Alyse and I *twyned* without your aid last night."

"From separate rooms." Alyse brightened as her sister blushed. "Although I don't think Amy expected it."

"Last night?" Jason looked between the sisters, his eyebrows raised.

"Before that," Amy clarified, her skin blotched to her neckline.

"Okay, that's funny." Nichole laughed at Amy and Jason's embarrassment. "Do you realize, with Bill and Kelly coming with us, there will be thirteen people scoping out the lay of the land."

"Scoping?" Jason raised a brow. "Will we need a scope?"

"Thirteen?" Alyse grinned. "That is a fortunate count."

"I thought it would be bad luck," Nichole replied.

"Oh no. The number thirteen represents the Divine flow of energy," Alyse explained. "*Mémé* always said thirteen was the perfect number for a coven."

"Really? Well, we can divide our coven of thirteen into three specific groups based on their abilities," Nichole informed them.

"What groups?" Jason asked.

"Artillery, for you, Merril and Jim. Battlemages for the elemental witches, and Spirit Seekers for White Eagle, Hunter, and–"

"You'll have changed groups. You stood with the Battlemages before, but with Hunter here to teach you more about your family skill, you would be a, what did you call it?" Amy asked.

"Spirit Seeker. I think you're right, but he hasn't done a lot of teaching so far."

In the corral, Bayard and Bernard climbed into their saddles.

Tom pulled the wagon to a stop between the pen and the house, set the brake and hopped to the ground. "You'll have the reins?" he asked Jason.

"I will."

Tom trotted past the wagon signaling to Jim and Merril in the corral.

After a few moments, Jim left Merril and approached the group by the wagon. "Merril says we're ready to go."

"Is that Midnight?" Nichole watched Merril settle into the saddle.

Beside Merril, Hunter mounted a brown and white paint.

"Yes, it is. Tom says Midnight is ready for a light workout." Jim took Alyse's arm and helped her to the wagon. "Oh, and he saddled Sugar for you."

"Awesome." Nichole hurried to Sugar, being careful where she stepped.

White Eagle and Waynoka crossed the back yard to the wagon as Nichole and Merril slowed to give Jim the reins to his gelding.

The rest of the riders filed past and rode down to the main road.

Jason assisted the shaman and his granddaughter into the wagon and saw them settled on the blankets Tom had stacked in the back. Then Jason climbed onto the bench and took the reins from Amy. "Let's go."

Nichole followed Hunter down the drive. They would ride roughly three hours to the hunting lodge. She reached back and pulled her wide-brimmed hat onto her head to shade her face. Riding gloves covered her hands. Her shoulders had finally finished peeling from the first Blackwood Jones encounter.

The Shilo Ranch looked desolate and abandoned as they passed. She glanced at her husband, but he just shook his head and looked away.

It must be hard for Merril to see his father's homestead stand empty.

A little less than halfway to Kiowa Crossing, Merril pulled ahead and pointed out the two-wheeled wagon tracks in the grass. "This trail will be completely gone in another year. When my father and I built the hunting shack, it was easy to maneuver with a wagon."

"We'll make it," Jason told him as he turned the horses onto the trail.

"Take it slow. The washout from the creek is just past the cabin, but we had rain yesterday. There's no telling what we'll find," Merril advised.

Nichole waited for the wagon to pass. "Remember to set the brake and watch for snakes," she called.

Jason gave her a horrified look.

"Too soon?" Nichole laughed and glanced at Merril.

His brows drew together, and he shook his head at Nichole.

"It was a joke."

"Not funny. You nearly died." Merril whispered, "Jason carries a tremendous amount of guilt over your carriage accident. As do I."

"Jason would have seen me locked up in a psych ward by your brother's mistress." Nichole shrugged. "I'm not going to walk on eggshells around my cousin."

"I'm going to get up front." Merril motioned forward, changing the conversation. "We're getting close."

Nichole followed him past the wagon and the riders staggered along the trail.

Bill and Kelly rode point.

"The shack is just after this scrub brush. See the creek? In the spring, the water winds close to the wagon ruts then turns back and runs behind the cabin. It crosses the path up there." He brought Midnight to a trot.

Nichole had Sugar match their pace.

The path through the summer grass turned southerly, and Merril pulled in on his reins. "You can see the cabin from here."

Roughly a hundred yards east of where they sat stood the small wooden shack. Brush along the dry creek behind the structure had grown to either side of the building, blending the shack into the growth. Bushes and saplings dotted the dry bed as it meandered toward the wagon path. Ahead, the route ended at the washout.

The others dismounted. A few hobbled their horses before walking the area. Others tied the reins loosely to the wagon rail.

Merril remained in the saddle beside Nichole. He rested his forearm on the horn and looked at her. "What do you think?"

"You used to come here with your dad?"

"My father and I built this together. We hunted deer and sometimes pheasant. Mostly we spent time here to try to mend our relationship after I returned home."

"Good memories then?"

"Yes. For the most part."

Hunter walked past them and stopped halfway between the cabin and the wagon. He crouched down and picked up several items from the ground, then nudged his flat-brimmed hat to the back of his head as he studied the foliage along the small creek. After several moments he walked toward Merril and Nichole. "We will need gunmen at each end of the clearing. There's a good line of sight from over there." He pointed to the line of brush they had already passed. "And a good place for me to set up. I'll be able to see our people coming."

"From that direction, the wagon won't get further than the washout." Merril pointed to the creek's intrusion on the wagon route.

Hunter nodded. "They'll have to run to the cabin from there."

"Who?" Nichole watched Jim lift Alyse from the wagon seat and hand her the cane. "Alyse couldn't get from the house to the stable this morning. How do you expect her to run across this field?"

Hunter studied Alyse's progress. "I don't know." He shook his head and turned back to Merril and Nichole. "But the monster won't follow anyone else. The women must lure Morago to the cabin and into our trap. With gunmen hidden along the creek bed over there, we should be able to stop anyone from following Morago to the shack." He shook his fist as though he rattled a set of dice and set off with his long strides toward the small cabin. He paused after several paces, then took another half-dozen steps. "This seems a safe distance. We can hold his gunmen back at the turn in the trail."

Nichole dismounted and followed Merril to where Hunter stood. "What's in your hand?"

Hunter held out his palm for her inspection. He held three pebbles—one large and two small ones. He crouched and cleared grass to display the prairie soil, then lined the rocks—small, large, small—then stood and dusted his hands on his trousers. "The sisters will need to draw him past this mark for me to spring the trap."

Chapter 25

Nichole Harris-Shilo

—

"Dusty but cozy." Nichole cleared a cobweb and toured the small cabin with Hunter, Merril and White Eagle. Merril hadn't exaggerated when he described the lodge. A one-room shelter with two camp beds and a fireplace.

Merril held the door, and they circled the outside of the structure. Not far from the tiny creek stood a lean-to large enough to protect two horses.

Nichole rounded the cabin beside Hunter. "You'll have White Eagle, Amy, and Alyse inside?"

"No. Only White Eagle will be caught in the trap with Morago." Hunter stepped around a yellow flowering bush. "Amy and Alyse must be clear of the area."

"How are they supposed to do that? There's no back exit." Nichole followed him back to the front of the shack.

Hunter raised a brow at Nichole. "They're witches. They perform miraculous feats on a scale I can't even comprehend. I must trust they will complete their task." He glanced down the side of the cabin and then peered into the interior. "Where's Waynoka?"

"There." White Eagle pointed toward the brush line.

While most of the group had returned to their horses, Waynoka and one of the twin brothers talked in the shade of a tall sapling not far from the road.

Nichole placed a hand over her stomach as it rumbled and sent up a grateful thought to Cookie and Henny who had tucked portions of food in each saddlebag.

Bill and Kelly spread blankets on the ground behind the cart.

Amy's uncle straightened the corner of the covering so that Waynoka could sit down.

"She likes him," Nichole stated.

White Eagle nodded. "Is he a good man?" The shaman enunciated each word carefully.

"Yes, he is. A very good man." Nichole and her companions crossed the open field to join the group.

"Which one is he?" Hunter asked. "I can't tell them apart."

"Waynoka is having lunch with Bernard." Nichole pointed the other direction. "That's Bayard over there."

"How can you tell, *fillette?*"

"Bay is more animated. He laughs and jokes. He also tends to become emotional." She looked back in time to see Bernard smile at Waynoka and offer her part of his lunch. "Bernard is serious and thoughtful."

"An interesting observation," Hunter whispered as they approached the wagon.

White Eagle departed their company and sat beside his granddaughter.

Nichole chuckled. "Look, White Eagle is checking out Bernard."

"You shouldn't stare." Merril handed Nichole a linen-wrapped package. "Let's find a spot and eat. We'll need to head out after lunch." He watched Hunter take a similar package from his saddlebag then signaled the Cajun to join them.

Hunter, Merril, and Nichole shared a lunch blanket with Jim and Alyse.

"When we get back to your ranch we can meet for a final assessment. Get everyone's thoughts on what we've seen today," Hunter said, then bit into a ham-filled biscuit.

"Nichole suggested we fall into three distinct groups." Alyse took a sip of water from her canteen. "After we finalize the details of the trap, I'd like to separate and practice our elemental skills with Amy and our uncles."

"What are the groups?" Merril asked.

Nichole swallowed her bite of sandwich. "Artillery, Battlemages, and Spirit Seekers."

"I need to show White Eagle my plan to trap the demon under a bowl," Hunter stated.

"I'll have Kelly or Bill set up a practice range for this distance." Merril pointed from the brush lined creek behind them to the washed-out road on the other side of the grassy meadow. "Then we'll need to determine where the monster is." Merril put his hands together and brushed away his biscuit crumbs. "It's best we return home after lunch, instead of taking the path on to Kiowa Crossing."

"Why is that?" Nichole asked.

"What if the demon is already there?" He indicated the group around him. "We're not ready to face him and his host."

"And I have not completed everything necessary to spring the trap." Hunter pushed himself to his feet. "We must proceed with caution."

"Besides, I want to get everyone's opinion on the area, and how confident each person is that the plan will succeed," Merril told them as they folded the blankets to return home.

***

Jimmy Leigh

—

Back at the ranch, Jim spread the map on the backyard table. He sketched a detail of the hunting shack and surrounding area to the side of the map. "The washed-out road is here. The cabin and the creek. There was brush here and along the back of the cabin." He spoke as he drew and then pointed to two places. "We will have gunmen here and here. The distance is no more than seventy yards. Bill, if you would place a few targets for this distance, we'll practice our aim and adjust the sights on our weapons."

"I must make a puppet for White Eagle," Hunter announced. "After that, I will set up the requested demonstration. Anyone who would like to watch is welcome to attend."

"I've had some ideas about how we can further disguise the fighters and shield Amy and Alyse as they draw the demon into the target area," Bernard added.

"For the next few days, we know what we all have to do." Jim took the map back to his room in the bunkhouse then returned to the yard.

With dinner and discussion over, everyone had broken into smaller groups and wandered off.

Jeanne and Lawna shook out the last few blankets and placed them beside the others on the wooden table. They gathered the dinner dishes and greeted Jim as they carried the items into the kitchen.

Alyse waited on the wooden bench. Her cane rested against her leg. "That didn't take long. I'm glad you came back."

He clasped her hand as he settled beside her. "How's your leg?"

"Numb. Useless. It's my back that aches tonight." She gripped his hand. "But I'll be fine by morning. It's just been a long day. You must stop worrying."

"I'll try." He schooled his face and changed the subject. "What did you think of Hunter's plan?"

Alyse shrugged. "I don't know the depth of his skill. If he and White Eagle can trap and hold the demon, then Amy and I should be able to finish him off."

"With *Fire* and *Earth*?"

"We've talked about how we accomplish that. My role is fairly straightforward." She held her free hand between them and wiggled her fingers. Flames crawled up from her palm and danced across her fingertips. She grinned at Jim through the fire then the flame disappeared. "It's the *Earth* part that raises concerns. Amy thinks she should drop a boulder on him."

"She'll figure it out." Jim chuckled. "She's smart."

"Oh, I know. Once Amy gets her mind fixed on a problem, she's tenacious." Alyse tipped her head and peered at Jim from the corner of her eye. "In fact, now that she knows she can move metal, she wants to practice shielding from gunfire. Of course, she wants Uncle Bern and Bay involved since they might be able to do the same." She laughed and looked toward the sunset. "At least moving metal, I can understand. But when she and Nichole discuss refracting light with water particles to attain mirror invisibility, they lose me."

"I don't even understand what you said."

Alyse turned and caught his stare. Her brows raised, and she laughed, wide eyes filled with joy. "The good part is, I couldn't do it even if I wanted to. She's the one that has to convince our uncles it would be worth a try."

"If I know Amy, and I do, she can be very persuasive."

"Hmm." Alyse leaned close to Jim and tipped her head back. "Let's see how persuasive I can be."

Jim's fingers trailed along the side of her cheek into the hair behind her ear, then lowered his mouth to hers. The brief touch of her soft lips was not enough, and he pressed his mouth to hers again.

Whether she had meant to speak, or simply take a breath, her lips parted.

Jim welcomed the invitation by tilting his head and stealing a small taste of her mouth with the tip of his tongue.

Alyse gripped the back of his neck and groaned. Her next breath sealed their lips.

Jim broke the kiss and raised his head. They were alone for the moment, but the ranch was full of people. What he wanted, what he ached to share with this woman would require an entire night and privacy.

Alyse rested her head against Jim's shoulder. "You make me feel things I've never... look, I have chills." She held up her forearm pimpled with gooseflesh.

Jim kissed the top of her head and wrapped his long arms around her shoulders. "I love you." He settled his cheek against her soft hair. "To be unable to defeat anyone or anything that intends you harm shatters my heart. What good am I?"

"Stop this." Alyse pushed upright and stared into his brown eyes. "I'm not defenseless. And regardless of how you feel, you're not the reason I will or won't survive this trial. There are thirteen of us. If I fall, it will not be because you failed me." She gripped his shirt with both hands.

"Hunter is deliberately putting you and Amy in harm's way. And though I understand his reasons, I hate him for it. I want to lure the demon across that field instead of you."

"But it can't be you." She released his shirt and smoothed the material flat. "And you should bless Hunter. There's not a single reason he shouldn't have ridden away from this mess with Sam and Cat. This isn't Hunter's fight. It's mine. That he stayed to offer his aid is a gift Amy and I can never repay."

Jim watched her face, able to interpret both her hesitation and her passion. She believed in herself and her elemental magic. Her only concern was the physical challenge. No one could help her make that run.

"Would you do me a favor?" Alyse threaded her fingers between Jim's.

"Anything."

Alyse smiled. "Hunter plans to demonstrate the glass barrier he created to hold Merril for White Eagle. I'd like to watch."

Beyond the well pump and the cottonwood tree, the old Indian's shelter stood shadowed in darkness.

"It's too dark to see my footing..." Alyse allowed her voice to trail off into a smile.

Jim steadied her as she came to her feet, then lifted her in his arms, cradling her against his chest. "I thought you'd never ask."

Chapter 26

Nichole Harris-Shilo

—

Stars appeared one by one on the eastern horizon. In the west, a final glimmer of light outlined the distant mountain tops. Nichole rubbed her chilled arms and wished for her wrap. As soon as the sun had set, the temperature dropped.

Merril and Jason carried good size rocks, from the border of Amy's garden to place in a ring around the fire. They dropped them in a pile in front of White Eagle's tent and went back for more.

"I can help." Amy held out her hand. With a wiggle of her fingers, the stones separated and rolled into a semicircle close to the shallow pit. "I need the practice."

"You don't need to wave your fingers," Bayard teased.

"It helps me focus."

Merril dropped another load of rocks and dusted his hands against his trousers. He pulled Nichole close and rubbed his warm hands down her arms. "You're chilled. Is that better?"

"Much. Thank you." Nichole relaxed against his warmth, comfortable now that his arms surrounded her.

Bernard and Waynoka arrived with a burlap bag containing several cow chips. Bernard tossed several into the pit. "I'll leave the bag behind the shelter. There's a large covered stack of bovine manure on the far side of the garden if you need more."

"Does anyone have a match?" Bayard asked.

"Can't you just light it with *Fire-magic*?" Hunter asked.

"No," Bayard explained. "We can't create elements, only manipulate an existing source."

Merril dug into his pocket, pulled out a wooden match, and flicked his thumbnail across the top. As soon as the spark flared, a flame leaped across the yard and into the fire pit. In moments, the earthy scent of burning manure, as well as heat and light, filled the small area.

"Thank you, Uncle Bernard, for lighting our fire," Alyse called from the darkened back yard. "Although I thought that was usually my job."

Jim emerged from the shadows with Alyse in his arms. He lowered Alyse to her feet beside Nichole.

"Grandfather would like to see your demonstration now," Waynoka smiled and lowered her eyes. She stood between White Eagle and Bernard near the side of the shelter.

"In anticipation of your request, I asked *Madame* Cookie for a drinking glass, which she has provided." He held up a Mason jar. "However, before I can begin, I must ask for something small and personal that belongs to your grandfather. It need not be an item of great value, only one he has carried on his person. Something that belongs to him."

White Eagle and Waynoka discussed the request.

Waynoka nodded and addressed Hunter. "Grandfather would like to know how this item will be used—in what magic?"

"Ah." Hunter grinned and lifted one of his grass dolls from a box at his feet. "I intend to make a connection between your grandfather and a doll that will represent him" He handed the handmade object to Waynoka. "That is one of myself."

A button from Hunter's jacket had been sewn to the center of the effigy.

White Eagle weighed the doll in his hand, chuckled, and held it up beside Hunter. He spoke briefly to his granddaughter and then laughed aloud.

Waynoka's smile lit her face. "Grandfather says he can see the likeness."

While everyone joined in the laughter, White Eagle closed his eyes and chanted, still holding the doll. By the time he finished, the group had grown silent.

He handed the grass doll to Hunter as he spoke.

"White Eagle has blessed your likeness and gives you his permission to proceed," Waynoka said.

Hunter accepted the doll, then withdrew an effigy with no adornment. "This will be White Eagle's puppet, but to complete the magic, I'll need the personal item."

White Eagle nodded, removed a strip from around his wrist and toyed with the shells and a small feather connected to the soft leather.

"This was a gift given to Grandfather by his wife, long ago," Waynoka explained. "He has carried it with him since she passed into the night sky. He would like you to use this for his soul-doll, in the hope that he may soon meet with his beloved wife again."

Hunter accepted the bracelet, then lowered to his haunches, setting the doll and the jewelry on the ground in front of him. From the box, he withdrew a small flask and poured a double-shot of whiskey into the Mason jar, then placed it beside the doll.

His familiar deep voice spoke a rhythmic chant in a language Nichole didn't recognize. Now and then a word sounded familiar to her ear, but the pronunciation was strange, and she couldn't be sure.

Hunter tied the bracelet to the grass doll then held the chest of the doll to the ground with one finger. With his other hand, he lifted the glass to the night sky and drank the potent liquor in a single swallow.

As he refilled the glass, he looked around the gathering. "Most of you were present the night Merril came home in the thrall of Morago's demon-spawn. I trapped our friend, and the fiend, under an invisible boundary created with glass." He picked up the jar and swirled the amber liquid. "The barrier can work in one of two ways. It can keep those inside the glass safe from outside threats, or it can trap someone on the inside and prevent them from leaving the confines of my ward.

"The spells are similar, but there is an important difference that must be understood. When we trap Morago, he will not be able to escape, but others may come to his aid. Preventing his allies from reaching him will be the work of the gunmen." His gaze moved from Merril to Jim and finally to Jason.

"I shall reverse the protective boundary I create around White Eagle, so he will come to no harm until he chooses to break the protective ward. Which would you like to see first?"

Nichole glanced around the gathering, and was startled to find Dessa, in her colorful robe, watching in silence from the other side of the fire.

The old woman's familiar gaze landed on Nichole. Dessa gave her a slight nod.

Hello, Granddaughter.

Nichole heard her voice—Dessa's voice—as though she spoke from beside her.

The others around the fire never looked toward the strangely garbed woman.

Nichole returned the nod to Dessa and was unaccountably pleased to see the spirit-woman smile.

"Grandfather would like to see the demon trap first. He requests you bind him inside your ward." Waynoka's eyes sparkled with excitement. She glanced from her grandfather to Bernard, then stared at Hunter as she rubbed her hands together.

"As you wish. This magic shall trap the demon Morago, forcing him to remain inside the boundary I set in glass. He will not be able to pass through the ward, but your bullets, your magic, and his allies may."

Hunter lifted his face to the night sky. "*Mèt Kafou mwen rele ou beni majik sa a.*"

A swirl of mist condensed behind Hunter and Carrefour stepped into the firelight. He bowed to Dessa and grinned a broad smile at Nichole. As always, he appeared dressed in finely tailored clothing. Tonight, there was a black satin stripe down the side of his trousers that matched his cutaway jacket. He swung his walking stick, resting the length over his shoulder as he leaned forward to watch Hunter's preparations on the ground.

How will you serve me so that I may serve you?

Carrefour's voice was as clear to Nichole as Dessa's had been. "Can you hear him?" Nichole whispered to Merril.

"Hear who? Hunter?"

Nichole shook her head. "I'll tell you later."

Hunter lifted the beaker and swirled the liquid.

"*Mèt Kafou, mwen sèvi ou ak likè.*" He downed the liquor, flipped the glass over, and covered the grass effigy of White Eagle.

"*Fèmen pòt l 'anndan an.*"

Behind Hunter, Carrefour straightened and threw his arms wide. He held the walking stick tight in his gloved fist and swallowed at the same moment Hunter drank the liquor.

"It is done." Hunter smiled at White Eagle's curious stare. "Reach for your granddaughter, but slowly. You don't want to break a finger."

White Eagle lifted his hand, and his face lit with delight. He spun around and measured the distance he could reach. He nodded and spoke excitedly to Waynoka.

"Can I touch him?" she asked.

"Yes. Anything can pass into the ward, but White Eagle is trapped inside." Hunter indicated the voodoo doll beneath the glass.

White Eagle pressed both hands against the invisible barrier, the pressure flattening his palms. His eyes beamed with excitement, and he nodded several times to Hunter.

Both Waynoka and Bernard reached in and touched White Eagle.

"There's nothing there." Bernard waved his hand above White Eagle's pressed palms.

"Yet there is. This trap will hold Morago. He cannot escape, but a bullet or *elemental-fire* may reach him." He chuckled at White Eagle's enthusiasm. "Are you ready to try the other way?" At White Eagle's nod, Hunter lifted the glass and released the shaman.

White Eagle searched the ground, a wide grin on his face. He grabbed his granddaughter's hand and motioned to Hunter as he spoke.

"Grandfather is pleased that the Shaman Hunter has shown him magic he has never witnessed. He thanks you," Waynoka translated.

"The pleasure is mine, *mon ami*." Hunter said to the old Indian.

Hunter poured a double shot of whiskey into the beaker. "Because we have no puppet for Morago, the trap spell will be set on a boundary." He looked at Amy and Alyse. "The magic will catch everything within a given area. You must be away before the trap is sprung."

"How far will they need to run?" Jim stood like an oak with Alyse leaning against him.

"If all goes as planned, from where the wagon must stop near the washed-out trail, pass through the cabin, and then beyond the creek behind. The creek will be the back limit of the ward," Hunter told him with an apologetic look at Alyse. He swirled the liquor and turned to White Eagle. "If you're ready, *mon ami*, I will demonstrate the ward I shall set around you."

White Eagle nodded.

"Step away from your grandfather." Hunter motioned to Waynoka and Bernard.

As Waynoka turned, she faced Dessa, and her eyes widened. She twisted her head to meet Nichole's gaze, a question in her eyes.

Nichole nodded and mouthed a silent, "Yes."

Waynoka must share her grandfather's gifts if she sees Dessa.

Did she see Carrefour as well? Did White Eagle? Nichole tilted her head toward the *Petro loa* behind Hunter and raised her brow at Waynoka.

The Indian woman tipped her head, grinning an affirmation.

They see and know more than they let on.

Carrefour had been leaning on his walking stick observing his nails. Now he edged up behind Hunter, to watch the Cajun's hands.

Hunter swirled the liquor.

"*Mèt Kafou, mwen sèvi ou ak likè.*" He swallowed the amber liquid, flipped the glass over, and covered the grass effigy of White Eagle. "*Fèmen pòt tout soti.*"

"I don't think *Carrefour* is doing anything, at least not that I can see. The magic is all Hunter's. The *loa* just watches," Nichole whispered to Merril.

"I can't see what you do. I take it Hunter's voodoo spirit is here?"

"*Carrefour*, yes. And so is Dessa." She hugged Merril and stretched to whispered in his ear, "Waynoka and White Eagle see the spirits too."

White Eagle stepped forward.

"Stop," Hunter cautioned. "If you step outside the ward, the spell will break. The barrier is invisible to you, but will stop anyone, or anything, from reaching you." He tipped his head at White Eagle while looking at Waynoka. "Try to touch him now. Move with caution."

Waynoka touched the barrier with one hand, and then with both. "I am impressed."

Both Bernard and Bayard walked around the ward.

"Nothing can penetrate?" Bayard picked up several clumps of dirt and tossed them at White Eagle. After the first few had bounced off, he threw with more force, exploding the clumps against the barrier. "Amazing."

"Does it block all of the elements?" Bernard asked.

Hunter nodded, then shrugged. "As far as I know, but we should find out."

"Bayard, don't use *Fire*," Alyse pushed away from Jim and leaned on her cane to walk to the campfire. "It's too dangerous. Use *Water*."

"We'll need to test them all." Bayard grinned. "But I have faith in our Voodoo priest."

"I am no priest." Hunter held his finger on the overturned Mason jar. "But I was taught the rites. One, such as I, would be called a *bokor*."

Bernard carried a glass of water to Amy. "Here."

Amy accepted the glass. "You could just toss the water at him."

"What fun would that be?" Bayard proclaimed with a playful chuckle.

Amy shrugged and lifted the glass as high as she could, closing her eyes. A cyclone appeared in the glass, twirled up in a tight spiral into the sky, then surged toward White Eagle.

He flinched as the water struck the barrier but stood firm. And dry. The rebounding water splashed everyone, and an arc of wet ground highlighted the boundary at the shaman's feet.

Hunter lifted the glass from White Eagle's puppet. "And that ends tonight's demonstrations." He rose with a slight smile to a round of applause. "Tomorrow, we shall begin in earnest to ready ourselves for the coming confrontation."

Chapter 27

Morago

—

Morago directed Vasquez to bring him small groups of men interested in working for Buckner. This time, the demon would take no chances. He placed one of his servants inside each man Vasquez brought who could carry a gun.

With the possession of his new host of gunmen complete, the sudden emptiness at the back of Morago's mind reminded him of when he'd been young, and alone. Before he'd captured his slaves by defeating them in battle and acquiring their small sets of skills.

He'd always considered his horde of demons endless, but in truth, there was an end to everything. Only one occupant resided in his mind now—the old witch, Chantal. Her considerable elemental magic had become his by right when he defeated her. As long as her soul remained his, so did her magic. In truth, the woman had grown so silent that at times, he forgot she existed.

Nevertheless, he had obtained what he needed. Twenty gunmen who answered to no one but him. They lingered in saloons, boarding houses, and bordellos nearby for Morago to give the command.

Morago eyed Violet as she managed the welcome room at the brothel.

Perhaps I should take my servant from the whore and secure another man?

After he had another drink, and given the matter due consideration, he decided against removing his thrall from Violet. She and his servant had formed a bond in much the same way as he and Randolph Buckner.

The woman and the demon were efficient and effective together.

He would also leave his demon-servants inside Albert Fielding, to observe the witch's lair in Denver, and the finch, who waited near June McKay.

Three additional men will make no difference.

Morago sipped his whiskey. From his chair in the small room, he watched through the door as men arrived to choose a companion for the evening.

As the longcase clock in the entry struck eight, Vasquez and Otis entered the bordello.

Morago had secured a room for Otis in a nearby hotel rather than allow him to stay at the brothel. Buckner had made that suggestion, based partly on jealousy over the way the women vied for Otis's attention. Morago, however, had agreed. The banker was skilled at manipulation, and when given a choice of partners at Buck's, he did not always choose the whore in Morago's possession.

The gunman and the banker wove their way through the half-clad women and came directly to Morago.

"*Jefe*, the horses and gear are ready," Vasquez said as he walked into the office. "I had to make deals with three stables, but it's done."

"Good." Morago finished his whiskey. He would miss liquor once he returned to the tangle of snake-demons with the witches' powers.

And sex.

He'd come to appreciate some of the physical pleasures afforded to humans which he'd not experienced in previous incarnations in the mortal world. He'd always been eager to leave this place before.

But not this time.

"I've decided," he told Vasquez and Otis. "We'll leave tomorrow for Kiowa Crossing. It's time to end this."

Otis poured himself a drink and sat across from Buck. "Do you want us to let your men know?"

"They already do." Morago smiled. "Why don't you enjoy an evening with Violet and stay here tonight. That way, you'll be on hand when we leave in the morning." He waved toward the lady's room. "It happens she's available this evening."

Violet leaned against the office door frame and smiled invitingly at Otis. She held out her hand. "Come along, Otis. Since this will be our last night together for a while, let's make it memorable."

Otis finished his drink and set his empty glass on the bar. "Well then, I'll see you gentlemen in the morning."

Morago watched Otis follow Violet upstairs. Nothing needed to be said, and yet, Morago felt the need to speak. "We'll meet here in the morning."

"*Si, Jefe.*"

"This time, they'll underestimate me."

Vasquez finished his drink and strode to the door. "I believe you." He tipped his head to Morago. "*Buenas noches.*"

When Vasquez departed, Morago closed his eyes and followed the silver thread to the demon-finch.

The bird slept in a bush near June's boarding house.

A nudge from Morago sent the yellow bird to June's windowsill.

Through an opening in the curtain, Morago watched the woman sink to her knees in her nightdress. She rested her elbows on the mattress, clasped her hands and closed her eyes.

Had he been there, he would have heard her thoughts. Her prayers. He would have drawn her dissatisfaction and disillusionment into his soul. Instead, he sent the tiny bird back to its resting place and poured himself another drink.

Before sunrise, Morago's men and Otis Pierce gathered outside of Buck's bordello. Vasquez held Big Buck's horse while Morago mounted. Directing the large animal without possessing the horse made Morago uneasy. He allowed Randolph to take the reins.

An hour into their ride, Vasquez reined his mount beside Morago. "We don't want to tire the horses, *Jefe.* We will need them again once we arrive in town to go to the ranch."

Morago slowed the riders' pace with a thought. "Anticipation drives me."

Vasquez chuckled. "Me too. Your victory will be a great accomplishment for us all."

If Morago could find no means to circumvent The Prophecy, then after he secured the elemental magic and returned to the tangle, a suitable reward would be found for this one's loyal service.

Vasquez did not fall back after delivering his advice about their pace. Instead, he continued to ride beside Morago.

Morago raised a brow at demon-Vasquez's presumption and studied the vaquero, reading his thoughts. There existed an indefinable quality in the duo he had never encountered before.

You sense an air of independence.

Morago scoffed at Buckner's opinion. How utterly absurd! His slaves were bound in servitude for eternity. Morago's grip was secure.

After awhile, Vasquez urged Morago to give the horses and men a rest break. Vasquez had provided trail food in each man's saddlebag, as well as water jugs for their mounts.

Morago accepted the advice with ill-grace and suspicion, even though Vasquez's forethought had likely saved his campaign before the battle had even begun.

Well before sunset, the group of twenty-two rode into the tiny town of Kiowa Crossing.

The gunmen passed the train depot as the sheriff left his office.

The lawman paused and watched the riders turn down main street. Then he casually stepped from the boardwalk in front of Morago's horse.

Buckner brought the mount to a standstill and raised his fist to halt the men behind him.

"Welcome, strangers." The sheriff thumbed his hat back and made a show of examining the large group. He flashed a smile as he spoke to Buckner. "Can I ask your business, friend?"

Randolph urged diplomacy, and Morago agreed.

Morago dismounted and extended a gloved hand to the sheriff. "I'm Randolph Buckner. Most folks call me Buck." He indicated Otis, who despite the long ride stood out among the Westerners by his posture and his clothing. "My companion is Otis Pierce. He's come all the way from Boston to speak with a friend of his. Jason Harris."

The sheriff took Buck's hand. "I'm Sheriff Wheeler." He stepped back and considered the gunmen behind Buck again. "This seems like a mighty large posse to bring to a discussion between friends. I don't want any trouble, either in town or out at the ranch."

"I understand." Morago nodded. "Apparently, a transaction between these men was incomplete when Mr. Harris left Boston. They've been in communication regarding the matter, but Mr. Pierce hasn't heard from his friend in a few months. He's come in person to check on his friend's well-being." The speech flowed naturally from Buckner's lips. Words he and Otis, along with Vasquez, had rehearsed over the last few days.

The sheriff's thoughts were as clear as if he had spoken. Ten dead men had been turned over to Sheriff Wheeler by a federal marshal a few days ago, killed in an attack on The Highlands Ranch. The connection between the dead men and the group before him appeared obvious to the lawman.

The sheriff knows we outgun him.

Otis dismounted and shook Sheriff Wheeler's hand. "Nice to meet you, sir. I've come a long way to talk to Jason. After our correspondence was interrupted last month, I knew I had to come and speak with him in person."

"Mr. Pierce." The sheriff smiled at the younger man. "I haven't seen Jason with my own eyes in several months, but I'm sure Marshal Kline would have mentioned if something was amiss with the family."

"I see." Otis glanced at Buckner and Vasquez. "I didn't realize a marshal had been at Jason's ranch."

"Yep." Sheriff Wheeler nodded. "He came through town just the other day."

"If I could speak with him, it would ease my mind with regards to my friend."

"Unfortunately, Marshal Kline is no longer in the area." The sheriff pressed his lips and turned to Buckner.

He's made up his mind to accommodate us as best he can. He trusts Otis.

"Do you intend to continue to The Highlands Ranch or stay in town?" He eyed the number of men again and shook his head. "We get a few visitors now and then, but there aren't enough rooms at the boarding house for your crew."

Buck smiled. "They are prepared to make camp nearby. Otis and I would be the only ones seeking a room for the next few days."

"Then you intend to remain in Kiowa Crossing?"

"Otis hopes to speak to his friend on neutral ground, so yes, we plan to stay here until they can complete their transaction."

"There should be rooms available above The Thirsty Mule." The sheriff pointed to a building with rocking chairs outside the door. "They serve food and liquor downstairs." The sheriff took a few steps toward the telegraph office. "As for your men, if they would care to set up camp south of the tracks, I'd be most appreciative."

The ugly feeling that stirred in the sheriff's gut was apparent to Morago.

He intends to telegraph the authorities in Denver and then placate us until federal deputies arrive.

With a thought, he brought the demon army behind him to alert. Morago didn't care if the sheriff died in a storm of bullets, or if he had to ransack the entire town, but it seemed a waste of resources. Some of his men could die, and there may not be replacements available.

If even one servant remained inside Morago, he would have possessed the sheriff immediately.

Perhaps I should take him myself.

As much as Morago enjoyed Randolph Buckner, the sheriff of this tiny hamlet commanded considerable power.

Not as much as we do, here and now. The sheriff fears us. Buckner reasoned.

From The Thirsty Mule emerged an obese man with thick double chins. White muttonchop whiskers extended down his cheeks from beneath his top hat. He teetered for a moment on the boardwalk, then made straight for the sheriff and Morago.

"Sheriff Wheeler, I see we have new guests in town." The portly gentleman offered his hand to Otis. "Cecil Cobb. Solicitor. Welcome to Kiowa Crossing."

"Otis Pierce. Investment Adviser at Pierce and Peabody in Boston."

"Boston? Perhaps you know Jason Harris?"

"As a matter of fact, he's why I'm here."

While Otis and the small-town solicitor became acquainted, Morago sent instructions to his servants.

Vasquez, accompany the men across the railroad tracks and set up camp. Send them in groups of five to dine at the town restaurant.

Sí, Jefe.

The men behind Otis and Morago turned their mounts and rode away down the main street, and across the railroad tracks.

"Is that a good place for my men, sheriff?" Morago smiled at the Sheriff Wheeler.

The solicitor and Otis's friendly conversation was having the desired effect on the sheriff. He relaxed.

The armed men are off his street, and he again feels in charge.

"Yes, that will be fine."

"If you haven't eaten, Sheriff Wheeler, please allow me to buy your dinner. We can discuss our business with Mr. Harris."

"As a matter of fact, I was headed to The Thirsty Mule when I saw your men ride in." Sheriff Wheeler fell in beside Morago and followed Otis and Cecil into the restaurant.

Up ahead, Otis and Cecil had their heads together.

Annoyed that he couldn't hear their conversation, Morago hurried to catch up.

Inside the restaurant, the waitress was wiping down a table. "Back so soon, Mr. Cobb?" She tossed the rag behind the bar and smiled at Otis. "Please have a seat." She indicated the two empty bar stools next to her.

"There will be four, Melinda." Cobb wiggled pudgy fingers over his shoulder at Buck and the sheriff. "We'll sit over here." He pointed across the room and removed his hat. The attorney navigated around two empty tables and hung his top hat on a wall hook.

Melinda followed the group to the table. "What can I get you, gentlemen?"

After the men had placed their orders, Cobb leaned forward. "I've been urging Sheriff Wheeler to bring both of them in for questioning. This appears a perfect opportunity."

"Both?" Otis tore a piece of bread from the basket the waitress had left on the table.

"There is some question as to the valid inheritance of The Shilo Ranch." Cobb lowered his voice. "The Shilo is a sister ranch to The Highlands Ranch, where Jason lives. Philip Shilo's recent death left the property to his two sons. It appears, based on eyewitness testimony, that one brother may have murdered the other."

"Now Cecil, there's no proof. We've been over this before." The sheriff nodded his thanks to the waitress as she passed out their drinks, then moved away from the table.

"Perhaps, but if Jason Harris left Boston with this man's money, and is now the attorney and accountant for both The Shilo and The Highlands ranches, he stands to gain a great deal by Kevin Shilo's untimely death."

The sheriff shook his head. "There's not enough evidence to arrest Merril, much less Jason."

"But you do have enough now, with the arrival of Mr. Pierce, to at least call them both in to answer a few questions."

Morago sat back in his chair, allowing Cecil Cobb to plead their case for them.

What luck! Cecil reeks of envy, and something else.

Buck leaned forward and concentrated on the plump attorney.

He's seen something that frightened him. Magic!

"If you want, Sheriff, I could send a couple of my men to bring Jason and the other fella back to talk with you." Buck slanted a quick look at Otis.

"No, no. That won't be necessary." The scent of cooked meat brought the sheriff's glance upward. "Thank you, Melinda."

The waitress placed a plate in front of each man. "You're welcome, Sheriff. Anything else?"

"No, dear. We're good." He cut into his fried pork chop. "I'll send a deputy over in the morning, and he can *invite*—" Sheriff Wheeler paused with the pork pinned to his fork and looked around the table, "—Jason and Merril to meet with us."

"Have them come to my office," Cobb instructed.

The sheriff chewed and swallowed. "I prefer my office, Cecil." He cut another piece of pork and narrowed his eyes at Otis. "I won't mention your name, Mr. Pierce. Whatever is between you and Jason has nothing to do with my questions for Merril about his brother's death."

"I understand, Sheriff." Otis took a sip of his beer. "Would it be all right if I speak with Jason outside your office?"

"You certainly can." The sheriff pierced his section of pork. "It's a free country, Mr. Pierce, but I don't want any trouble in town."

Chapter 28

Nichole Harris-Shilo

—

Nichole rested her hip against the porch rail and waited for the bark of a rifle to echo again across the ranch.

Bill and Kelly had set up the firing range some distance from the house along the south road, but Lloyd had already come to her. Twice. The repeated gunfire bothered a few of the horses.

She sipped a cup of hot tea and sighed.

The men would have to move their target practice even further away. They wouldn't like that, but sound traveled quite a distance in the dry summer air.

Turning her back to the road, she observed her friends rehearsing their magic spells.

The battlemages had taken over the side yard beside the porch. Amy and her uncles cast water vapor around Alyse in an attempt to make her invisible. So far, they had only succeeded in soaking her in mist.

Nichole chuckled and took another sip of tea.

Alyse shimmered and faded, only to reappear moments later, her soaked skirt clinging to her legs. "Am I supposed to get this wet?"

"More like this." Amy lifted her hand and Alyse glimmered for a moment, then disappeared.

"But will there be enough water to work with at the cabin?" Bayard asked.

"We had rain the other day. We should be able to pull from the soil even if the creek bed has run dry."

Bernard bent, picked up a handful of dirt, and tried to squeeze it into a ball. "We should carry canteens to be safe." The dry soil spilled from between his fingers.

"Can I move yet?" Alyse's disembodied voice held a hint of annoyance.

Amy dropped her hands.

Alyse reappeared. Her skirt and hair stripped of moisture. She hobbled with her cane to stand beside Amy and her uncles. Alyse had pushed herself to improve her mobility although she still relied heavily on the cane. Her imbalance worried everyone, especially Jim.

"Let's give this a break. After lunch, I want to go with Jim and Jason to the shooting range." Alyse proposed. "I can't move metal, but I can throw fireballs at targets."

"That reminds me, Bern and I will need to prepare a small fire near the hunting lodge."

Nichole downed the last of her tea.

Hmm, firing range. I've nothing better to do after lunch. I'll go with Alyse.

The spirit witches had little to prepare.

Hunter had shown his skill and outlined the plan, finished his puppets, and collected the necessary glass bowls from Cookie.

With naught to practice, Nichole was left to sip tea, listen to the echo of gunfire, and watch the James family prepare for battle.

A slight movement on the porch caught her attention and Nichole pushed away from the rail.

Dessa stood beside her, observing the witches. Her hands folded serenely against her gown. "I thought we should talk, you and I." She dipped her head. "I'm sorry I frightened you at the bridge. I assumed Alexander had told you about me."

Nichole studied the spirit.

Dessa hadn't changed much from when Courtney had last seen her, and yet in many ways she had. The strength of her voice was the same, but now she spoke with an accent Nichole associated with tropical islands rather than her familiar southern drawl. "He didn't, but that wasn't the problem." Nichole bit her lip and rubbed against the shivers that ran up her arms. "I recognized you."

"You recognized me?" Dessa's dark brows rose to the edge of the colorful headscarf. "How is that possible?"

"You know I spirit-walked back from a future life, right?"

"Of course. A descendant of Alexander." Dessa's eyes widened. "You knew me in your other life."

Nichole nodded. "Your accent was different, and you were—real."

"Little girl, I assure you, I am very real."

"But I could touch you." Nichole tapped Dessa's shoulder and pulled her hand back. "Holy sh—."

"Less vulgarity, please." Dessa tossed her head and smiled to lessen the rebuke. "What did I say to you—when we last spoke—in your other life?"

The teacup rattled in its saucer as Nichole set it on the rail. "You wanted to know if I was the one who called about the room for rent." She turned away from Dessa and watched Amy and Alyse follow the men into the back yard. "You talked me into staying at the house when I would have left. You helped me find the photograph of Merril and me."

"I wonder why?"

"If I were to guess, I'd say you wanted me to return here."

"Yes, of course. But why would I want that?"

"To be with Merril. To reunite me with my soul mate." Nichole's voice softened, "To be less alone."

"That doesn't sound like me." Dessa shook her head. "I'll have to give this more thought." She walked forward, down the porch step to the side yard and disappeared.

You've given her quite a puzzle. Carrefour lounged against the corner of the house.

Nichole wrinkled her nose at him. "It's rude to eavesdrop."

His laughter faded as he stepped into the shadows.

Beyond where Carrefour had lounged, dust hung over the south road. The men were returning from target practice.

Nichole picked up her empty cup and carried it inside, passing the long table as she hurried down the hallway and into the kitchen. "The men are coming back."

Cookie added several of the apples Hunter had brought back from Kiowa Crossing to the lunch baskets, placing them alongside thick slices of cheese and fresh baked bread. "I've got Jeanne and Lawna spreading the blankets. We're ready for them."

Lunch would be served in the back yard, as it had been since White Eagle had arrived.

"Nicki?" Merril's raised voice sounded from the front door.

Nichole set the cup and saucer down and returned through the passage. The tone of Merril's voice quickened her pulse with alarm. They met in the dining room. "What's happened?"

"Sheriff Wheeler's deputy found us at the practice site. The sheriff wants to speak to me about Kevin's death."

"What? After all this time?"

"I'm sure it's nothing. A formality." He tried to smile and shrug it off, but Nichole knew him too well.

Jason moved up to stand behind Merril. "He wants to see me too."

"You?"

"I smell Cecil Cobb all over this." Jason slapped his gloves down on the table. "This is everything that fat rat threatened me with."

"But why would Sheriff Wheeler agree to this now? He knows you had nothing to do with Kevin's death."

From outside, a piercing cry for help halted their questions. Nichole rushed through the kitchen and out the back door, Jason and Merril close behind her.

Both Alyse and Amy were on the ground with Bay and Bern beside them.

"She fell against me and I couldn't catch her." Alyse cradled Amy's head against her chest. At least she landed on top of me, or she would have cracked her skull."

Bernard lifted Amy from her sister as Bayard steadied Alyse and helped her to her feet.

"Let me." Jason took Amy from Bernard and pulled her into his lap. "Amy?"

Her eyes were open, vacant, and unblinking. Every few seconds she twitched as if she were dreaming.

"She must be having a premonition." Nichole sank to her knees beside Amy and took her hand. "We're here Amy." She looked up at Merril. "Would you get a damp cloth from Cookie?"

Hunter, Waynoka, and White Eagle rounded the corner of the house and hurried to the huddled group.

White Eagle nodded and spoke to Waynoka.

"Grandfather says she receives visions from the Great Spirit." Waynoka moved around the group until she stood beside Bernard.

Nichole took the cloth from Merril and wiped Amy's face. "You're safe, Amy. Ride it out, girl. You got this."

Jim, Bill, and Kelly emerged from the kitchen.

"Where did everyone—Alyse!" Jim opened his arms as she rushed to him. "What happened to your sister?"

Alyse shook her head. "She cried out then fell. I tried to catch her, but I have no balance." She held up her cane.

"A vision." Merril said.

Jim nodded.

On the ground, Amy took several deep breaths cradled in Jason's arms.

"She's coming out of it." Nichole washed Amy's hands with the damp cloth. "Come on, Amy."

Amy blinked several times as tears filled her eyes and streaked down her cheeks. She gasped and tried to sit up.

Jason steadied her. "Easy, Amy."

She slapped the towel away and gripped Nichole's wrists. "The demon's in Kiowa Crossing."

"You saw him?" Hunter asked.

Amy took the cloth and wiped her face. "No. I saw the train station. A pit opened across the railway from the town. Things slithered in the dark. It was repellant, and I didn't look in." She lifted her gaze to Nichole. "I should have."

"Not necessarily." Nichole held her cold hands. "What else did you see?"

"Not much more. But I had the sensation of being drawn in, of anticipation. The demon is expecting us."

"Let me help you." Jason rose and set Amy on her feet and assisted her to the bench.

"The sheriff must be part of this." Nichole met Merril's gaze. "That's how the fiend knows you'll go to town. But why you and Jason?"

Merril lifted his hat and ran his hand through his hair. "They could hardly call in Amy and Alyse for questioning."

"It's a ploy to separate us." Hunter surveyed the group with a smile on his lips. "But this is what we want. For the beast to believe we're vulnerable."

"When does Sheriff Wheeler want to speak with you?"

"Now, or as soon as possible. Since lunch is ready, let's eat and discuss what we should do," Merril suggested.

"Eat yes, but we already know what we will do." Hunter took one of the cheese and fruit baskets from Cookie.

The eager anticipation in his eyes filled Nichole with hope.

Hunter lifted his voice and spoke to the people gathered for lunch. "The demon calls, and we, *mes amis*, shall answer."

Chapter 29

Nichole Harris-Shilo

—

"I'll let Kelly and Bill know it's time." Bayard jogged toward the bunkhouse.

Bernard took a step to follow his brother then turned to Hunter. "Two wagons? Six horses?"

"We have four bound for Kiowa Crossing—" Hunter began.

"Five," Nichole corrected.

"Make that six." Jim's arm remained firm around Alyse's shoulder.

Hunter swept his jacket back and placed his hands on his gun belt in aggravation. "We can stage a surprise attack without Nichole. But you, *mon ami,* you will fire the fatal shot. You must be ready when the demon arrives."

"I won't leave Alyse."

"Yes, you will." Alyse pushed against his ribs. "Hunter's right. The most dangerous part will be when we reach the cabin. You'll protect me best by being prepared for our arrival." She held out her hand to her sister. "Help me upstairs, and we'll change our clothes."

Amy helped Alyse up the backstep.

The two black cats that had been playing in the yard raced past their ankles and slipped inside when Amy opened the door.

At the top of the stoop, Alyse called back to Jim. "We'll be right back. Don't leave before we return."

"He won't," Hunter assured her. "We'll stay together until the turn-off to the cabin." Hunter spread his gaze between Jim, Jason, and Merril. "Let's go over where everyone will be when they draw the demon into our trap one last time."

Merril nodded to Hunter and kissed the top of Nichole's forehead. "You'd be safer with Jim and Hunter."

Nichole wrapped her arm around Merril's waist as they walked to the bunkhouse. "Perhaps, but we'd be apart. We'll meet them at the cabin, and until then, you'll have to put up with me."

"A trial of which I never grow weary."

Inside the bunkhouse, Jim spread the leather map across Kelly's bed.

Hunter pointed to the split in the road south of The Shilo. "This is where we will separate, where we turned the other day. Jason and Merril will take Amy and Alyse through town, springing Morago's trap and drawing him back to ours." He tapped an area across from the shack. "I'll be here. It's the best view of the front of the cabin and provides some cover in the tall grass beside the road."

He moved his finger to a second location. "Bay, Bern, Bill, and Kelly will be our main line of defense. They'll set up here. It's the closest cover to the washout. Their job will be to keep the demon's gunmen at bay."

He touched the third location. "Jim, I need you here with Waynoka. She has her grandfather's spirit sight and will be your eyes."

"Where do you want Merril and me to go?" Nichole asked.

"Ride past the brush on the far side of the cabin and dismount." Hunter sketched her path with his finger. "You'll circle back to me but stay hidden. Merril, if you would, join Jim."

Jason touched the penciled in buildings of Kiowa Crossing. "We'll turn around near the station."

"I should be with Alyse," Jim argued.

Jason slanted his gaze to Jim. "Between Merril's guns, Amy and Alyse's magic, and Nichole's ability to see demons, we'll be fine."

Hunter indicated the washed-out road near the cabin. "The tricky part will be the run from the wagon to the cabin. Morago won't want Amy and Alyse killed by gunfire. He'll want to do it himself with their grandmother's magic. They must not engage him before they draw him into our trap."

"They won't," Jason assured him. "I'll get our wagon and meet you at the house."

Nichole stretched to give Merril a kiss. "Bring Sugar with you to the porch, my love. I'm going to check on Amy and Alyse."

"Yes, sweetheart." Merril kissed her lips then turned back to the map. "Wouldn't I be better used with Bill and Kelly? I could turn in here and join them ..."

Merril's voice faded as Nichole hurried from the bunkhouse and past the corral.

Amy and Alyse waited on the porch, dressed in identical black dresses and sun bonnets.

"What's with the black?" Nichole glanced down at her brown divided skirt and tan blouse. "Did I miss the memo?"

"We want to look identical." Alyse brushed at her skirt. "Our appearance won't give pause to the demon or his spawn, but it may unsettle anyone not possessed by the beast."

"We were going to wear white, but thought we'd appear sacrificial." Amy tucked a stray curl beneath her bonnet. "Black has the added benefit of hiding bloodstains. Jason and Jim would have hysterics if the tiniest drop of our blood gets spilled," Amy explained.

"You're ready for this?" Nichole asked.

The sisters shared a look.

"Although my family hid the real reasons from me," Alyse glanced at Amy, "I've trained for this day since I was a child." She stepped forward leaning on her cane. "I want to get on with living, instead of training to fight." She looked across the yard to where the men were mounting up. "I've found someone to build a life with. I want the demon destroyed."

Amy opened her parasol. "I'm ready to use the magic I always considered useless. Now, I manipulate metal and cast shimmering reflections." She smiled at Nichole. "I'm terrified, but I'm ready."

At the sound of horses approaching, Nichole turned. "Alright then, let's do this."

***

Morago

—

Early the next afternoon, Randolph Buckner took a seat at The Thirsty Mule with Otis Pierce and Cecil Cobb. While Buckner broke bread with his new friends, Morago sulked in the background, impatient for news from the sheriff.

Near the end of their meal, Sheriff Wheeler's deputy entered the restaurant and sauntered to their table. "Excuse me, gentlemen. The sheriff asked me to come by and let you know I delivered his summons this morning—more of a request, actually—to Jason Harris and Merril Shilo."

"And?" Buckner's body sat at attention as Morago moved forward to take command.

"Both men, and a couple of their workers, were at target practice along the road. They agreed to meet with Sheriff Wheeler but didn't know when they'd be able to come to town."

"And you let that stand?" Buckner's short sharp tone bit with authority. "You should have demanded they return with you."

"I have no warrant for their arrest." The deputy sheriff narrowed his eyes at Buckner, then glanced at the other two men at the table. "Please remember, this meeting is a courtesy, requested by Sheriff Wheeler."

"How many men were with them?" Morago wiped his napkin across Buck's lips and set it aside.

"Only a few. I didn't take a count." He touched the brim of his hat. "Enjoy your lunch."

Morago rested his sight on the deputy's departing back. The more of the witches' guardians who came to town, the better. He intended to erode their defenses and reduce their numbers, as they had reduced his. Without a doubt, his servants could murder the handful of men the deputy described.

Perhaps you should consider taking these men hostage.

Randolph Buckner's suggestion flickered across the demon's mind.

Why ever would I do that?

To draw your prey to you. I've used this method successfully in the past. If you have one of the witches' husbands, she will come to you. I promise.

Let us see how this plays out. Given the opportunity, we shall attempt to capture them.

With a thought, he sent instructions to the gunmen across the tracks.

Do not shoot to kill. We want to take these men alive, if possible.

Sí, Jefe, demon-Vasquez replied. *Come outside. There are travelers on the road heading for town.*

Morago pushed back from the table. "It seems our guests may have finally arrived."

Both Cecil and Otis stared at him.

"How do you know?" the attorney demanded.

Otis rose and followed Buck to the door without comment.

Rising dust along the north road into town drew their attention.

"There are women with them," Otis commented as the wagon and riders drew closer.

Morago remained near the building while Otis stepped into the street to meet the newcomers.

***

Nichole Harris-Shilo

—

Nichole pulled back on the reins to slow Sugar as they approached the sheriff's office. She walked her horse beside Alyse.

"Isn't that Otis Pierce?" Amy touched Jason's arm and nodded at the man crossing the street to intercept the wagon.

"It looks like him." Jason set the brake as the man approached.

When their gazes met, Otis tipped his head. "Jason."

"Otis Pierce. Not someone I would expect to find in Kiowa Crossing. What brings you here?"

"I came to see you. Step down. Let's have a drink."

"Now's not the time, Otis."

"I need the money back, Jason. The loan. I need it now."

"I don't have your money, and even if I did, you'd never see it." Jason's voice dropped to a hiss. "You set me up to buy failing stock—to prop up those bonds so your father could make thousands." He shook his head, and his voice grew in volume along with his anger. "No. We signed no agreement or note for that money. And then, you turn around and blackmail me! I owe you nothing."

Otis clenched his fist. "Your questionable ethics extend to more than the money I'm owed." He addressed Merril. "I hear you've maneuvered yourself into a position of authority for two large ranches. You won't want to jeopardize that."

As Jason and Otis argued, Nichole's attention was drawn to the two men who stared at them from across the street.

Cecil Cobb and another man stood in the shadow of the overhang in front of The Mule.

A sick feeling ran along Nichole's nerves. "Over by The Mule. The big man near the door is demon-owned."

Ignoring Jason and the man he argued with, Merril urged Midnight forward several paces. "I recognize him from Denver, but I don't know who he is."

Sheriff Wheeler opened the door to his office and tipped his hat. "Good afternoon, ladies. If Jason and Merril would step inside, I'm sure we can take care of this matter in no time. The Mule would certainly be a comfortable place for you ladies to enjoy a glass of fresh lemonade and wait for your men." He eyed the twins, and his brow rose, but he didn't comment.

Amy pointed across the railroad tracks. "The pit that I saw was over there."

Across the tracks, a large group of men mounted their horses.

"Sheriff, it seems we'll need to discuss your matter another time." Merril tipped his head toward the men on horseback coming across the rails into town. "There's a lynch mob headed this way."

"They're all demon-controlled." Nichole turned Sugar around. "We need to go."

"Now wait just one minute—" Sheriff Wheeler reached for the bridle of the nearest horse, but the animal lifted its head.

Jason released the brake, shook the reins, and turned the wagon around on the tight street.

As they picked up speed, they passed the men in front of The Thirsty Mule.

Cecil Cobb's red face and double chin waggled as he shook his finger at Jason. "You'll not get away with this."

The big man beside Cobb stepped into the sunlight. A slithering shadow circled him. He didn't have the same worn-out look Hunter had when Nichole had first seen him. Morago inhabited this man, but something had changed.

"Go!" She urged Sugar forward.

As the wagon gathered speed, Amy and Alyse's bonnets blew back. Their coiffed buns shredded, and their hair streamed behind them in the wind.

Nichole and Merril followed Jason and the twins north along the road.

Nichole rode the long straight trail with her waist low over the saddle. Her head close to Sugar's neck, she kicked the horse's haunches. "Come on baby, go. Haw!" She glanced back through the dust, immediately sorry she had.

The gunmen had gained on the wagon. In the quick quarter-mile, they'd lost a lot of ground.

They ride like the wind, while we follow a wagon.

Beyond the thunder of their hoofbeats, the silence unnerved her. "Not shooting?" she called to Merril.

Why haven't they tried to kill us?

Merril nodded at the girls in the wagon as his horse pounded the ground next to Nichole.

Of course. They don't want to risk hitting Amy or Alyse.

The sharp crack of a pistol told a different story, and they both lowered their heads.

"Pull ahead," Merril yelled. "The turn."

Nichole nodded in understanding and glanced back at their pursuers. There were too many men. Their small band of fighters could never hold off this many.

Amy and Alyse crouched on the wagon's footboard and peered over the back of the seat, their long dark hair whipped around their faces.

Alyse's face was pale with anguish.

Amy's fierce with determination.

Merril flagged his arm and shouted, "The turnoff." Then Midnight shot past Jason to take the lead.

The wagon creaked and shook at breakneck speed.

Nichole's horse pounded across the dry dirt, yet she couldn't help but chance another look back.

The demon-possessed gunmen raced right at their heels.

Ahead, Midnight shot off the road to the west.

Jason pulled the reins to the side without slowing. The wagon bumped off the road and rose on two wheels. When it came back down, the back wheels threw dirt and fishtailed, but Jason shook the reins for more speed, and the wagon straightened.

Not sure of the distance to the washout, Nichole urged Sugar ahead. For less than a quarter-mile, Sugar raced alongside the wagon.

Amy faced forward now, braced between the box rod across the front of the wagon and the edge of the seat at her back. Her concentration focused on the road ahead. She never looked at Nichole.

Alyse glanced over at Nichole through her streaming hair. Fear pulled her features into a horrified grimace. Her eyes fixed on the riders close behind them.

The closest pursuer urged his horse beside the cart and jumped, landing on his side in the back of the rocking vehicle. As he rose to his knees, he drew his pistol from his belt.

Alyse wiggled her fingers, and a gust of wind lifted a blanket from the wagon bed and covered the man's head.

Before he could fight his way free, Alyse delivered a punch of air to his midsection. He tumbled from the back of the cart to his death under the hooves of his brethren.

Frightened, Nichole held tight to the reins and urged Sugar past the wagon, past the team of horses, and back on the trail behind Merril.

He'd lost his hat during the chase, and his hair tangled around his face when he looked back at her. Catching her glance, he signaled for her to catch up, then pointed.

The washout loomed fifty yards ahead.

Nichole knew what her role was—jump Sugar over the wash, and ride into the shelter of the bushes on the far side. Dismount. Find Hunter.

However, the wagon was moving too fast to stop, and Jason wasn't slowing down.

Midnight took the jump, and then Sugar. As they raced toward the brush along the creek on the other side of the clearing, Nichole turned in her saddle, desperate to see the wagon.

Alyse had her head down. She held the edge of the seat, her back to the road.

Jason and Amy shared a long look, then Jason threw the reins in the air.

What the fuck is he doing?

Nichole would have slowed, but Sugar had taken the bit and followed Midnight past the open ground in front of the cabin toward the dry creek and foliage ahead.

The two horses pulling the wagon jumped over the washout, bumped together, but kept their footing. The metal bolts that held the pole between the horses to the cart came undone, and the horses raced away to the west, dragging the bar and reins behind them.

The wagon's front wheels fell into the shallow ditch, halting its progress.

Alyse's scream echoed across the clearing.

Nichole caught a last glimpse of Amy, arms extended, jaw clenched with determination.

The back end of the wagon rose in the air, flipped over and landed on this side of the creek, upside down, in a whoosh of dust and dirt.

Chapter 30

Nichole Harris-Shilo

—

"No!" Nichole sawed on Sugar's reins, but she had passed the foliage. She couldn't see her friends through the thick cloud in the air around the wagon.

The overturned wagon stymied the gunmen. They circled their mounts in confusion.

Gunfire, from the nearby copse, added to their disarray.

Nichole pulled hard on the reins to turn back, but Merril, already dismounted, grabbed Sugar's lead. "No. Don't go out there. Let Amy and Alyse handle their part. Look."

Out of the dust cloud, Amy and Alyse struggled forward toward the small cabin. Dirt covered their hair and clothes.

Alyse attempted to keep up with her sister, but her limp slowed her down.

Amy put her arm around Alyse and together they disappeared into the cabin.

Merril pointed Nichole at Hunter. "Help him." He slid his rifle from the strap on Midnight's saddle and ran down the bush line to Jim and Waynoka.

Hunter lay on his stomach watching the cabin. He had cleared the area before him within arm's reach. In the dirt, he'd etched the creek behind the hunting lodge and created an effigy of the cabin out of bark strips and sticks. In front of his tiny replica, the open space ended with three small stones.

Nichole dropped to her tummy beside him. "I saw you put down stones like that the other day."

Hunter nodded, never taking his eyes from the clearing. "Come on, you bastard. Go after them." Beside his hand was Cookie's best glass mixing bowl.

Carrefour paced behind where Hunter lay in the tall grass.

The dust around the wagon dissipated as it rose to the east on the slight afternoon breeze. Jason lay near the broken cart, face turned away, still as death.

"Oh no," Nichole whispered.

"Easy," Hunter told her. "If he doesn't move, they'll ignore him."

"What if he's hurt?" A trickle of sweat ran down Nichole's neck and between her breasts.

Hunter didn't reply.

The big man Nichole had spotted on the boardwalk in town dismounted and stepped forward. The shadowed aspect of a coiling snake twisted around him. He strode into the clearing.

"Morago," Hunter murmured.

Morago paused in front of the hunting cabin. A look of satisfaction spread across his face. "You should come out and meet me, ladies," he called. "Let's put this Prophecy to rest, once and for all."

"A few more steps," Hunter murmured.

Carrefour crouched beside Hunter.

The gunmen who accompanied Morago did not advance. Several of them were down, their humpbacked demons clinging to them as the men clung to life. Those still in the saddle returned fire toward the nearby thicket.

Morago paced forward several steps. "Then I'll come in and drag you out." He took another step toward the cabin.

Hunter flipped the glass bowl over the cabin and pebbles before him. "We have him."

Carrefour stood upright. His anticipation showed in a smile so gleeful, it raised his cheeks and caused his shifting eyes to slant.

The effect of the barrier on Morago was immediate. He spun around and looked to his demon-gunmen. "What? No!" He tried to return to his men, but he rebounded when he encountered the invisible barrier.

His gunmen stopped returning fire at the trees as a dozen or more of their number toppled to the ground. Their demons sprang free attempting to reach their master.

In an instant, Carrefour was among them. He snatched the lesser demons from the air, balled them in his fist, and popped them into his mouth. He ignored the demons who remained with their human host.

"Why isn't he taking them all?"

Hunter understood her meaning. "I don't think he can. Their hosts shield them. Carrefour can't touch them."

Morago spun around. His glare focused on the cabin. He stalked forward, raised his arm, and a ball of flame arched from behind the copse of trees, and across the clearing into his hand. The big man twisted the tiny spark into an inferno of rage and hate. With a guttural cry, he launched the massive storm of flames at the shack.

Wood and stone exploded with the force of the fireball. Parts of the structure flew upward slamming into the boundary, only to rain down, scorched and burning, to the ground.

Inside the bowl, under Hunter's hand, the tiny cabin exploded as well, revealing a small glass covering White Eagle's doll.

Amidst the broken and smoldering rubble, White Eagle stood, majestic in his white burial robes and feathered hair ornaments.

Dessa crossed the devastation to stand beside him.

Missing from the destruction were Amy and Alyse.

"I don't understand—" Nichole began.

Morago stalked toward the dignified Indian shaman. "What is this?" he snarled. In full possession of Buck, Morago kicked a cot. He turned over the second one. "Where are they?" he yelled and twisted around, seething with rage.

On the other side of the clearing, Carrefour continued to collect demon-spawn, either as the host died or when the demon abandoned it.

At least ten men lay retching on the ground with the aftereffects of possession.

The gunfire from the thicket had ceased.

"Now." Hunter urged White Eagle, though the old man couldn't hear him. "Do it now."

Morago whirled. He searched the area with his scathing gaze until his chin lifted. "I recognize your scent, human." He stalked directly toward the tall grass where Hunter and Nichole lay hidden. Held by the containment, his lip rose as he snarled in contempt, "I know it well."

The shadowy snake writhing around the host expanded in size as the demon grew in anger. "Is this some miserable trick of yours?" He threw out his hands and blasted the interior of the glass barrier with pure elemental magic. "You will know my rage."

The bowl beneath Hunter's hand shattered.

"Oh, shit." Nichole scrambled to her feet and stumbled back from the approaching monster.

Between Morago's hands grew a ball of fire, fed from the flames of destruction behind him. With a shriek, he launched the orb of blazing hatred at Hunter and Nichole.

Halfway to Nichole, the burning missile changed direction and streaked toward the wagon.

Alyse, her black gown covered in dust, caught the flame with one hand. The fire doused as she fell against the wagon.

Visible now, Amy huddled protectively over Jason.

From the debris behind White Eagle, two sparks of light lifted from the rubble. Alyse's familiars, in their faerie form, streaked across the distance and fell like stars on either side of Alyse.

Identical black wolves, larger than Nichole remembered, sprang from the sparks of light and landed in a crouch, their hackles raised.

"Now I have you," Morago whispered as the snake uncoiled, prepared to jump to Alyse.

Hunter rose to his knees, lifted his arms as his spirit shed the confines of his human frame. His specter ignored the demon's human host and intercepted the serpent Morago as it launched itself toward Alyse.

The spirits tore at each other, shredding the ether substance of the other. Neither willing to give quarter.

The shot glass over White Eagle's doll splintered as the shaman crossed the protective barrier Hunter had placed around him.

Beside White Eagle, Dessa screamed, "Carrefour—our bargain!"

Movement to her left caught Nichole's eye.

Merril raced towards her, gun in hand, while along the creek bed, Jim raised his rifle.

"Wait." Waynoka placed her hand on Jim's forearm. "Hunter has engaged the demon in the spirit world. The monster could pull Hunter's spirit with him when he flees to my grandfather."

"What?" Jim looked from Waynoka to Nichole and Hunter. "He's right there."

Nichole pointed to the clearing. "He's not. His spirit is out there."

Carrefour stepped from a sudden swirl of shadows beside the snake. He grabbed the serpent by the throat and pushed him back into his host. *You are mine, demon.*

Hunter continued to grapple with the snake.

Get back, you fool, Carrefour yelled at Hunter and shoved him aside.

"Can you reach him?" Waynoka lifted her voice to Nichole.

Nichole dropped to her knees beside Hunter and wrapped her arms around his chest. His body was stiff and hard. She laid her cheek against his shoulder blades.

Hunter? Alexander? Step away. Let Carrefour have Morago.

In the clearing, Hunter's spirit bellowed his rage and dove at Carrefour and Morago, knocking them away from Alyse, and closer to the remains of the hunting shack.

Cat needs you. I need you. Come back.

Hunter's spirit staggered as Carrefour forced him back a second time.

Go, chwal. I release you. Our bargain is done.

Carrefour wrapped his arms around both the demon-snake and the host.

Leave the demon to me.

Hunter's body sagged in Nichole's arms as his spirit returned. He inhaled shuddering breaths and stared vacant-eyed at the sky, dazed and blinking. Then he coughed and struggled upright. His attention focused on the clearing.

White Eagle had crept forward while the demon engaged Hunter and Carrefour. He placed his right hand on the shoulder of Morago's host, his voice lifted in his death chant.

"Now, Jim," Nichole called.

Jimmy Leigh looked down his gun-sight and squeezed the trigger.

The bullet found its mark in the big man's temple. The side of his head sprayed outward as the body crumpled to its knees.

White Eagle's eyes stretched wide and his back arched, as both Dessa and Carrefour dove into the shaman behind Morago.

"White Eagle has the demon," Nichole tore her eyes from the old Indian and looked to Alyse and Amy. "You can end this now!" she yelled.

Beyond the wagon, Bayard and Bernard watched from the edge of the thicket with Bill and Kelly. A minuscule trail of smoke behind them spoke of the small campfire they tended. In unison, the brothers raised their arms and fire flew from their hands to Alyse.

She gathered the flames, wrapping them in her arms until she pushed a fiery orb out with her hands. Tears streamed from her face as she screamed, "I'm sorry, White Eagle. Forgive me."

The blaze engulfed White Eagle.

Amy flattened her hands, palms to the ground, and closed her eyes.

The soil under White Eagle's struggling figure rippled, becoming liquid. The shaman gained control of the demon at the last moment and crossed his arms and raised his chin just as his head sank beneath the ground.

Amy and Alyse continued their magic, forcing air and fire into the conflagration below the soil, pushing the demon deep into the earth.

Nichole ran across the clearing to Jason.

He sat beside Amy holding his head with his hand.

Blood trickled from Amy's brow, and Alyse's gown hung torn at the waist. They continued to press the demon into the soil, burning away any form of life that could be buried in the ground.

As Nichole reached the wagon, movement in the distance caught her eye.

A lone rider raced away across the prairie. A demon-hump firmly attached to his back.

It doesn't matter.

Nichole touched Jason's head. "Are you okay?"

He nodded. "Amy's protection spell could use a little work."

Merril, Hunter, Jim, and Waynoka followed Nichole.

Bernard and Bayard led the way as the four men in the copse jogged to join the others at the overturned cart.

Waynoka's lips trembled, and tears at the loss and bravery of her grandfather streaked her face.

Bernard surprised everyone when he wrapped the Indian woman in his arms.

Hunter took a step toward the empty rubble and held up his hand. "It's done. The demon is defeated."

"How do you know?" Alyse cried, maintaining the flame.

Nichole reached over and touched both Amy and Alyse. "Because the spirits have come to say goodbye."

Hunter placed his hand on both Jim and Merril's back.

Waynoka released Bernard but remained close enough to touch. Then she held out her hand to Bayard. "Your mother wishes to make her farewell."

In the clearing, two spirits walked down a long passage.

Alyse ceased to press her fire magic and dropped to her knees beside Amy. "*Mémé,*" she whispered.

The elegant white-haired woman stopped first at her sons. "Thank you, my beloved sons. So strong and skilled, grown to be honest, loving men. My heart swells with pride. You've given your lives in the service of your nieces." She paused, and tears glittered in her eyes. "Now, you should find a life of your own. A life to cherish. Go with my love and my blessing."

Bayard released Waynoka's hand and fell to his knees, sobbing.

Kelly placed a comforting hand on his shoulder.

The statuesque shade approached Amy and Alyse.

The twin women knelt on the ground as Nichole touched their shoulders.

"I love you, my darlings." She looked from Alyse to Amy. "I love you, both. Such strength and resolve will inspire your children in tales for years to come." She acknowledged each person with her gaze and bowed her head. "I thank you all." She turned and looked fondly at a glowing corridor behind her. "Now I shall see my Sully again. It has been far too long."

Jim tipped his head, at a loss for words. "Ma'am."

White Eagle bowed to Waynoka and spoke.

"He greets his beloved granddaughter and asks her not to grieve." Merril translated softly. "He now goes to meet his wife in the green fields, a gift of the Great Spirit, which he has been looking forward to for many years now."

Together, the spirits returned to The Passage. They vanished just as the last rays of sun disappeared from the tops of the brush.

Bernard looked over the head of the grieving woman in his arms, to his nieces and his brother. "I doubt they would want us to grieve too hard or too long."

Waynoka lifted her face to Bernard and she brushed tears from her face.

"After all, *mère* is free from the demon's grasp, and her granddaughters have fulfilled The Prophecy of the Twins by vanquishing the demon in fire and earth." He pushed a stray strand of silver hair from Waynoka's face. "And your grandfather walks again with his beloved wife."

Nichole hugged Merril and watched the James family come to terms with their loss and their victory.

"It's time to go," Jason told the group after the tears were dried "We won't make it home before full dark."

"We can't leave yet," Amy replied as she touched the blood on Jason's brow. "There are injured people."

A number of the gunmen had revived enough from the possession to capture horses and ride away. But there remained a half-dozen men with bullet wounds too hurt to ride. Two of the hired gunmen were dead.

Amy and Alyse treated the injured men, who in turn fled as fast as possible from the horror they had witnessed.

"What do you want to do with the corpses?" Jim asked Merril.

"Let's move them under the wagon to keep the animals away. I'll let Sheriff Wheeler know where they are."

Chapter 31

Nichole Harris-Shilo

—

A constellation of stars painted portraits in the sky as they rode up the incline to The Highlands, but the lanterns illuminating the veranda and side yard displayed the best picture of all.

Home.

Lloyd waited beside the corral. "Turn your horses into the pen." He opened the gate and waved the riders inside. "Tom and I will see to them. Y'all look tuckered out."

As they walked back to the house, Nichole took comfort in Merril's arm around her. Fear and torment no longer ruled their lives. The Prophecy of the Twins had ended. The demon returned to whatever hell he called home.

Inside, Cookie shooed the men back out to the well pump to wash while the three women climbed the stairs to freshen up in their rooms.

Alyse followed Amy and Nichole up the stairs, leaning heavily on her cane. "Did you injure your leg?" Amy asked.

"I don't think so." Alyse rubbed her hand from her knee to her ankle. "My leg troubles me more when I'm tired."

"We should have asked Waynoka to come in with us," Nichole worried.

"I saw her talking with Bernard." Amy shrugged one shoulder. "She's devastated at the loss of her grandfather. Although she knew what we planned, talking with his shade broke her heart."

"She'll be lonely tonight in her shelter," Alyse predicted.

"No, she won't." Nichole shared a smile with Amy. "I doubt she'll be alone at all."

Alyse's eyes widened. "Waynoka and Bernard?"

"Don't tell me you didn't notice?" Amy pressed a damp cloth to her face. "They've been inseparable since she arrived."

"I've been distracted." Alyse plucked at her torn dress. "I'm going to change." She limped out the door and down the hallway to her room.

"I should too." Amy decided.

Once the women had changed, they came downstairs to find the table set for ten.

Alyse raised a brow at the table settings. "Not outside?"

"No," Jason looked up from pouring the wine. "Waynoka assured us she would like to have dinner inside." He picked up the next glass and tipped the bottle. "She went to change."

Jim held out his hand to Alyse, then tucked her fingers around his arm. "Lean on me."

"Always." Her lips curved, and her face broke into a brilliant smile. "I can't believe it's over."

After everyone had taken their seat, Bernard rose from his chair at the foot of the table. "Before we eat, I'd like to propose a toast." He raised his glass. "To exceptional friends." He looked at each person seated at the table. "Thank you for your help today.

"To those who are no longer with us. The spirits. From the one who foretold The Prophecy to my mother, as well as those who paid the ultimate price vanquishing the demon. May you rest forever in the Goddess' light." He raised his eyes to the ceiling and nodded.

"We've dreaded this day for what seems like forever. Without all of you, we would not be where we are tonight." He lifted his glass. "To friends."

"To friends." Glasses clinked around the table as Bernard resumed his seat.

Cookie brought in a large platter of fried chicken, followed by Jeanne with a bowl of greens, and Lawna with a tray of thick sliced cornbread.

When dinner was finished, Merril asked Bernard, "The spirit who spoke to you today, was that your mother?"

Bernard took a sip of wine and swallowed. "Yes. Chantal James."

"She must have been a remarkable woman," Jim observed. "To have raised men such as yourself and a granddaughter, knowing one day you would face such a horrendous trial."

"She urged you to find a life of your own." Nichole tasted her wine as she studied the James brothers. "Any idea what you want to do?"

"Actually, yes." Bayard folded his napkin and placed it on the table. "Bern and I have decided to return to making furniture."

"You're going home?" Alyse set her glass on the table, her brows raised.

"No, and yes." Bayard teased. "We shall begin our new business here. Most likely near Denver. With the growth we observed the day we arrived, there should be plenty of customers who need to furnish their new homes." He lowered his voice, and the happy grin fled from his face. "But I do intend to return to the farm. I need to take stock of what remains, perhaps bring some items back with me. We left in such a rush..."

"While Bay travels to the farm, I shall find a suitable building in town." Bernard addressed Nichole, "Would it be possible for me stay at your house in Denver while I search for a place of our own?"

"Of course," Nichole agreed. "Whatever you need."

Waynoka straightened in her chair; her hand rested in Bernard's on the tabletop. "I too shall remain in Colorado, for now. I have no family waiting for me on the reservation." Her shy eyes lifted to Bernard.

"You will always have a home with us," Bernard assured her.

"Congratulations." Merril squeezed Nichole's hand. "We couldn't be happier for you."

After the well-wishes for Bernard and Waynoka were done, Nichole turned to Hunter. "And what are your plans?"

Hunter swirled the last of his wine in the glass, then gazed at Nichole. "I'll ride to Kiowa Crossing in the morning and telegraph Judge Anders. I need to let him know I intend to accept the position of federal marshal. I hope to partner with Sam."

"And what about Cat?" Nichole urged.

"As for Miss Catherine Kline, we shall see." He emptied his glass and winked at Nichole.

"Uh-huh." Nichole grinned at Hunter. "So, you'll return to New Orleans right away?"

"Yes. Although I know Sam will take care of my sweet Roulette." Hunter chuckled, grinning as he explained, "I have a horse which is very dear to me. I miss *ma belle fille, la Roulette.*" His face turned somber. "However, I must first return to Denver and compensate the stable for the lost horse. After that, I shall catch a train for home."

"I will miss you." Nichole blinked at the burning in her eyes. "I already miss Cat. Please say you'll come visit us."

"Of course we shall. And you must visit N'Orleans. She's a beautiful city."

Merrill nodded. "I'll ride with you to Kiowa Crossing. Jason and I still need to speak with Sheriff Wheeler."

"I wonder if Otis Pierce remains in town, or if he fled after you killed the demon." Jason pushed back from the table.

"The man you spoke with on the street?" Nichole asked.

Jason heaved a sigh. "Yes. An old friend from Boston."

Jason and Amy shared a long look, then Jason smiled at Nichole. "Otis is a fool and a manipulator, but underneath, he's not a bad man." Jason raised one brow. "If he stays away from his father and gets a second chance to be his own man, he could make something of himself."

"I never trusted Otis," Amy stated. "All he wants is money."

"I know." Jason smiled and took her hand.

Alyse sat forward. "I guess that just leaves me." Her gaze strayed around the table and stopped on Jim. Her smile widened. "I'd like to stay with my sister if that's acceptable with Merril and Nichole. I find I quite like having one." She grinned at Amy.

"You're welcome to stay as long as you like." Nichole shared the jubilant smile between Alyse and Jim.

Jim raised his glass to Alyse. "To magic and beautiful women."

Chapter 32

Nichole Harris-Shilo

—

After dinner, Bernard, Waynoka, and Bayard excused themselves. Dropping eyelids and measured movements seemed the theme for the night. Amy and Alyse walked arm in arm up the staircase, with Jason trailing behind his wife and her sister.

Nichole drank the last of her wine and pushed the glass toward the bottle near Merril's elbow. "Pour me another glass, would you love?" As tired as she felt, she couldn't go upstairs and miss spending one last evening with Hunter.

"I should head off to bed myself," Jim said.

As he came to his feet, Dessa stepped from shadows into the room and stood at the end of the table.

Jim halted halfway up, his eyes wide. "Um."

Merril fumbled with Nichole's wine glass.

"It's all right." Nichole steadied the glass. "This is Dessa. She's—family."

"My *arrière-grand-mère*," Hunter clarified as he came to his feet and greeted the spirit with a bow. "Thank you for your help today."

Jim lowered himself back to his seat. "Miss Dessa." He acknowledged the spirit.

Dessa bowed her head to Jim. "The honor is mine, Ancient One." When her head rose, her eyes sought Hunter. "Carrefour has returned to his home." She smiled at both Hunter and Nichole. "He informed me I have an unusual and interesting family."

"Now that it's over, what bargain did you make with him?" Hunter asked.

"To keep your life and soul safe in exchange for all the demons he could capture."

"Did he get Morago?" Nichole asked.

"No." Dessa shook her head. "Morago's destiny was determined by The Prophecy. Even *Maître* Carrefour could not alter that." She strolled beside the table and stopped at Nichole's chair. "I've given much thought to our conversation—about how I helped and perhaps even encourage you—to spirit-walk back to your previous life."

"To reunite with my soul mate." Nichole reached for Merril's hand.

Dessa chuckled. "I doubt my motives were—altruistic. I was never much of a romantic." She tapped her fingernail on the table. "But I must have had a reason. One my future-self trusted I would come to understand and act upon, at this time." She grinned at Nichole. "I now believe I know why I led you to discover your strength and desire to return to this time."

Nichole gripped the arms of the chair as Dessa leaned toward her.

Dark eyes captured and held Nichole's in their magnetic gaze. "You had no training in our skills because your family died when you were a young child."

Nichole nodded. "That's true."

"Therefore, when you passed from your future time, Hunter's line ended."

Nichole glanced at Hunter, then back to Dessa. "Yeah. I guess so."

"I believe that is the reason I assisted in your reunion with Mr. Shilo. Tell me, child, how did your father perish?"

Nichole took a sip of water. "Courtney's parents died in a—traveling accident. They boarded an airplane in New York to attend my father's conference in Scandinavia. Something happened over the Atlantic Ocean, and everyone on board was lost."

"I believe we can stop that tragedy from happening."

"Stop the plane from crashing?"

"Nothing so grand. But we can change your parents' course."

Nichole's stomach tightened into her throat. "What...." She swallowed. "How?"

"Write a letter to your father. One he would know was from you and would consider seriously. Urge him not to... not to..." Dessa fanned her hand toward Nichole.

"Urge him not to board the plane?" Nichole supplied.

"Exactly." Dessa nodded. "A new path and a chance I would like you to take."

"How will we know if your plan is successful?" Merril asked.

"Nothing will change for us, of course. This event has yet to happen, but for Courtney, the difference should be profound." She gripped Nichole's hand. "Think of it—a life lived with a mother and father, perhaps siblings. Courtney's young life would be much, much different than the one you remember."

Hunter reached across the table to Nichole. "Her plans are never without consequence. Be assured—you will be the one who pays the price."

"I understand." Nichole nodded to Hunter, then looked back at Dessa "And yes, I want to try."

"You must remember, this will only work if your love for Merril is strong enough to choose him over the family you must leave behind. Regardless of whether or not your parents live or die in the..."

"Plane crash."

"You will still have to return to this life to write the letter."

Nichole looked at Merril. "I would always choose you. Always."

Merril went into the office and brought back a sheet of paper, an envelope, dip pen, and ink.

Nichole dipped the pen and thought for a moment, then scratched ink onto parchment for several seconds.

Dear Daddy,

This is not a hoax or a lie. It's me—Courtney—writing to you from the future, and from the past.

You once told me the ghost in my room wouldn't hurt me, and if she scared me, I could tell her to leave, and she would. Do you remember? You might have spoken those words to your little girl last week, but for me, it's been more than fifteen long lonely years.

Please believe what I tell you now...

When she finished, she held one corner and waved the paper in the air to dry the ink. "I think this will do it."

She folded the missive and slipped it into the envelope and addressed the front with her father's name—Russell Veau. She held up the envelope. "Now what?"

"We must make sure he receives your note before his death. When did he die?"

"September 2, 1998." A date Courtney saw written on every inheritance document and certificates her entire life. The day her life changed.

"Then it must be delivered in August," Dessa said.

"The Western Union Company will hold mail to deliver on a future date," Hunter said.

"We can do better than that." Jim held out his hand from across the table. "I'll deliver it myself."

Nichole lifted the envelope to Jim.

Merril reached out and pushed her hand down. "What happens if she decides to stay with her family instead of coming back—to me?"

"If she doesn't return to write this letter, her parents will die just as she has foretold." Dessa tilted her head and studied Merril and Nichole.

"But if this works, they would be alive. I wouldn't have to write this letter," Nichole argued.

"No, child. They will be alive because you were here to write the letter. By taking this action, you will create a paradox. The warning must always be given, in order for your family to survive." Dessa hesitated with a glance toward Hunter and then spoke, "I must caution you, if this works you will both gain and lose a great deal in a single instance. It will be—unsettling."

"More than unsettling, *fillette*," Hunter whispered. "But the price may be one you would be willing to pay to protect the lives of those you love."

Nichole looked at Jim.

His hand remained open and extended across the table. "I'll convince your father to heed your warning. I'll make sure he understands the consequences."

Nichole nodded and placed the letter in Jim's hands. For a split second, nothing happened. She turned questioning eyes to Dessa as a new set of memories flooded her mind.

Courtney played on a swing set. Her father pushed the seat from behind. "Higher daddy, higher!"

A younger brother lay swaddled in her mother's arms. "We named him Connor. Do you like that, sweetheart?"

A bearded man set a present on the floor. When they tore the colorful paper away, and the lid opened, she heard the boy beside her shriek with delight.

"It's a puppy, Courty! A puppy! Oh, wow, look Courty, for us!"

"I know this memory." She blinked and realized tears rolled down her face. "The first to return after the carriage accident—of receiving a puppy. I thought the little boy was Jason, but it couldn't be. It was—oh God, my sweet little brother, Connor."

As new images continued to pour in, they etched a new map of Courtney's life in Nichole's memory. From the surface of her mind to deep within her soul, a love of family she had never known blossomed.

A little brother Courtney had kissed goodnight and taught to read. She had comforted him when kids at school said cruel things about their father's TV show.

Never again would she and Connor throw a ball across the yard, play board games late at night, or scare each other while they watched old horror movies.

Nichole sucked in a long breath of air. The little boy had needed her, and she'd been there for him. But no more. The young man she remembered would need to find his way without his big sister.

She reached a trembling hand toward Merril.

To hurt the man she loved by telling him about the sudden ache in her heart would do neither her nor Merril any good. He would never know how precious her family had been to Courtney, or how deep the pain of their loss cut into her heart.

Tears ran freely down her cheeks as thoughts of her mother returned. Mom had helped her pick the perfect prom dress and guided her in choices of the heart. Scolded her for coming in late and taught her to bake a cake.

If her sweet mama could have met Merril—even just once—but she never would.

Her body began to shake, and Merril pulled her onto his lap.

Courtney had given up a father who taught her the ways of spirit magic, encouraged her to help others, to value herself, and to follow her inner voice.

He would never dance at her wedding, never shake Merril's hand, and she would never get to wrap her arms around his neck and kiss him goodbye.

The thought of how her death would affect them crushed her with their grief.

At least they live. Losing me is part of the price we had to pay.

"Daddy," she whispered between quivering lips. "I'll miss you."

Her price—a lost and broken heart—would take time and Merril's love to mend.

Dessa sank to her knees before Nichole and took her hands. "This is what I hoped you'd do. Change the fate of the Veau line, but the cost to you is immeasurable. I'm sorry, child." Dessa placed Nichole's hand in Merril's. "There is comfort for you here, and memories you can always cherish, knowing you are the reason they will live."

Nichole rested her forehead on Merril's shoulder and cried for all she had lost and all she had gained. In the end, she knew she would make the same decision again and again.

"I love you, Nicki," Merril whispered.

His declaration brought another storm of tears. Grateful tears. Joyous tears. When the storm passed, and Nichole lifted her head, they were the only ones in the dining room.

"Tell me," Merril whispered. He kissed the side of her face. "Was it a good life?"

"Oh Merril, Courtney's life was precious and full. So fresh in my mind right now—it hurts. I'll miss my family—her family—for the rest of my life, but I could never make a different choice when it comes to you. You're the reason the sun rises, and the world turns.

"You." She pressed her finger to the skin above his heart. "Your heartbeat beckons through The Passage to my soul, and it will always lead me right back here, to you."

Chapter 33

Jimmy Leigh

—

Present day – Fort Worth, Texas

Jimmy Leigh rested against the leather headrest as the limousine driver wove his way through Dallas traffic. Jim touched a button near his hand, and the opaque divider slid shut with a swish. He pressed the second button, and a ring tone chimed from the surround-sound speakers.

"James and James, attorneys at law," a pleasant voice informed him.

"Greta James, please."

"May I tell her who's calling?"

"John Larson. She's expecting my call."

"Certainly, sir. Please hold."

The relaxing rhythms of smooth jazz filled the back of the limo.

Jim placed his hand on the box beside him. A gift between siblings, one only he could deliver.

The music paused, and a woman's sensuous voice addressed him, "Good morning, John."

"Hello, Greta." He glanced out at Reunion Tower. "I hope you're ready. We're almost there."

"I'm on my way down."

The line disconnected as the limo pulled to the curb. Moments later, the door opened.

"Thank you, Sal." Greta folded her long legs into the seat across from Jim, and the car door closed. "You look handsome."

"Black continues to be my go-to color."

"John, John, John." Greta shook her head and grinned. "Here are the documents you asked for. You're sure about this?"

Jim opened the large brown envelope and slid a driver's license, a passport, and several credit cards in the name of Jacob London into his large palm.

"Is the name all right?"

"Huh? Sure. The initials are what's important."

"So now you simply become Jacob and stop being John?"

"That's how it works." He stared out at the traffic and lowered his voice. "How it's always worked." He returned the documents to the envelope and shoved them into the side pocket of a leather briefcase beside his leg. "I stopped being Jimmy Leigh the day Alyse died. I intend to bury John Larson beside Aubrielle."

"And you become Jacob London?"

"That's right. As a bonus, I get to keep the monogrammed towels and luggage. And I can stop graying my hair."

"You put gray in your hair?" Greta raised one delicately contoured eyebrow. "I have to say—a touch of silver adds to your already abundant charm."

Jim chuckled.

Greta's phone pinged, and she pulled the device from her bag. "It's Grace."

"Tell her I said hello."

Greta nodded. The ride continued in a companionable silence while she texted with her twin.

At the gate to the cemetery, the limousine stopped, and Sal spoke to one of the security guards Russell Veau had hired to keep reporters from disturbing his daughter's funeral.

The window beside Greta lowered, and she handed the guard her identification. "Greta James and guest," she said. "He's not with the press."

"ID please," the guard said to Jim.

Jim handed the guard his John Larson driver's license.

The man studied the photo then handed it back to Jim. "All right."

Outside the window, several news vans and reporters were broadcasting from the funeral of a minor celebrity's daughter.

The uniformed man stepped back, and they entered the cemetery grounds.

"Will Russell remember you?" Greta asked.

"I don't know," Jim replied with a thoughtful frown. "I only spoke with Russell Veau once, when I delivered his daughter's letter, seventeen years ago." As the vehicle stopped, Jim straightened his tie. "It would be easier if he did."

Sal opened the door and helped Greta out.

Jim climbed from the opposite door then picked up the box.

The few mourners allowed to attend were preparing to depart. Two young women hugged an older woman and a young man before they hurried across the grass to their car. Only the immediate family remained. The father, mother, and son watched as Greta and Jim crossed the narrow, paved access drive and approached the family.

Courtney's remains had been cremated. There was no casket or open plot beneath the temporary canopy. Instead, a small garden bloomed with life in the corner of the Veau family area. Courtney's marker and sealed urn sat amongst Texas wildflowers and natural stones. A concrete bench completed the garden. A peaceful place for remembrance and reflection.

Set on a cloth-draped table inside the small shelter, was a photograph of the beautiful, dark-haired young woman, surrounded by cut flowers and plants.

The last to leave, the minister shook Russell Veau's hand and departed.

Courtney's mother stood protectively beside a tall dark-haired teenager, Courtney's sixteen-year-old brother, Connor.

Russell had gained a little weight, and his hair had thinned and turned silver. The loss of his daughter, and the foreknowledge her death would occur, had taken its toll on the spiritualist.

Courtney's father held out his hand to Greta as she and Jim arrived at the service site. "Greta James. Thank you for coming. I am surprised, though. I hadn't expected to see you today."

"I'm so sorry for your loss, Russell." Greta kissed the air beside Russel's face and stepped to his wife. "Susan, and Connor, is it? You have my deepest condolences."

Jim held out his hand to Russell Veau. "John Larson."

Russell took Jim's hand, and his eyes narrowed. "I believe we've met."

"Yes. A few years ago."

"Courtney was young—just turned four—but I remember you well." Russel tilted his head as he studied Jim. "My God, you haven't changed."

"A bit grayer, I think." Jim released Russel's hand and stepped back. "It's good to see you again, sir. I'm sorry for your loss."

Russel ran a hand over his tired face and glanced at the photograph of Courtney. "Her letter warned us this would happen and that this would be her choice. Still, I wish I had one more day with my little girl."

Jim studied the photo. Courtney had looked remarkably similar to how he remembered Catherine Kline.

"She missed you as well but leaving was a sacrifice she had to make." Jim looked at Connor. "Especially for her brother."

"They were close," Russel watched his wife and son as they spoke with Greta. "Inseparable, in fact. He's taken her death quite hard."

"I have something for him, from his sister, if you'd allow it." Jim lifted the box. "She kept a diary of her life as Nichole Harris. Before Nichole passed, she asked me to make sure her brother received the journal and a photograph."

"She asked you to deliver it?" Russell's eyes widened.

"Initially, she only asked me to deliver the letter," Jim explained. "Many years later, she gave me the journal and the photo for Connor. She wanted me to make sure he received both after her death."

"I hope this isn't more bad news, Mr. Larson." Russell thinned his lips and backed away from Jim, anger apparent in his bearing. "Do you know what it's like to live each day knowing a person you love dearly will die before you?"

"In truth, sir," Jim murmured, "I do."

"Courtney failed to include the details or date of her death, only asking that I withhold her letter and my foreknowledge of her death from her."

"Mr. Veau," Jim pleaded, "you're not the only one with a history or magic in their lives. Your daughter trusted me with the most important thing she ever had. A thing she'd been willing to die to protect." Jim sighed and blinked tears from his eyes. "Please give me your forbearance for a few moments. I'll gladly share my story with you, but today is about Courtney." Jim lifted the box. "And her younger brother. She hoped to lessen Connor's grief with a gift."

Russell Veau nodded and stepped aside.

Both Susan and Connor studied Jim as he approached.

"Mrs. Veau, my name is John Larson. Your daughter made arrangements for a gift to be delivered to her brother, Connor, today."

Susan cast a swift glance at her husband, who nodded, then she stepped back.

Jim looked down into the dark blue eyes of Courtney's brother. "Perhaps we could sit and talk for a moment?" He moved to the concrete bench and sat down.

Connor followed but remained standing. "You have something from Courtney?"

"I do." Jim contemplated Russell Veau who spoke with his wife and Greta, then smiled at Connor. "How much has your dad told you, or taught you, about his gift."

"The spirit thing?"

"Yes."

The young man shrugged. "I've seen spirits too. He's not the only one with skills."

"Your sister had those abilities as well. In fact, Courtney spirit-walked into her previous life."

"Yeah, Dad showed me her letter yesterday morning. He said she sacrificed herself to warn him and save us."

"That's true, but she didn't just die, Connor. She lived a long and happy life as Nichole Harris. She and her husband had many exciting adventures. They even knew an ancestor of yours, Alexander Veau. But despite her full life, she thought about you and missed you very much."

Connor sank to the bench beside Jim. "She did?"

Jim nodded. "She wrote to you, in her journal, throughout her life. And when she was very old, she made arrangements for the journal and a photograph of Nichole Harris to be delivered to you."

Connor glanced over at his parents and lowered his voice. "The journal and the photograph are for me?"

"Yes," Jim assured the young man. "To share or not. The choice is yours."

Connor took the box from Jim. "Thank you." He opened the lid and lifted the sepia-toned photograph in an oval metal frame. A beautiful blonde-haired woman sat between two men. "Is this her?"

"Yes." Jim nodded and cleared his throat. "She talked about you a lot, and I could tell the two of you had been close. Connor, leaving you was the hardest thing she'd ever done, but she never regretted her decision. She doesn't want you to regret it either."

Connor put the photo back on the journal and ran his fingertips along the leather binder for a moment. Then he closed the lid and gave Jim a tearful smile. "I won't. But I'll still miss her."

"I know you will," Jim whispered.

Russell, Susan, and Greta left the pavilion and walked slowly toward the cars along the access road.

Susan carried the photo of her daughter from the shelter table. She looked back and called, "We'll be at the car, Connor."

"Okay, mom." Connor stood and held out his hand to Jim. "Thank you."

Jim took the young man's hand as he rose to his feet. "You're welcome. And if you ever want to talk, or have any questions about your sister, your dad's attorney, Greta James can get in touch with me."

As they followed Connor's parents and Greta to the cars, Jim shaded his eyes from the sun and glanced back at Courtney's peaceful garden.

Beside the large funeral wreath stood Dessa. Dressed in mourning black with a lavender orchid adorning her jacket, she carried a bright bouquet of white daisies and yellow roses threaded with yellow ribbons. With slow deliberation, she placed the flowers in the deep concrete cup beside the ornamental urn.

She raised her gaze to Jim and tipped her head, then slowly walked away from the canopy and garden, vanishing among the tall gravestones.

A wide satin ribbon woven through Dessa's bouquet quivered in the breeze and then unfurled to display the old spirit's last message across the summer garden.

Jim ran a hand through his hair and stilled the tremor on his lips as he read the words printed in blue on the bright yellow ribbon.

Beloved child—Thank you.

Sneak Peek at Patriarch

The Soul of the Witch Saga continues in Book 6:
Patriarch

Chapter 1

Harbor Delight

Ayden MacKenna

Boston, September 1874

Ayden stepped from Revere's Tavern and paused on the narrow walkway. Although the day had been seasonably pleasant, the sun's recent departure took with it the day's warmth. East, across the harbor, darkness obscured the horizon while high clouds changed from pink to orange to purple overhead.

He gave a nod to the ever-present coven companions who still shadowed his every move.

Let's give them something new.

Instead of heading uphill into the city or south along the harbor, he turned and strolled north, adjacent to the pier.

Ayden didn't recognize the men who followed him tonight. They weren't the ones who had jumped him the night of the Boston fire with their friend

Gordy, nor had he seen these individuals come into the tavern these last few weeks.

Perhaps they wore a glamour like Jason's friend, Lisbeth.

The skill required to create glamours had to be as complex as the skills needed to perform in-depth healing. Anyone could throw a fireball, even those not particularly skilled with *Fire*, but healing took both *Fire* and *Earth* and more than a scant knowledge of the human body. Ayden's mother spent years as a healer—a midwife—but only strong enough to ease pain and slow blood loss during birth.

A glamour would take a great deal of *earth-skill*, Ayden imagined. Then again, he honestly had no idea how Lisbeth changed her form so convincingly.

When Jason had recognized Lisbeth in Revere's the night of the fire, she appeared to Ayden as a large, broad-shouldered man. Remembering that encounter, he realized he could not describe the face she wore. She had worn a hat; that much was certain. She'd pulled it low on her forehead and fled after Jason called her name. But did the face have a beard? What had been the hair color? There was more to creating a glamour than simply changing what other people saw—it also appeared to muddle what they remembered.

A convenient skill. I'd like to speak with this Lisbeth about it.

He glanced back at his unwanted companions, noting their features, then looked forward, setting their faces to memory.

If I can remember their face, I'll assume it is indeed theirs and not a skill-crafted visage.

At the curve in the harbor road, several dozen angry men had gathered in the street. Shaking their fists, they yelled obscenities and threats toward a three-story building across from the pier.

Although Ayden rarely walked this direction, he knew of this place—a brothel that catered to diverse sexual tastes and the occasional outlandish perversion. Men would sometimes come into Revere's to eat and sometimes gamble but, at the end of the evening, they'd often take their winnings up the street to Harbor's Delight—or Har-De's—as a few locals dubbed it.

Ayden slowed.

Mob mentality chilled him. He'd seen a man torn apart by an angry crowd in India for stealing a loaf of day-old bread for his family.

He knew of no *mind-magic* that would calm an angry throng, then or now.

One of the outraged men approached the closed entrance. "Come out and face a real man," he yelled, then nodded back at his friends, who shouted and urged him on. He downed a gulp from the half-pint whiskey bottle in his hand then threw it at the door. Glass shattered, and the spectators roared their approval. "Ya filthy sodomites—come out, or we'll burn you out!" He kicked the entry until the wood splintered, and the door flew open. Instead of rushing inside, the man retreated to the safety of the angry crowd.

The coven members who followed Ayden moved forward, their interest piqued by the powder keg of violence before them. They stood, captivated, two feet behind Ayden.

"This is turning uglier by the minute," Ayden said over his shoulder to his watchers.

"Don't talk to us," one of them murmured, his attention on the scene unfolding before them.

A match flared within the crowd, and then a lighted kerosene lantern was hurled toward the broken door. The lamp struck the casement and burst into flames.

The angry mob cheered.

Where are the harbor patrols?

Movement on the third floor caught Ayden's attention.

Robert Prescott stepped onto the balcony, surveyed the angry mob in the street while he tucked in his shirt, and then returned to the room.

"Damn." Ayden turned to the men behind him. "There's a man in there I need to get out unharmed." He looked from one man's glare to the other. "You can watch if you want, but lift one single finger to interfere, and I will kill you without hesitation or remorse. *Do you understand me?*" Mind-magic drove home the warning. *Do not test me.*

Both men paled and took an involuntary step back.

Ayden didn't wait for their response.

First, the Fire.

He took control of the flames in the doorway, stretching them across the entry as a barrier and containing the spread.

No one comes in.

The brothel sat on an oversized lot. Unruly bushes and saplings grew along the side and back of the establishment.

As Ayden darted into the high weeds and made for the back door, gunshots sounded in the street.

Surely, Robert understands the danger and will try to escape.

Ayden paused at the corner of the building and looked toward the back door.

Three partially dressed women escaped down the back steps and ran into the tall brush behind the establishment.

Ayden suspected a trail led across the overgrown lot behind Harbor's Delight to the street on the other side.

A man with a long rifle emerged, scanned the area, and lifted his weapon toward Ayden.

"I have a friend upstairs." Ayden lifted his hands and stepped into the small yard. "I mean to see him escape unharmed."

The rifleman lowered his weapon slightly. "Name your friend."

"Prescott," Ayden responded.

Behind Ayden, one of the coven thugs hollered, "He went this way," to the overexcited crowd.

Anger flared inside Ayden. His eyes closed for a moment as he reached for his two unwanted companions.

Only one of the followers remained, leading the group of angry men through the bushes to the back door and Ayden.

Ayden raised one hand and clenched his fist. Water flowed from between his fingers, down his arm, and onto the ground. "A promise made."

"Everyone out." The guard yelled over his shoulder into the building, dropping to a crouch as gunfire erupted from alongside the building.

There was no cover other than the overgrown brush behind the tavern. Ayden ran across the exposed yard, crouched behind a bush in the weeds, and watched the back door.

Several men escaped the building and sprinted across the yard into the foliage along the path. Then Robert stood in the doorway. He spoke to the man with the rifle, nodded, and raced out the door.

"Robert!" Ayden rose to intercept him as they both ran for the narrow trail.

A flurry of angry shouts and gunfire erupted from the side of the house.

A molten fist struck Ayden in the back and threw him forward onto the ground.

"Ayden, what in God's name are you doing here?" Robert gripped him and urged him to his feet. "Come." He pulled Ayden's arm across his shoulder, taking his weight, and lifted him forward onto the narrow path.

Behind them, the rifleman on the back step gave cover fire as he ran to the path.

Ayden's shirt and pant leg were already slick with blood, and the material clung to his skin. "I've been shot."

"I saw that." Robert exited the trail and hurried across a cobblestone street and then down a path between two buildings. "Unfortunately, that will have to wait for the moment. Are you in much pain?"

"Some. I'll manage."

Robert released Ayden beside a door as he fumbled through his pocket. "I have the key here somewhere. Ah!" Robert unlocked the door, pushed it wide, and then gripped Ayden's jacket. "Inside, quickly."

The rifleman raced behind them between the buildings, and followed them in. "What a disaster." He closed the door and then set the rifle beside it.

Robert bolted the door and directed Ayden toward the back through aisles of cargo crates. "How did this happen?" He pushed open the office door and pointed to a sofa along the wall. "Have a seat, I'll find bandages." He paused as the other man entered the office. "Halstead, this is Ayden MacKenna—a friend of Margaret's." Robert gave Halstead's shoulder a pat as he hurried out of the office. "Ayden, this is Halstead Coffrey, an old friend of mine."

Halstead offered his hand to Ayden. "Call me Hal."

"Nice to meet you, Hal." Ayden tried to lift his right arm to take Hal's hand, but the pain in his side prevented it.

Hal withdrew his hand and stepped back, nodding toward Ayden's injury. "I almost shot you myself." He helped himself to the liquor on the sideboard, poured a drink, and handed it to Ayden. "How bad is it?" He motioned toward Ayden's side, then returned to the open cabinet and poured himself a drink.

Ayden downed the shot and set the glass on the side table. "I'm not sure how to answer since I've never been shot before." Ayden chuckled and then winced. "I'm not dead, so there's that. I'm fairly certain the slug passed through." He unbuttoned his shirt with his left hand, but the wound was high on his right side, beneath his arm, and it hurt too much to twist out of his shirt.

Robert returned with the bandages and placed a pile of folded cloth strips on the low table in front of Ayden. "I'll bandage this as best I can, but we must take you to Margaret."

"No." Ayden rolled his good shoulder as Robert pulled the sleeve of his jacket and shirt past his elbow and then off his left hand. "What can she do?"

"It isn't what Margaret can or can't do." Robert removed the jacket from the injured side and then pulled the bloody shirt from Ayden's wound. "Sorry."

Ayden winced as the stuck cloth tore away. He looked down at his side and felt hot bile crawl up his throat. "Goddess. Margaret can't fix this."

"She can sew a straight seam, which is more than either Hal, or I can do." Robert lowered his voice, "But it isn't Margaret per se; it's the salve Amy left us." His voice dropped to a whisper, "It works like... *like magic.*" He held Ayden's gaze.

Ayden's brows rose in understanding. "Even so, Revere's is much closer. I don't think I can manage the trip to Beacon Hill and back tonight."

Robert wiped the blood from Ayden's back and side. "Hal, under the sideboard, there's a bottle of grain alcohol. Pour a bit on these pads."

Hal came to the settee, looked at Ayden's gunshot wound, and shuddered. "Jesus." He took the pads and returned quickly, handing them to Robert. "I'm going to step out." He downed the rest of his drink, set the glass on the table, and left the room.

"No stomach for blood?" Ayden asked.

Robert shook his head. "Not precisely. Hal is averse to other people's pain."

"He was going to shoot me."

"He didn't know you then. It's difficult to explain." Robert stared at Ayden. "Are you ready?"

"Yes." Ayden ground his teeth as the alcohol burned into his raw flesh. "Enough!" Ayden finally shouted.

Robert removed the alcohol-drenched pad and replaced it with absorbent gauze. "I'm blaming this entirely on you, of course. Running into a maddened crowd, getting shot, refusing to go to Margaret for treatment." He wrapped long strips of linen around Ayden's chest, then tied the ends together. "What were you doing there anyway?"

"I happened to walk in that direction when I left Revere's. I saw the angry crowd and then you on the balcony. I thought to help you escape."

"I appreciate the sentiment, and I'm sorry you were injured on my account." Robert's gaze kept returning to the amulet Ayden wore on a chain around his neck. "That's a very unusual pendant. Where did you find something like that?"

Ayden lifted the stone. "It was a gift I received while in India."

"The color flares with a life of its own."

"Not unlike fine fire opals, although this stone, whatever it is, is not an opal."

Robert nodded and gathered the bloody scraps of material, tossing them into a tall trash bin. "I wonder if there would be a market for jewelry like that in Boston."

Ayden gripped the jewel in his fist. "This is one of a kind, I believe."

Hal returned with a white garment folded over his arm. "I found a shirt that should fit." He shook it out, held it up, and tossed the clothing to Robert. "I don't think it's one of yours."

"No." Robert examined the shirt. "Where did you find this?"

"In a big basket at the back of the closet."

"A costume?" Robert speculated.

Hal shrugged, picked up his empty glass, and carried it to the sideboard to refill his drink. "It was the only one wide enough at the shoulders." He turned and gazed at Ayden's bare torso. "But it will be too large at the waist."

"That doesn't matter." Robert helped Ayden get the shirt on over his bandages, then picked up his jacket as Ayden buttoned the shirt. "And now the coat."

Ayden grimaced as he came to his feet. His head felt light, and his knees weak, as though the single shot of whiskey had gone to his head. Blood already soaked Robert's carefully applied bandages.

Robert acted as valet and slipped the jacket onto his arms and shoulders. "I'll see you home."

"That's not necessary. Revere's is only a couple blocks away."

"Nevertheless." Robert pulled on his jacket. "I'll hail a cab from there and head up the hill."

Ayden paused at the door. "Nice to have met you, Hal."

"Goodnight, Ayden." Hal lifted his glass. "Goodnight, Robert."

"Lock up behind us," Robert reminded him, then led Ayden to the warehouse door.

Outside, the night had turned chill, and a mist seeped across the town from the harbor.

"Hal lives there?" Ayden asked as they headed south along the empty street.

"He does. There's a living space above the office. I'd charge him rent, but honestly, having someone there at night is one less guard I must pay."

"Does he work at Harbor's Delight?"

"He provides security several nights a week, or he did. I have a feeling that mob may have torn Har-De's to the ground."

The connection between Robert, Hal, and Harbor's Delight made no sense to Ayden. He was having trouble keeping pace with Robert physically, and his thoughts were wrapped in a hazy gauze. His side burned and throbbed, and he could sense blood seeping from the bandages down his leg and into his boot.

I can stop the bleeding once I'm alone—I think—but I need to rest before I try.

"Is this your door?"

Ayden nodded and pulled the key from his pocket.

Robert unlocked the door, gathered Ayden in his grip, and helped him into the room. "The chair or the bed?"

"Bed."

"Do you want me to help you undress?"

"No. Just let me be." Ayden struggled to keep his eyes open.

"I'm going to wedge this towel next to you to staunch the bleeding."

An uncomfortable wad was shoved against his side, but he didn't complain; he didn't have the energy.

"Ayden, try to stay awake. I'm going to get Margaret."

Chapter 2

Balm to Cure

Margaret Prescott

"Margaret!" Robert's voice echoed up the stairs as the front door flew open and banged against the entry wall.

Margaret shut her book and came to her feet. "What's wrong?" She looked down the stairs at her distraught husband. "Where's your hat?"

Robert ran a hand through his hair. "I'm not sure. What does it matter?" He started toward the back of the house, then stopped and looked up at Margaret. "Ayden's been shot. I need Amy's best salve and bandages. I need Wrigley to hitch up the carriage—" He spun and headed to the back of the house.

"Robert, slow down." Margaret tossed the book onto the window seat of the reading nook and hurried after him, thankful she hadn't undressed for the evening. "Where is Ayden?"

"At Revere's, in his room." Robert stalked through the kitchen and out the door. "Wrigley!"

"Robert, stop. I need more information. How badly is he injured?" She followed him down the back steps and into the yard.

Robert raised his fist to pound on Wrigley's door when it was snatched open. "I hear ye. Like as not the whole hill heard you too."

"I'm sorry, but this is an emergency. Ayden's been shot, and I need to take some of Amy's salve to him." When Wrigley didn't move, Robert raised his voice. "Right now, man. This is life and death." He waved his hand in the air, stomped to the carriage house door, and jerked it open. "Never mind, I'll rig it myself."

Margaret and Wrigley stared at each other in stunned silence for a moment. Margaret couldn't remember the last time she'd seen Robert this upset. "I'll gather bandages and the salve. I have it in the house." She spun on her heel and ran up the back steps into the kitchen. "Don't let him leave without me."

"What's the matter?" Peg stood in the opening between the kitchen and the dining room.

"Ayden MacKenna's been injured. Run upstairs and gather a basket full of sterile bandages. I'll need pads to staunch blood, long binding strips, and anything else you think I might need for a bullet wound. Hurry."

Peg ran for the stairs.

Margaret opened the remedy cupboard and reached over several packets and vials until she felt the mason jars with Amy's liniment. Careful not to knock the other items from the cabinet, she withdrew two jars, one at a time.

Peg returned to the kitchen with a large, hinged picnic basket over her arm. She lifted the lid to display sterilized bandages, a hooked needle with silk thread, and a vial of alcohol. "Will this do?" She flicked her wrist to light all the lamps in the kitchen and then sat the basket on the table for Margaret's inspection.

"Perfect." Margaret slipped the two jars into the basket and then lifted the container.

"I'll carry the bandages; you get your coat." Peg took the handbasket from Margaret's grip and headed outside.

Margaret pulled one of the gardening jackets from the wall and slipped it on as she followed Peg into the yard.

Behind the carriage house, Wrigley tightened the girth and checked the breast collar and breeching. "Good boy, Hob. Easy now." He climbed onto the high seat and arranged the reins.

"We have to wait for Margaret," Robert said as he opened the door.

"I'm here." She handed the basket to Robert, took his other hand, and climbed into the vehicle. "Peg, can you close everything up?"

"Yes, ma'am," Peggy called.

Robert pulled the door closed and shouted out the open window to Wrigley, "Let's go!"

It wasn't long before the transport pulled to an abrupt stop in front of Revere's Tavern.

Robert opened the vehicle door, jumped down, lifted the basket from the seat, and then helped Margaret to the ground. "The door to his room is this way." Robert indicated the narrow alleyway beside the tavern. "There won't be room to turn," he called to Wrigley.

"I'll back the carriage in."

"You can do that?"

Margaret yanked his jacket sleeve, "Take me to Ayden."

Robert nodded and took Margaret's arm. "You're wearing the gardening jacket?"

"The whole time. You just now noticed?"

At a door beside a darkened window, Robert pulled a key from his pocket and stepped inside. "I left a candle burning. I haven't been gone that long. Ayden, are you in here?"

When Ayden made no answer, Margaret flicked her wrist, and both a candle on the dresser and the kerosene lamp beside the bed sprang to light."

"Good Lord, Margaret. You startle me when you do that."

"Sorry." Margaret crossed the small room to the bed and dropped to her knees. "Ayden? Can you hear me?" She shed her jacket and then caught her breath at the amount of blood soaked into the towel wadded beside him.

"Is he... dead?" Robert queried hesitantly.

When Robert spoke, Ayden rolled his head, murmured something unintelligible, and struggled to open his eyes.

Wrigley entered the room, closed the alley door, and walked to the foot of the bed. "What are you waiting for? Turn him over and apply the salve. You don't need his permission."

"He's coming around. Ayden?" Margaret shook his shoulder gently. "I'm here to take care of your wound."

"Wrigley, take his feet and help me turn him." Robert slid his arms beneath Ayden's back. "The damage is on his right side."

When they lifted, Ayden's eyes opened, and he exclaimed with pain, "Ah!"

"Yup. That woke him up." Wrigley pulled off Ayden's boots. Blood dripped from his right boot and his sock was soaked with red. Wrigley glanced up and met Margaret's worried gaze.

"He's lost a lot of blood." Margaret tossed the blood-soaked towel from the bed behind her and reached for the basket.

I hope Peg packed the larger scissors.

Ayden murmured, "I dreamed of you."

Margaret looked over at Ayden and brushed his hair from his forehead, laying her palm across his brow. "You have a fever." His skin was hot and dry to the touch.

"Fire dancers burn my soul."

"And you're delirious."

His half-lidded gaze followed her as she worked, cutting away his borrowed shirt. "You're so beautiful."

"Hush, Ayden. Robert, hand me the alcohol." When she looked back, Ayden's eyes closed again.

"This is going to sting, but I must clean it before I stitch the wound. Ayden?" No response.

"You best take a good grip on him, Rob, before she pours the spirits on that bloody mess. He's like to cock up and smack her a good one." Wrigley gripped both ankles.

Ayden struggled against the pressure on his shoulders and legs.

Margaret placed the soaked pad of alcohol on the wound, and an agonized scream tore from Ayden's throat.

Margaret choked back a sob but held the pad in place as she murmured, "I'm sorry, Ayden. I'm so sorry. Almost done. I'm sorry."

Ayden muttered to Wrigley at the foot of his bed, "I'm awake now. I won't strike her."

"I still have to stitch the wound," Margaret leaned forward, then sat back with a sigh. "But I need more light."

"Robert, through the door behind you." Ayden tipped his head back to view Robert. "Follow the aisle—Harry behind the bar—he'll get what you need."

Robert nodded, sniffed, and wiped his face.

"This wasn't your fault," Ayden said, then closed his eyes again, his face gray.

"Your fault?" Margaret stared at her husband.

"I'll get more light." Robert shook his head at Margaret and mouthed, "Not my fault," then left the room.

In moments, Harry surged into the room. "What have you done now, Mac?" The lamp he carried brightened the room. He stopped beside the bed, rubbed his mouth, and started aghast at Ayden's bloody side.

Robert followed with a lamp as well and held it above the bed.

"Very good. I'll be quick." Margaret drew the ragged edges of Ayden's torn skin together and pressed the sharp tip of her hooked needle through them.

Ayden flinched but held still, eyes closed, his face ashen.

Margaret finished the tiny stitches, then sat back on her heels. "I need to see where the bullet went in. Wrigley, can you help Ayden roll onto his other side?"

"I can roll," Ayden assured her.

"Nevertheless." Margaret tipped her head at Wrigley to help, and the older man steadied Ayden's shoulder and helped him roll.

"The back is not as bad," Margaret murmured. Her hand shook as she reached for another alcohol-drenched cloth. She'd never seen someone lose so much blood and live.

"He's out again," Wrigley told her.

Margaret nodded and cleaned the entrance wound. "This isn't bleeding as much. The opening is small and should close well on its own. Amy's salve and a bandage is all this needs." She dipped two fingers into the light green salve and applied it to both the stitches on his back and the hole in front.

Blood continued to ooze through the stitches, and she bit her bottom lip to stop it from quivering.

I can't lose him again; dear Goddess, be merciful.

The folded pads covering the wounds would need to be strapped in place.

Together, Robert and Wrigley lifted Ayden's shoulders from the bed, and Margaret, with Harry's help, passed long strips of binding cloth beneath him several times.

When Margaret was satisfied the bandages would remain in place, she nodded to the men.

With care, they eased Ayden down on his left side.

"The ointment will make him sleep. Hard." She looked at Harry. "He won't be any use to you for a few days. If he wakes, offer him water or weak tea."

"I will." Harry nodded. "How did he get shot?"

"You heard about the ruckus down at Harbor's Delight..." Robert asked as he followed Harry out of Ayden's room.

"I want to stay with him," Margaret confessed to Wrigley.

"I know you do, but you know you can't. It's a shame we don't know a healer who could mend this."

"Amy would have been more help than I've been tonight." She pushed a strand of hair out of her face with the back of her wrist, then brushed a tear from her cheek.

"Maybe. But she couldn't care for him like you have. That must count for something." Wrigley came around the bed and held out his hand to Margaret. "Let me help you up."

She took his hand and then shook her head. "I can't feel my legs."

Wrigley wrapped his arm around her and helped her to her feet. "I've got you. Just hold on until the feeling comes back."

Margaret nodded as her legs began to tingle. She gazed down at Ayden. "What if the salve doesn't work?" Laying on his left side, he faced away from her. "Has he stopped breathing?"

"He's breathing." Wrigley helped Margaret to the single chair in the room. "Keep wiggling your toes."

"Should we have called a physician?" She wiped another tear. *What is wrong with me?*

"And what would they have done? The same as what you've done, probably less. Or worse, try to bleed the poor man. No. You've done well."

Robert returned to the room and looked from Margaret's tear-filled eyes to Ayden. "Is he...?"

"He's fine. Sleeping or unconscious from blood loss. We've done all we can," Wrigley picked up Margaret's gardening coat. "We should go and let your daughter's salve do its work."

"We don't know if it will work at all!" Margaret grabbed the handkerchief Robert offered and covered her face.

"It works on horses, small animals, and me. It helped heal that nasty cut from the leather knife." Wrigley offered, holding out the tiny scar on his hand.

"That was small compared to this." Margaret stood and approached Ayden's bed. "I should stay."

"Harry will look in on him, and I daresay, there are any number of ladies asking after his health. He'll be fine." Robert stepped past Margaret and locked the outside door. He picked up the basket from the bedside. "Is this everything?"

"Yes." Margaret took her coat from Wrigley and put it on. "I'd feel better if Peg came to check on him. At least she's skilled." With one last look at Ayden, she followed Robert from the room.

The Soul of the Witch Saga continues in Book 6:
Patriarch

Also by

Soul of the Witch Saga

Prodigy – Book 1

Pyromancer – Book 2

Passage – Book 3

Prophecy – Book 4

Paradox – Book 5

Patriarch – Book 6

—

J.L.'s Timeless Quest

Aubrielle's Call

The Corsair's Tempest

Hawthorn and Mistletoe

—

The Hunter Chronicles

Hunter's Gamble

Hunter and Lily Graham

The Kid in Black

Penelope's Heart

All of these stories take place within the same shared universe.

About the Author

C. (Connie) Marie Bowen writes paranormal romance and historical fantasy set within a richly layered, persistent universe. Her award-winning novel *Passage* launched the *Soul of the Witch* series, introducing a world where magic, loyalty, and sacrifice intertwine.

Bowen's stories span multiple series, with characters crossing paths and timelines within the shared universe of the Soul of the Witch Saga. Figures such as Hunter from *The Hunter Chronicles* and J.L. from *The Timeless Quest* play meaningful roles within this interconnected world.

Born in Denver, Colorado, Bowen grew up with a love of ghost stories and storytelling. She now lives in the greater Chicagoland area with her husband and two rescue pets, Abigail and Rousseaux.

Visit https://www.cmariebowen.com to explore her connected series and learn more.